I0692745

TRUTHSIGHT

MIRIAM GREYSTONE

CITY OWL
PRESS

TRUTHSIGHT
Outcast Mage: Book One

CITY OWL PRESS
www.cityowlpress.com

Cover Design by Mibl Art and Tina Moss. All stock photos licensed appropriately.

Edited by Heather McCorkle.

Author Photo by Fox and Owl Photography.

For information on subsidiary rights, please contact the publisher at info@cityowlpress.com.

Print Edition ISBN: 978-1-9447280-4-5

Digital Edition ISBN: 978-1-5337525-6-7

Printed in the United States of America

This book is for my Mother and Father,
who have always loved me so fiercely,
and believed in me so much.

PRAISE FOR MIRIAM GREYSTONE

"TRUTHSIGHT offers unusual details that keep the reading experience fresh; an infant earth spirit running amok in Rowan's house is a moment not soon forgotten."
- *Publisher's Weekly*

"A fun, fast-paced read with a compelling main character, excellent world-building, and refreshingly unique mythological creatures. Greystone delivers an impressive start to an intriguing new series."
- *Leah Cypess, Author of MISTWOOD*

"From the first page, TRUTHSIGHT reaches out insistently, drawing us into hidden corners of our world, into shadowy places populated by pixies and centaurs, by harpies and elves—all with plenty of magical qualities to fascinate us, all with enough humanity to seem utterly real. It is fast-paced, and suspenseful. It is also heart-breaking, funny, terrifying, and passionate. It is, in the end, deeply satisfying. It is not to be missed."
- *B.K. Stevens, Agatha-, Anthony-, and Macavity-nominated author*

"TRUTHSIGHT is a compelling debut novel with a smart, forthright heroine, a good-hearted but rough around the edges hero, and a unique approach to supernatural creatures. Not the sweet little fairy type either. Like humans, they run the spectrum from kind to vile. But vile is good when it makes you squirm. Not to mention appreciate the heroine's toughness that much more."
- *Michelle Markey Butler, Author of HOMEGOING*

ONE

THE PIXIE WAS VERY CLOSE TO SHOOTING ME.

I took a deep breath and tried to sound calm.

"If he moves while I'm working, the damage could get much worse," I explained. "It can be you, or it can be Jason. But we need to do this fast, and someone is going to have to hold the boy down."

Not much taller than the length of my hand, Grenalda crouched on the exam table in front of her son's crumpled body. Her chest heaved from the effort it had taken to carry him here in her arms. Blood smeared the colorful bits of woven bird feathers she wore as clothing, and her eyes were wide and panic-stricken. She kept her right hand up, poised over her shoulder, stretching her fingers toward the dart-blower strapped across her back. We were humans, and though she might have no choice but to come to us for help, she made it perfectly clear that she didn't fully trust us.

"Why can't you just bandage him up?"

"His head wound is simple—we'll wrap it and it will heal just fine. But his leg is broken. If we don't fix it correctly, the bone will heal crooked. He'll limp for the rest of his life."

My chest burned and I still wore my scrubs from my shift in the ER. I hadn't eaten since breakfast, which I vaguely remembered choking down while driving to work at around 5:00 AM. Now dark had nearly fallen, and the chill early evening air streamed in through the thrown open doors of the converted barn that sat on the edge of my property. Usually, I had a break between a shift in the county ER and the arrival of the first patient to my night clinic. But Grenalda's boy couldn't wait for treatment. I blinked and tried to focus on the small creature glaring up at me.

"Very well," she announced, after a long pause. "Dr. Jason may hold him. *Gently*. I will watch." She launched herself into the air and came to hover just over my shoulder, her eyes narrow as she watched my every move. Jason had moved with impressive speed, setting out everything I might need on the table. The magnifying equipment I used when working with our tiniest patients was waiting, as well as an assortment of salves and bandages. I ran my fingers down the small boy's body, checking to make sure there weren't any injuries I had missed.

"All set?" I asked Jason.

He lay his hand over the boy's chest, holding the child's arms down and his body still. "Ready when you are, Amy." He nodded, and I set to work.

The most difficult thing would be not using too much force. The boy's bones were so thin that it was hard not to break more while trying to set the leg bone he had already injured. The child's eyes flickered, open and then shut. He made a sharp, high-pitched sound of distress that sounded like the mewl of a kitten.

"What is wrong with him?" Grenalda demanded, her voice breaking even as her eyes flashed and her fingers tightened around her weapon.

"Nothing," I replied, working hard to keep my voice even. "Setting bones is a nasty business. We have clover leaf on hand to give for the pain, if he fully regains consciousness. But if I move quickly, this can all be over by the time he wakes up."

But the boy's cry of pain had pierced my heart, and as I spoke my conscience twisted uncomfortably inside me. *It doesn't have to be this hard. I could heal this boy with a touch. With barely a thought. No need for pain or fear. He could be whole again already.* But I shook my head to dispel the thoughts, and leaned closer to my work. *No,* I told myself. *Those days are over. If I use my touch to heal him, then in two or three days I will be dead. They would find me. And then who would heal him the next time he falls? And Grenalda and her son are not the only ones who need me.*

"Almost done," I announced, more for my own comfort than for anyone else. Grenalda hovered just over my shoulder, her eyes flashing as she watched my every move. Any time her son made a pained sound, her hand flitted back toward her dart blower.

I had once asked a pixie to pay me with one of those darts, instead of my usual fee, so I could run some tests. The poison the darts were dipped in was powerful stuff. Not enough to kill a human outright, but enough to lay you flat and leave you with the mother of all headaches when you woke up a few hours later. I hoped sincerely that my evening wouldn't end with me unconscious on the floor, a dart the size of a bee sting buried deep inside my neck.

"He was trying out his wings?" I asked, not looking up from my work, but hoping to help her relax.

"No, he is not old enough to even try flying. He was jumping through the branches with his friends."

I nodded, wishing I could ask his name. But I knew Grenalda would not want to tell me.

"Well, the bone broke cleanly. Once we have it set, his natural healing abilities will take over. It should heal up as good as new."

When I had the bone in place, Jason took the wood we kept for splints, and managed to cut some into small enough pieces to fit Grenalda's son. Two hours later the child was dazed but awake. He sat with his tiny legs sprawled out in front of him, chewing on some clover, his eyes unfocused as he gazed blearily around the barn.

"It should mend quickly," I assured his mother. "In a few weeks bring him back and I'll check to see that all is well."

She was like a different creature, now that her son was out of danger. She stood on the table top beside me, her wings fluttering slowly and her eyes soft. She shook her head. "I feared the worst, when I heard him crashing through the leaves."

"Don't worry," I said. "He'll be recklessly leaping through the branches and making you furious again in no time."

"It is fortunate that I have that to look forward to," she commented, and I saw the corner of her lips curl up in a smile. Then she turned toward me, her expression suddenly business-like. "Now. We must discuss payment."

"Ah. Yes," I answered, distracted, my eyes were still fastened on her son.

He gazed up at me, his small, pointed chin making his face look almost alien, his bead-black eyes unblinking. "One stone, then. You can bring it in a month, when you bring him back for me to check on his progress."

"One stone?" Grenalda's voice faltered, and I glanced down at her. Her wings, which had been fluttering in a soft, careless way behind her, went suddenly rigid and still.

"For my time and labor," I said hastily, forcing myself to look away from the boy, anxious to reassure Grenalda and correct my mistake. "But then a second stone for the supplies I used to design the splint, and to cover your follow-up appointment. Another blue one, perhaps, like this." And I motioned to an especially uncommon stone on the necklace I always wore while I was working in the clinic. The necklace was a long, two-tiered gold chain, covered with rows of smooth, rounded beads. Shining red jasper hung next to golden amber, and blue lapis dangled beside deep purple charoite.

"A blue topaz!" Grenalda exclaimed. Her eyes widened as though with indignation, but her shoulders immediately relaxed, and her wings regained their rhythm. "Your rates are very high, Dr. Amy!"

I shrugged, turning my eyes back to the boy. "Next time let the bone heal crooked, if you don't want to pay." I turned my head toward her a fraction of an inch, and our eyes met.

I winked.

Grenalda let out a snort of laughter which, coming from her, sounded almost musical. "Fine, then. I will bring you the stones in a month."

"Until then just make sure he stays off that leg as much as possible. Are you able to fly him home?"

"I will have to stop to rest frequently, but we can manage."

I wished I could offer to help, but knew that was impossible. She would never allow me to know the location of her home. Even suggesting such a thing would be cause for much suspicion.

"Okay, Grenalda. I'm glad you came."

"I'm glad you are here, Dr. Amy." She arched an eyebrow and smiled wryly. "Despite your exorbitant prices."

Just then her son began to stir, moaning a little and trying to get to his feet.

"Don't stand, love; let me carry you," Grenalda chirped, swooping over to his side and trying to gather him up in her arms.

But he squirmed and pushed away, looking over his mother's shoulder to stare at me again with those bright, feverish eyes. He opened his mouth, and at first I thought the hoarse, sing-song sound he made was a howl of pain. But then I understood the words.

"Run, run," he wailed, his eyes riveted to mine. "But still they come."

My heart froze, and suddenly everything in the barn seemed to go perfectly quiet and still.

"Hush, child," Grenalda said, stroking his cheek to try to calm him. "I'm sorry, Doctor, although you are the one who gave him the clover. He gets like this sometimes. Likes to pretend that he has foresight." Grenalda clucked and shook her head affectionately. "His grandmother did have the gift, but he is much too young. We'll see if it manifests when he's older. Until then we'll have to just put up with the dramatics."

Neither the boy nor I paid her any attention.

"A hundred mouths, a million teeth," he shrilled, his voice rising till it broke. "Stone and bone deep underneath." His eyes were locked onto mine, and I could see that he trembled.

"Enough, little one. You're tired and you need rest." Grenalda looked back at me, the smile instantly fading from her face. "What is it, Doctor? Are you all right?"

"Fine," I managed to whisper, though my mouth was dry and my lips felt numb. "I'm just fine, Grenalda. Thank you for asking."

"I'll get him home so he can sleep the clover off. No," she insisted, when he feebly tried to push away her hands, finally managing to gather him into her arms. "We're really going. You're delirious, and you're going to frighten the poor doctor."

He was heavy, and she bobbed and weaved a bit as her wings buzzed and she lifted up into the air. The boy struggled fretfully in her arms, craning his head over her shoulder to look back at me as she flew away. He cried out something I couldn't hear, and then, just as they were disappearing into the dark, his voice echoed back to me, high-pitched but clear.

"Three days more, and they're at the door," he wailed. "Run and run. But still they come."

TWO

FOR A MOMENT I STOOD FROZEN, STARING AT THE DARK THAT suddenly seemed to be pressing itself up against the cheerful light of the barn, trying to find an opening to force its way inside.

It isn't real, I told myself firmly. *He was high on the clover, and spouting nonsense. I'm safe here. I've always been safe here. They won't find me.*

"A patient showing up before the sun even goes down. I guess I got back in the nick of time." Jason's voice came from behind me.

"I know," I said, turning to face him, and trying to force my lips to smile. "I heard your truck pull up in front just as she was flying in the door. I didn't even get a chance to say hello before things got crazy. How are you? I didn't know when you'd get back. How did it go?"

"Pretty good. I think."

"You look different."

"I do?" He spread his hands out and glanced down at himself, grimacing as though bracing for bad news. "How? In a good way?"

"Yeah." I paused, my eyes searching his face, trying to find words that would match what I saw in front of me.

Jason had been gone for three weeks, and there was no denying the change in him. He stood straighter, his shoulders thrown back, more at ease with himself than I'd ever seen him. He was still lanky and slender, but he seemed a bit softer too, not quite so much like a medical student used to skipping at least two meals a day. His sandy blond hair was pushed back, away from eyes that seemed brighter, the light blue color contrasting with skin that was now deeply tanned. He looked...good. Happier than I had ever seen him. I knew he was close to my own age of twenty-seven but now, somehow, he looked younger. "Maybe it's that you look more like yourself. Have you been sleeping?"

"No." He smiled, dropping his eyes to the ground. "Not at all. I did all the things you suggested, Amy." He looked back up at me, his soft smile growing into a grin. "You have no idea how much it's been helping me."

"I'm incredibly glad," I said, wanting to pump my fists in the air or wrap him in a fierce hug, but forcing myself to stay still. "I *knew* we'd figure it out."

I can only assume that it's difficult to find out that you aren't fully human, when you always thought you were. Growing up, Jason had always been sickly and miserable, but he had never known why. The humans who raised him hadn't known how to help. I had done everything I could once I got him to trust me enough to tell me his symptoms, but nothing seemed to fit. We still weren't sure exactly what he was—but after months of effort we had at least come up with a good theory of what might make him finally feel well.

"I ate the sunshine," Jason explained, the wonder still fresh in his eyes. "I drank moonlight. I stood with the trees for days, not moving, not saying anything, just being with them. It was wonderful. I've never felt so good."

"I really want to hug you," I admitted, raising my arms but holding them back. "Is that still all right?"

Many preternatural folks don't like human touch, and a hug, the feeling of being enclosed and locked into a human embrace, can be outright painful. I hung back, not sure how much had changed, afraid of hurting him. But Jason laughed and threw his arms around me. I buried my head in his shoulder and breathed in the smell of dirt and old leaves, and air as fresh as daylight. He felt more substantial to me, as I hugged him, less like a good gust of wind might blow him clear away. I could feel the muscles of his arms through the smooth fabric of his shirt. He leaned down, resting his head against mine, curling his arms around my back.

Something changed in the air between us, and suddenly the embrace was too much. I took a step away.

"I've missed you," I admitted, folding my arms across my chest.

"I can tell," Jason answered, looking at me a little more closely than I liked.

He smiled. I looked away.

"Don't take offense or anything, Amy, but you kind of look like shit."

I hit him on the shoulder, laughing to hide a grimace.

"I know I do. Thanks for pointing it out, though. I guess I've gotten soft, having you around for so long. I don't remember how to do it all alone."

But my laugh hadn't fooled him.

"No, Amy. Really." He leaned his face down close to mine and put a light hand on my shoulder. "Are you all right?"

I drew a deep, slow breath, trying to ignore the warmth of his hand through my shirt. I looked him straight in the eye.

"I'm fine," I lied, and prayed to God that his ability to sense dishonesty hadn't blossomed along with the rest of him. Life would get complicated quickly if Jason suddenly knew every time I took liberties with the truth. What if he realized Amy wasn't my real name? "Just a little sleep-deprived."

If he could hear the untruth in my words, his face didn't reveal it. "Why don't you turn in early tonight?" he suggested. "You've been running this place all by yourself for weeks. I can handle it on my own for one night. You should rest up a bit."

I hesitated. After the pixie boy's outburst, the quiet and dark of my house didn't sound all that inviting. But I really was exhausted. And Jason wanted to help.

"Are you sure?"

"Trust me." Jason smiled. "I learned from the best."

"All right, thanks." It was easier to give in than to argue. And it would make him feel better to take care of me, for a change. "I'll just walk to the back for a minute first. I want to call and check in on Finar and his wife."

"Oh." Jason's eyes tightened. "How have they been doing?"

"Fine. For now." I shrugged. "They always do fine at this stage. When her water breaks—that's when all hell will break loose."

"What will you do?"

"First, I'll drive like hell to be there. Then I'll do anything I can think of ... even though it won't be enough." I shook my head. "I told them, before they tried, that I didn't know what was wrong. That I wouldn't be able to stop it. They knew the dangers. It was their decision."

"I don't understand how he can risk his wife." Jason's fist tightened convulsively. "He knows perfectly well what will happen."

"She knew what she was doing, too, Jason. They made the choice together." I laid a hand on his shoulder. "You have to understand—their people are dying out. In all of North America, there have been a total of two live centaur births in the last decade. Their kind are going to disappear. They believe they have to try."

"I guess I can understand. It's just such a harsh, harsh thing."

"Life is always harsh," I murmured. "No matter how hard we try not to notice. I'll be back in a minute, 'kay?"

"Sure thing."

I reached up to switch on one of the dozens of paper lanterns that dangled from the ceiling as I turned and headed toward the back of the barn. Usually our patients waited for the cover of night before venturing out to us, but Grenalda had come when it was barely twilight. I hadn't even had time to turn on all the lights before she arrived.

I walked the long length briskly, forcing my mind to focus on what was real and in front of me. As my eyes ran over everything, I felt a surge of happiness. The clinic was real, and safe. And I had built it. Where once there had been a row of horse stalls now stood four large patient rooms. I had done all the work myself, knocking down the walls to combine every two stalls into one. Each room had a door that shut, so the patients, who sometimes did not naturally get along well together, had privacy from each other. I had learned that lesson the hard way, after an unfortunate incident involving a gnome and a harpy who came face to face inadvertently. That night I had discovered both that the walking sticks most gnomes carry can double as surprisingly effective weapons, and that keeping certain patient populations separate from each other made my life a whole lot easier.

Each room was a different color. White is traditional for hospitals, and I was sick of it. So we had the blue room, the pink room, the purple room, and the green room. It made it easy to tell them apart, although I had once had a male centaur refuse the pink room on the grounds that it wasn't befitting his dignity. I *had* drawn a few flowers and butterflies on the wall in there, so I kind of saw his point, and I switched him to another. The brownies loved it, though, which made me feel a bit better.

I leaned over the rainwater barrels, checking to make sure they were full, and opened the fridge to make sure we weren't running low on our stocks of wild herbs, flowers, and honey. We also had several large Tupperware containers, all carefully labeled and filled with different types of dirt.

When I got to the center of the clinic, I stopped for a second to check on the waterfall. It had been my idea, and building it had been surprisingly fun. Soon after I had opened the night clinic it had become apparent to me how frightening it was for many of my patients. Even in a barn, with the doors open wide and the night air pouring in, many of them felt trapped and uneasy in anything resembling an enclosed space, especially one built by humans. So I made it feel more like the outdoors. I brought in potted trees, coaxed ivy to grow on the rafters, and finally built the waterfall. I had found smooth gray stones that weighed nearly as much as I did out by the river, and hauled them here in my truck, one by one. I poured the cement myself. When it was done, I had stocked the water with fish that were native to the area. For a while I even had frogs, until I realized that one of my patients had been eating them when I wasn't looking. I didn't replace the frogs—but I did make the troll pay me back for the free meal.

When I got to the library in the back, I pulled the door shut behind me. Strings of drying herbs hung, crisscrossing from the ceiling. Their pungent smell mixed with the smell of old books and dust, as the study was crammed, wall to wall, with every book on supernatural creatures I could find that was the least bit worth reading. I never knew what was going to walk through my door. Or fly, or leap, or materialize, for that matter. I made it my business to prepare as much as I could by becoming a lay expert in folklore, and the truth was that I loved the old, far-fetched tales, and enjoyed the challenge of trying to parse out the nonsense from the occasional gems of truth.

I slid my cell phone out of my pocket and dialed. Most of the patients who came to the clinic wouldn't be able to touch a man-made, technological device like a phone without suffering serious physical harm. But centaurs, being half-human, had a much higher tolerance for exposure to manufactured materials and, when necessary, could even use a device like a phone for short periods of time. It was a mark of the love Finar had for his wife that he hadn't argued with me when I pressed the prepaid phone into his hand so we could maintain contact. He had even agreed to stay within an hour's drive of the clinic as she neared the end of her pregnancy. Though, of course, they would not tell me where until they actually needed me to come. Like all supernatural creatures, their need for secrecy was deeply instinctual and at times shockingly fierce.

Finar picked up after only half a ring. "Hello?" he answered. "Doctor?"

"Hey there, Finar," I said, keeping my voice low and calm, and speaking slowly. "It's me, Amy. I'm calling to check and see how you both are doing. How is Crinea today?"

"Tired," he said. Male centaurs usually had deep, bass voices, but Finar was young, his beard still patchy, and his voice was high-pitched in his anxiety. "She sleeps so much. It makes me worry."

"Is she waking up to eat?"

"Yes."

"Is she eating normally?"

"More than usual, actually."

"Well, that's a good sign. And when she does wake up, does she seem confused at all, or is she her normal self?"

"She seems like herself. Nervous, of course, and emotional. But still her."

"All right. And there hasn't been any bleeding?"

"No." I could hear his shudder through the phone. "No bleeding."

The word "yet" hung unspoken in the air between us, but I kept going, keeping my voice cheerful. "Then I don't think it's anything to be concerned about. Her body is working really hard right now, growing that baby and staying strong. I'd say let her sleep as much as she wants to, as long as she's getting enough food and drink."

"How much longer do you think it will be?"

I half-laughed. "I don't know. You're the centaur. Shouldn't you know better than me? What do the stars tell you?"

"They tell me nothing," he answered, and I could hear despair in his voice. "When I look up, I see only blackness. The stars tell me nothing at all."

"Well, the best guess I can give you is anywhere from a month to six weeks until she's ready to deliver. But I'm far from an expert on centaur gestation."

Only silence came from the other end, and pain shot through me as I wondered if he was crying.

"Just call me," I said softly. "Whenever you think the time is coming, okay? I'll come."

"It may be in the middle of the day," he protested, his voice a bit thick. "Your work at the hospital…"

"I'll be there." I let the cheerful facade fall away. "I will be with you, and with her. And anything that can be done for her, and for the baby, will be done. I promise, Finar. I will do whatever I can."

"I know you will. Thank you, Amy. I'll call."

I hung up, shoved the phone deep in my pocket, and stood for a moment, rubbing my eyes. I felt dried out, stretched thin. The pain that always skulked in my chest throbbed, making my shoulders ache and my stomach roil. I stretched my arms out and cracked my knuckles. There was nothing else I could do for them —not right now. I wouldn't let myself think about them, or the pixie boy's warning anymore tonight. Jason was right. I had to rest.

When I found Jason leaning over a table with a handsaw, cutting wood into very small pieces, I asked, "You're sure you'll be all right on your own?" Presumably, he was preparing for the next time we had a pixie for a patient. I loved that he thought ahead like that. It was part of what made him so good at this.

"Go. To. Sleep," he said, frowning at me when he looked up from his work. "I don't want to have to treat you if you collapse. I have a strong suspicion you'd make a lousy patient."

"All right. Fine. I'll leave you alone." I turned and headed out. "The outside lights never got turned on. Do you want me to flip the switch on my way to the house?"

"Light 'em up!" he called out after me. "And eat some real food before you crash. Seriously, Amy. Not that green-seaweed-smoothie shit you chug all the time. A sandwich. You could even get crazy and cook yourself some pasta."

"Yes, Mother," I replied, turning back toward him just long

enough to stick out my tongue before letting the barn door swing shut behind me.

I strode out to the light switch that controlled the multi-tiered rows of Christmas lights that hung, stretching from the barn doors all the way to the edge of the woods. Jason sometimes referred to them as our landing lights, but I think on average more of our patients came by foot. The lights did act as a kind of runway, though, or welcome sign, gently guiding the patients right up to the barn's front door. I grinned as I switched on the big, flashing "Merry Christmas" sign too. The lights were easily visible from the road, so I had to make them look natural. Anyone driving by would laugh and think I really had gone native, leaving my Christmas lights on all year long like a good South Dakotan.

As I came up to the steps to my house, a high-pitched barking greeted me. A small ball of fur and dirt hurled itself in my direction, wiggling joyfully and trying to jump up high enough to lick me on the face.

"Yes, I'm happy to see you too. Down, Pip. You're getting dirt all over me. Down!" I held my hands out in front of me and tried to ward him off as best I could.

I had attempted to teach Pip not to jump up on people for a while, but eventually I'd given up and just learned how to dodge more effectively.

"You're filthy again," I commented, when he stood still long enough for me to get a real look at him. "What a shock. What was it this time? Did you get into the swimming hole or go digging in my herb garden?" Pip stared intently, his body quivering slightly, and yelped back at me. The best I could figure, he was part pug and part Australian Shepherd, both noble breeds that should never, ever, be mixed together. He danced around me, wiggling his tailless rump and leaping in the air, so ugly that he was beautiful.

I reached down and scratched behind his ear before opening the kitchen door so he could dart inside. He jumped up on the couch and settled down into his favorite spot, while I headed for the stairs.

I had told Jason I would eat, and I wished that I could keep my word, but the pain in my chest made eating impossible. I liked to think that he would have understood if he knew about the pain that I always carried inside me, but he didn't know about that. No one did. I just had to get to bed.

I took off my scrubs and threw them into a pile at the foot of my bed, sighing with relief as I slipped into the soft flannel nightshirt I always left hanging on the bedpost. I pulled the clips out of my hair and bent over, letting the mass of tight blonde curls tumble over my face. I tugged a brush through them a few times—hair this curly didn't need an excuse to snarl, and once it did I had little patience for sitting and working out the knots. Then I slid between the sheets, relishing the smooth, cool fabric on my skin.

I ought to sleep, I thought, but instead I turned and picked up the thick notebook on my bedside table. I flipped through the worn pages quickly, my eyes scanning the alphabetized, handwritten entries as I went. The list of supernatural creatures, both those I had actually encountered and those I had only read about, was very long. I found the entry for Pixie and quickly made a few new notes. When I finished, I flipped through the journal at random, letting my eyes wander as my heart sank.

Jann. Kelpie. Kobold. Leshy. Leucrota. Next to each of these entries the note was scrawled in red ink on the margin: *presumed extinct*. I had written it over and over again, until almost all the pages in my notebook were lined in red. There were just as many entries marked as being *in rapid decline*.

My finger lingered over the centaur entry, and I shook my head as I thought of Finar. I loved the clinic, and loved what I did there more than any other work I could ever imagine doing. But sometimes I felt like I was standing on a beach, cold, wet, and alone, watching the tide roll away as I clutched uselessly at handfuls of water, trying desperately to somehow hold the sea in place. I knew that sometimes I was able to do my patients real and lasting good; but there was no denying they were fading. The preternatural creatures simply couldn't hold their own against the rapid expansion of humanity. I could patch up broken arms and mend torn wings as much as I wanted to, but I couldn't keep their species from dying out.

I shoved the notebook away from me and turned off the light. I curled into a ball under my blankets and closed my eyes, focusing on my breathing. This was the most dangerous time of day for me. The time when no one needed me, when I was alone in the dark. This was when thoughts—that were usually drowned out by the bustle of my days—could finally swim to the surface of my mind and circle there, like sharks closing in on a kill.

Sooner or later, they will come. Even here, in the middle of nowhere, where no one knows your true name or recognizes your face. Eventually, they will find you.

Fear swirled in me, and the fire in my chest burned hotter.

This life isn't really yours, and you don't deserve it, not after what you've done. And when the past does catch up with you, how many more will be hurt because of you?

I let myself reach up and rub the spot just under my breastbone where the pain was the worst. In general I suppressed that habit—I was well aware that it made me look like I was in imminent danger of a heart attack and, since all of my co-workers were medical professionals, was probably unwise to do when I could be observed. But I was alone, and for the moment I didn't have to hide. *Enough!* I told myself. *I'm safe here. All this time, and they haven't found me. I haven't done anything to attract their attention. I'm safe.*

I forced the memory of the boy's warning down. I had to get my mind under control. If I wasn't careful, soon I would be nothing but a small, quivering ball of guilt and tears and pain. But I'd been fighting back self-reproach and panic for a long time now, and I had learned what to do.

I drew breath into my lungs, over and over, forcing my mind to stay blank. I tensed the muscles in my toes, and then relaxed them. My calf muscles came next. Slowly, I moved up my body, forbidding my mind to think of anything but the gradually increasing feeling of relaxation as it crept up and up my limbs. When sleep finally did come, it was a dreamless, dark wave that swept around me and swallowed me whole. But somewhere in the darkness, a small voice wailed a warning, urging me to run.

THREE

A FAINT RINGING WOKE ME WHEN THE SUN JUST BEGAN TO RISE. Blinking the sleep out of my eyes, I ran down the hall, sliding in my socks on the smooth wood to the kitchen counter, where I had left my cell phone the night before.

The phone switched to messages just as my hand touched it. Hurrying down the hall and already reaching for my clothes, I dialed him back.

"Finar? It's me. What's going on?"

"It's happening. Just like all the others." Hysteria bubbled just beneath the surface of his voice, and his tone grew higher-pitched with every word. "I thought we would have more time, but it started about an hour ago. She woke up. She was in pain, and now..." The voice that had built to a scream dropped almost to a whisper. "There's so much *blood*."

"You have to stay calm," I snapped. I couldn't let him give into the fear. I needed him to stay functional. "We knew this might happen, and you can't let yourself panic. Your wife is counting on you to take care of her right now. You've got to keep calm, and you cannot allow her to give up. Do you understand?"

"Yes."

"Okay, I'm coming right now. Where can I find you?"

His voice steadier, he gave me directions to a spot I knew was about a thirty-minute drive away. "That's the closest you can get by car," he explained. "I'll meet you there, and show you through the woods. You'll have to walk the rest."

"Fine, but don't you come. Send someone else to meet me. She needs you now, and you shouldn't leave her side."

There was a moment's hesitation.

"Are you sure?"

"Finar, I don't want to frighten you, but I need you to understand that I don't know what is going to happen. I haven't seen this before, but you've told me what has happened to the others. I really don't think you should leave her. Not even for a second." We both understood the warning that lay beneath those words.

"All...all right, Amy. Someone else will come to guide you."

"I'll be there as soon as I can."

"Please, hurry," Finar answered. Then in a voice so low that I could barely hear him, he added, "And be *careful*, Amy."

He hung up before I could ask him what the hell that was supposed to mean.

I pulled on a long-sleeved tee-shirt and tied on a bandanna to keep the hair out of my eyes. I had two bags packed with medical supplies waiting for me by the front door of the barn. I had packed them the day Crinea had told me she was pregnant. She had come to me just after dawn, and stood with hoofed feet splayed wide and her eyes flashing. All centaurs are battle-minded, but that was the first time I saw the warrior in Crinea. She lifted her chin high in the air, challenging me to question her decision, a slight tremor in her voice the only thing that gave away her awareness of just how much she was risking by attempting to carry this child.

I sprinted out to my truck, ignoring how running sent small slivers of pain slicing through my chest. I hefted my bags into the back and jammed the key in the ignition, not bothering with my seat belt. I stomped on the gas, sending gravel flying as I whipped out of my driveway. I didn't worry about speeding—there were few cops around here, and those that were in the area all knew me on sight. They knew I was a doctor, and if they saw me speeding, they assumed I had good reason.

I drove like I was on autopilot, knowing almost instinctively where to turn. In the years I had lived here, I had made a point of getting to know the area well. During those first months, before I had opened the clinic, I had spent every day I had off from the hospital wandering, letting myself get lost in the shadows of the back roads, testing to see how far they would take me. I used all that knowledge now, bumping my truck down roads that were little more than twin brown tracks, hurtling down gravel drives that wound along the edges of brown fields. I had no time to enjoy the pale blue shade of the sky, or pause to appreciate the coolness of the early autumn breeze. One of my patients was dying.

Finar had told me to come to a small, deeply shaded clearing that melted into the shadows of the Black Hills. The drive should have taken me thirty minutes, but I drove recklessly enough that when I spun into the clearing only twenty minutes had ticked by. I threw the door open and scrambled out before the truck had fully shuddered to a stop.

I turned my back on an empty clearing to retrieve my bags.

When I turned back around, a centaur stood not two feet from me, a spear in his hand, his lips pulled back from his teeth in a silent snarl.

I froze, my eyes taking in the creature that towered over me. I knew instantly who he was, though of course I had never seen him. The centaur chief was huge. My eyes were even roughly with his chest, just above the place where the chestnut brown fur that covered the horse portion of his body gave way to the leather-thick, brown skin that was his human half. He was old, older than any creature I had ever met before. I could see it in his eyes, though his not-quite-human face appeared not more than forty. His human half was still as a statue, the thick brown braids that fell down his back unmoving, but his horse half gave his true state of mind away: his hooves pawed the ground, as though preparing to charge.

It had not occurred to me, until that moment, that Finar might have called on my help without the approval of his chief. But I should have guessed. Centaurs are fiercely secretive, and they are fighters. Exposing themselves to an outsider, especially at a time of weakness, would be unthinkable to many. Add to that the hatred and distrust towards humans that many supernatural creatures carried with them always, and it made sense that the chief was angry. That he had come to greet me, though, and the fact that he had not struck already, suggested that he was willing to consider letting me see Crinea.

All this I saw in a single instant and then, deliberately, keeping every other part of my body utterly motionless, I turned my face aside.

I knew without a doubt that the chief was more than willing to kill me and that he was, in fact, very close to doing just that. Meeting his eyes was out of the question. It would have been a challenge, and he would have seen himself as perfectly justified in cutting me down right then. But dropping my eyes would have been equally disastrous—it would have been a submissive move, a confession of weakness. And someone weak could not be trusted with the secrets I was about to see. Looking to the side made me vulnerable; it gave him the opportunity to strike if he chose to. But it was also an expression of trust, making it clear that I did not expect him to hurt me, and that I had nothing to hide. Full minutes went by. Sweat trickled down the back of my neck. I was determined not to speak— I had to let him be in charge, and to tell me what he needed me to know before he would let me help his people. I did not blame him for his distrust. Crinea was weak and vulnerable, and with so few centaur babies surviving birth, the baby in her womb was inexpressibly precious not just to her and her husband, but to their people as a whole.

"So," he said in a deep baritone that would have been beautiful if it had not been soured by a sneer, "here stands the great doctor, come to rescue one of my own. The miracle maker, who says she can do what no one else can do, whose wisdom is so much greater than our own."

"I promised no miracles," I said, still keeping my face turned away.

"Didn't you?"

"No, sir." It bothered me that I did not know how to address him. Should I call him chief? Your Majesty? Great-big-horse-man-in-charge-of-all-things?

Sir seemed the safest bet.

"I told Crinea I would do all I can for her, and I will. I cannot promise it will be enough."

He took a step closer to me, and I could feel the suspicion rolling off him like heat, could smell the sweat that trickled down his chest. His voice lowered to a growl.

"Why are you really here, Doctor? Why have you come at the time of our weakness, to pry into our secrets?" His words grew faster as he spoke them; he was working himself up into a rage. "To see a people, once great, as it crumbles from within?"

"I came to help Crinea and Finar."

"Lies!"

"I am not lying." I fought to keep calm, though I could feel myself starting to tremble. If I lost control of my emotions, the whole situation could spiral downward very quickly. "I'm just trying to help."

"You are a spy."

I winced, old pain shooting through me. I tried to take a deep breath, but my chest felt tight and constricted.

"No, sir. You are mistaken."

"You have come to discover our hidden places, to bring proof of our existence to your tribe, so they might attack us now, when we can no longer fight nor flee!"

"I am not a spy, and I have no tribe. I am alone!" I cried, and God help me, I could not stop the raw desolation that crept into my voice as I said it. Beside me, the centaur's hooves stilled for the first time since I had seen him. "Please, just listen to me! I have no desire to know any of your secrets, or to share information about you with anyone else. I only want to help Crinea, who is currently *bleeding to death*. We don't have time for this." I risked a glance in his direction, but the snarl was gone.

He was listening.

I quickly turned my face away again.

"Listen, you don't have to trust me. Just let me go to her. When it's over, you can ask me all the questions you want, and if you don't like my answers, you can kill me. But let me do what can be done, before it is too late. Please," I added hastily, remembering that I was speaking to the chief.

He paused again, but this time the silence felt thoughtful.

"What is in the bags you carry?"

"Medical supplies," I answered.

"You brought so much?"

"I do not know what Crinea might need," I explained. "I brought as much as I could." And then, guessing what he might be wondering, I added, "I brought no cameras, nothing that could make a recording. I left my phone in the car. You can go through everything, if you want to."

Another pause.

"I will take you to her," he said at last, his words slow and formal. "But I take no responsibility for your well-being, and I cannot promise your safe return. Do you accept me as your escort on these terms?"

"I do. Thank you," I said, and my chest loosened enough for me to draw a full breath. I picked up my bags. "We need to hurry."

FOUR

I SOON REGRETTED TELLING THE CHIEF TO HURRY, AS I PELTED AFTER him through a maze of black-barked pines and rocky soil, gasping for breath. I tripped, over and over again, afraid to look down at the ground and pick my footing carefully for fear that he would disappear altogether out of view. Outside the woods the early afternoon sun shone, and the chill of the morning was giving way to the warmth of day. But gloom hung beneath the thick shade of the trees. I did not see the clearing until I stumbled into it, and the chief put his hand out in front of me to bring me to a halt. I hardly needed his warning, though. The sight I found brought every muscle in my body slamming to a stop.

I had never dreamed there could be so many.

I had known for a while that there was a herd hidden somewhere deep in the Black Hills. The first time a centaur had stumbled, scowling and red-faced, into my clinic, I had not really been surprised. Any time you have a large area with few people and large swaths of still-wild land, it is almost a given that a few centaurs will stake a claim and make their homes there. But I had never imagined the herd could be this huge. My eyes darted back and forth across the sea of tan and black and brown. There must have been two hundred, maybe three. They stood packed in together, forming a tight semi-circle around a long, narrow cabin that leaned against the rocky hillside. They all faced it, some with their eyes fastened on it intently, others with their eyes closed and their faces turned up toward the sky.

They all moved.

Like the surface of water disturbed by a storm, they rocked from side to side, waving their heads back and forth as though in slow, drawn-out denial. A sound rose up from them, a deep, rumbling noise, magnified as it rose from countless throats. They hummed, their wailing song a lament that held no melody or rhythm.

"My God," I whispered. "What's wrong with them?"

"They are in distress."

"This is because of Crinea?" I breathed, my eyes locked onto the sight, almost missing the chief's answering nod.

"She is ours to protect, and the child she carries—it too is ours, to keep safe from harm. And we are losing them, as we have lost so many." He growled, the noise a harsher, more savage echo of the humming song of worry his people sang. "We are warriors. If I could meet our enemy on the field of battle, I would rip it to shreds. But this is an enemy I cannot see, and my people are dying." He shook his head, and started to lead me through the crowd. "Come," he said. "It may already be too late."

When we entered the shelter, it was not the blood that shocked me. There was a lot of it, and I was painfully aware from the first moment that, other complications aside, the blood loss alone was enough to be life-threatening.

But it was the stillness that chilled me.

Finar stood several feet away from his wife, his face turned upward with eyes closed, as he rocked slowly from side to side. A female centaur, who I assumed was meant to be the attendant for the birth, knelt next to Crinea. But she was doing little more than stroking Crinea's hair and humming to her softly.

Crinea lay on a bed of straw at the far end of the shack, her legs writhing in slow, pained movements, as though trying to escape her fate. She was significantly smaller than her husband, and more slender than most centaurs, who tended to be thick and muscular. Her coloring was lighter than her husband's, too, the horse portion of her flank tan and golden, the thick braids that hung from her head chocolate brown. She saw me when I walked in and tried to speak, but no sounds came when her lips moved. Her pain had carried her, weak almost to the point of death, to a place without words.

The chief stood right beside me, but I had stopped worrying about him and his glowering disapproval the moment I stepped through the door.

I turned to the shell-shocked Finar, grabbed him by the shoulders, and shook him.

Hard.

At my side the chief's whole body went suddenly rigid and still. Clearly he didn't like my handling one of his people—but I didn't much care. He hadn't killed me yet; that told me how badly he wanted Crinea to live. I figured it was unlikely he'd kill me before I got a chance to try to save her. Finar blinked his eyes rapidly and focused in on me.

"A...Amy?" he stammered. "What...what are you doing?"

"Snap out of it." I took a step closer so I could glare up into his face. "You don't get to lose it yet. Your wife hasn't given up, Finar. Look at her. Look!"

His eyes dragged with a terrible reluctance to his wife, who lay covered in blood and kicking uselessly.

"She's moving," I said. "She's breathing. You had damn well better pull yourself together and go hold her hand. She needs you now, and you won't be able to live with yourself later if you make her go through this alone."

Finar, his eyes still cloudy, nodded and moved closer to his wife.

I turned to the centaur woman. "Who are you?"

"My name is Melia, Dr. Amy. I am the midwife of our tribe. I have done everything for Crinea that I know how, but you can see that her difficulties are far greater than my skill."

I went over and knelt by Crinea's side on the rough dirt floor, pushing the sweat-drenched hair back from her face with one hand as I took her pulse with the other.

"When did the contractions start?"

"Just before sunrise. The bleeding began almost immediately."

"How far apart are they?"

"Almost four minutes from one to the next."

"You've seen this before?" I took Crinea's hand in my own, turning it from side to side and peering at her nails.

"Yes. Many times. We tried to call you quickly."

"Her heart rate is elevated," I said. "And her breathing is labored. Her skin tone is off, too, and the skin on her face and hands is too pale. Crinea?" I called, putting a hand against her cheek and angling her head towards me. Her eyes were so dilated that I wasn't sure she could really see me at all. "Do you feel dizzy?"

She nodded.

"Okay. Hang on. We're all here, and we're going to take good care of you. Do you see Finar, Crinea? He's right here, beside you. Melia, I need my bags. They're by the door. Would you bring them to me, please? Chief?"

"Yes, *Doctor*?" he asked, his voice full of sarcasm so heavy that it was practically a threat. His eyebrows rose almost to his hairline, as he added, "Do you have an order for me, as well?"

"Could you, *please*, tell your people outside to stop making that horrible noise?"

"They are in distress."

"I understand. But the sound is so loud that it is making the walls of this place vibrate. I want her to hold on to hope. It is hard to convince her to do that when everyone outside is already singing a dirge. Could you just get them to do something different? Sing her a hopeful song maybe? Anything?"

The chief looked at me for a long minute, and this time I met his eyes. He was stronger than me, and more powerful. When all this was over, he might very well decide to kill me, and there was nothing I could do to stop it. But here, in this room, I was in charge.

"I will see what can be done."

"Thank you." I said, flashing a large, forced smile. I had learned long ago that snapping at the people around you during an emergency never made things better. Which is not to say that I always managed to remember that in the heat of the moment—just that I knew it was true.

Finar came up to the straw pallet and knelt on the other side of his wife. He held his hands up in the air, away from her, as though afraid that anything he did would make her pain worse.

"Good, Finar. Thank you," I said, pretending not to notice his distress. "I want you to hold her hands and talk to her, okay? I need to check something." I pulled a dropper and a small vial from my bag. "It should be fine," I muttered to myself, as I slid a syringe into Crinea's arm as gently as possible. "I took a sample just two weeks ago, and the results were normal." But it was with a sure sense of dread that I let the drop of Crinea's blood drip into the vial of liquid. "That's. Not. Possible," I cursed, watching the small drop of red as it dispersed into a thousand miniscule particles that floated to the top of the vial and danced on the liquid's surface. "That can't be right."

"What is it, Doctor?" Melia asked, but I just shook my head.

"Sorry, hold on." I grunted. "I must have done something wrong. Let me try it again." I pulled a second vial from my bag, and a fresh syringe. "Two weeks ago she was completely fine. There's no way…" But the second drop of red was just as traitorous as the first. The results were exactly the same.

Melia leaned close, gazing at vial. "You are testing her blood? For what?"

"For iron," I explained, setting the vial down on the ground and pressing my fingers against my temples. "You can become anemic during pregnancy. It's quite common. The baby needs iron for building its body, and it gets pulled from the mother's system as the baby's body develops. If there isn't enough even in the mother's system, sometimes there can be birth defects." I gestured towards the vial. "The drop of blood is supposed to float slowly to the surface. If it floats too fast, you know there isn't enough iron in the mother's blood. Severe cases of anemia can cause a woman to bleed to death during delivery. But this...this shouldn't be possible."

"What do you mean?" Finar looked back and forth between me and Melia. His eyes were red, his cheeks flushed and blotchy. "What's the matter with her blood?"

"It's like it's turned to water." I tried to keep my voice calm and factual, even as I gazed at the floor, at the bright red pools of blood gathering beneath her flanks that suddenly made sense. "Like all the iron was sucked out of it. Suddenly. I don't know how that could have happened. I've never seen anything like it."

"It's the baby." I couldn't help starting at the sound of Crinea's voice. I had thought her incapable of speech. Her voice, strained and a bit hoarse but still forceful, took me completely by surprise. "He's been changing," she said. "I could feel it. Growing...so much. It's made me too tired. He needed everything I had. More than I had. Is he alive, Doctor? Is my baby all right?"

"Let me check on him," I said. "Crinea, I just want you to stay calm, okay?"

But as I pulled out my stethoscope and leaned in close to Crinea's swollen belly, my own heart pounded wildly, and fear rushed like waves inside my ears. I wouldn't be able to save her. There was no way I could. Even if I had a whole hospital at my disposal, even if I had been able to set her up with a succession of blood transfusions, she was too far gone. With results like that, she should be dead already. She couldn't have more than a moment or two left. There was no time to do anything, and I couldn't think. I closed my eyes, hoping that it would seem that I was focusing, rather than trying to pull myself back from the edge of panic.

"Do you hear a heartbeat, Amy?"

"Yes, Crinea," I stammered, looking back into the deep brown eyes, suddenly clear, that stared at me. "The baby is definitely still alive. I can hear the heartbeat, and he's kicking. The movements aren't frantic, either, which is another good sign."

She nodded, as though I had merely confirmed something she had really known already.

"I don't have much time left. There's nothing you can do for me; you must know that already. But this baby is strong. He wants to live—and you can save him. You'll have to cut him out, though. I have no strength for pushing."

For a second I just stared at her. I had no idea what to say.

"No, Crinea," Finar said in an agonized whisper, clutching her hand as though, by squeezing tightly, he could hold the life inside her. "You must not give up!"

"I am not giving up, my love. I am fighting the battle that may yet be won. I am sorry, brother," Crinea said, turning her eyes to the chief. "I am leaving. I wasn't strong enough, after all."

"You have fought bravely." The chief's voice was thick, and love flashed in his eyes.

I gasped quietly as I suddenly understood. Of course! Crinea was his sister.

"It is we who have failed you. Go in peace, with your honor a cloak around your shoulders, and our love a shield upon your arm. Enter the land of our ancestors with pride."

"Tell our son..." Crinea's gaze moved back to Finar's face, and a slow tear leaked from her eye. "Tell him he was loved. Loved fiercely. Tell him that he will have a warrior's spirit at his right side every day of his life. My soul will be his guard."

"I will tell him."

Crinea's eyes widened, and her fingers tightened convulsively around Finar's.

"I can't see," she whispered, and for the first time I heard fear in her voice. "My sight is gone. Finar?"

"I am right here, my love. Right here, beside you!"

But her eyes rolled back in her head, and her body went limp.

"Is she dead?" Finar cried.

I leaned in, my fingers pressing her neck. "Her heart is still beating, but she won't feel anything now. And she won't wake up again."

"You must do it," the chief said, stepping closer. "You must do as she said. Quickly!"

With numb fingers I pulled my bags closer, and fumbled through them, finding what I needed. I had lost patients before. Their faces were part of the landscape of my dreams, the sobs of their loved ones a song that played, always, somewhere deep inside my heart. But it had been a long time. And Crinea was different.

"Wait a minute. Wait," I whispered.

My fingertips began to tingle. It was an old feeling, a beloved sensation, but still strange.

I had not felt it for so very long.

I looked down at my hands, flexing them. It had felt unthinkable just a few hours before. Now it felt as though I had always known that this would happen. Hadn't I said as much to Finar, days ago? Hadn't I promised him, more than once, that I would do *everything* I could?

"Why are you wasting time?" the chief roared, rage and grief making his whole body vibrate. "Save the child! If the baby dies, your life is forfeit!"

"One minute," I answered, his rage sliding off me as if it meant nothing. I didn't look up at him.

I knelt in the dirt next to Crinea's limp form, and laid my palm against her chest. With the pixie boy's cry still ringing in my ears, I knew exactly what this decision would cost me. And in that moment, I didn't care.

My eyes slid out of focus, and a shiver slithered up my spine. I could see it, on the edge of my field of vision; a minuscule dot of silver that shimmered and beckoned. It was always there. Waiting. It had been years since the last time I had laid claim to my birthright. I had tried hard to forget—but I hadn't. As I focused on the speck of silver, it grew, larger and larger, spreading until it was the only thing I could see. I closed my eyes, and reached out for the silver in my mind. Almost immediately, I could feel it running through me, like rain pouring down on the surface of a parched desert. A delicious coolness ran through me.

There had been times in the past few years when I had half wondered if I still remembered how to call to it, if perhaps, like an unused muscle, my ability to access the Source had atrophied, dried up and fallen away. But, with a sense of relief so profound that it bordered on pain, I felt it all come back. A surge of awareness flung itself at me, like a dog leaping up against a master who has been gone for far too long, and the lavender-rose-freshly-turned-dirt smell of magic.

I opened my eyes. I could *SEE*.

I half-laughed as I looked around the room. I had forgotten how right, how truly beautiful it was. Nothing had changed, but everything was different. Finar and the chief and everyone around me were edged in glinting light.

I swiveled my head around and looked, really looked, at Crinea. With my Truthsight I could see that sores covered her arms, her legs, and her face. Each a great, gaping, silver hole, some larger than my palm and some no bigger than a nickel, every one of them lined in angry, painful red. They dripped molten metal rather than puss, and her flesh steamed and burned as the drops of silver ran down and down, until they seeped into her belly. Her chest fluttered fitfully, and I could see right through the tortured skin on her chest to her barely beating heart. I had almost no time. If her heart stopped and her soul left, then there would be truly nothing I could do.

I reached down and slowly, reverentially, stroked the ground, summoning what I needed from deep within it. It wasn't hard. The earth is full of iron, and it rushed up to me when I beckoned, coating my fingertips, bubbling to the surface until I had to reach down and cup my hands, bringing them up, brimming and full, to smooth the silver, molten substance over Crinea. I worked swiftly, and messily, splashing the stuff on her as quickly as I could, watching without breathing until one of the smaller holes was filled. As soon as the silver reached the top, the sore closed and puckered, and wretched skin grew, stretching thinly over the breach.

It wasn't pretty, but it was working.

I picked up speed, working frantically to close the sores and restore her strength. I wasn't sure how much time was passing, and I could hear, like rain on the rooftop, a distant patter of words falling all around me. Some were angry, some pleading; I couldn't make out more than that. But no one touched me, or disturbed my work. Whatever it appeared to them that I was doing, they seemed at least to believe that I was helping. As I worked, more metal splashed onto Crinea's belly, and the form curled within her grew fuller, and then developed a shining outline of its own. I looked down and saw him, the not-so-tiny baby, the outlines of his body snapping in and out of focus. I caught my breath, amazed, and stared for a moment, as his forms took shape and solidified, first one and then the other. He was a marvel. Something new—a true miracle. No wonder he had drained his mother dry, when he was building up a little body so complex. But as I watched, I saw his form set.

"Are you ready, little one?" I whispered, and on that plane, where he and I could see each other truly, I saw him nod.

"Melia?" I managed to call out in a real voice, a voice the others could hear. "Be ready!"

I pushed gently down on Crinea's abdomen, imagining myself creating a wave inside her body. The baby rocked up and forward. I could see his small arms reaching out, could see four tiny legs kicking as the crest of a small silver wave lifted him up and carried him towards life. Melia cried out as his head pushed out into the open. I pushed down again, and the next moment he was safe in Melia's hands. Through the haze a weak, neighing cry told me he was awake, and breathing. But I could not turn. The child was whole and healthy, but Crinea still barely hung on. The holes in her skin had filled, but the skin that covered them was paper-thin, and weak.

I knelt beside Crinea and slowly ran one finger down the length of her arm. I could feel the cells of her skin like tiny, individual beads beneath my touch. I felt where the fabric of her flesh was rent, and slowly, carefully, I began to mend it. This was where my skill truly lay, my great gift that I had missed so much.

My fingers traveled down the length of her body and back, and every second that I touched her I came to know her better, came to see her more clearly, inside and out. I felt the fracture in her right leg, a bad wound from long ago that still pained her now and then. I knew her unpredictable temper, her propensity for going into rages, and her fear of closed spaces and of being left alone. I knew her love for Finar and for her people, which I saw as a smooth, shining rock, nestled in a crown atop her head.

Then the truer, Truthsight version of Crinea sat up, and looked at me.

Her Truthsight self was beautiful, but also frightening. I had always known she was a warrior, but the version of her face I saw now was drawn in lines hard and savage, with eyes all black and staring straight at me. The cloak of honor she wore was thickly made of animal skins, and hung heavy on her shoulders. A deep, puckered scar, that was not visible in reality, ran from her right shoulder all the way to the center of her chest. Tight-fitting bracelets ringed her arms, covering her like armor. She looked all around her, as though she did not know where she was. I wondered what she saw, what the Truthsight would show her. Her hand reached for the knife at her belt.

"What is happening?"

"You are safe, Crinea. I am healing you, and am nearly done. You will survive this."

Crinea nodded, slowly, but her eyes darted around the room as though searching for enemies, and her grip on her knife did not relax.

"What is this place?"

"We are still in the shed," I explained to her, though my lips did not move and no one else could hear me. "But you are seeing it, and me, truly now. It is called Truthsight. Everyone who uses Truthsight sees something different—something that is unique to them. But whatever you see is the truth. You have access to it now because, while I heal you, we are linked. I had to tap into the Source to save you."

"Is that you, Amy?" she asked, looking at me strangely, and my heart sank. I could see others in Truthsight, but not myself. And apparently my true self bore so little resemblance to the woman I was trying to be that I could not even be recognized.

"Yes, it's me."

I didn't want to know, and yet, somehow, I could not help but ask.

"What do you see?"

Crinea leaned closer to me, tilting her head to the side as she studied me.

"I see a tree beside a river. I see a silver fish, nestled high up in the branches of the tree."

I snorted. Who would have thought that the Truthsight of a warrior centaur would be so poetic?

"Why aren't you in the water, Amy?" Crinea leaned in towards me and, linked with her as I was, I could feel worry fluttering inside her. Me. Us.

"The river is your home. There." She pointed over my shoulder to a place behind me, and I stiffened. I knew what she was seeing. Every part of me wanted to turn and look.

But I could not.

Crinea went on. "You should be there. I can sense that. It is silver, just as you are. Fish die in open air."

"I can't." The words choked out. I couldn't lie to her. Not here, in this place.

And then, because I was weak, because I couldn't help it, because I missed it so very much, I turned to look at the river. It was just as I remembered it. Whatever had changed in me over the years, my Truthsight still saw the Source in exactly the same way. The silver water rushed along, the surface smooth and shining, the sound as it bubbled over the rocks more beautiful than any other sound I could imagine. A moan of regret and bitter longing escaped my lips. Crinea had been right. I was so thirsty for home.

"You have to go back, Amy," Crinea urged me, but I only shook my head, my eyes still fastened on the water.

"But you'll die!"

"I know. I should die. And I will. But not because of that."

Crinea ground her teeth in frustration.

"But why not? Why can't you?"

"Because of them," I whispered, and gestured at the forms I had known would come. Their heads pushed up out of the water, their faces taking form through the molten silver. One after the other, like seals poking up out of the stream, they came to the surface, and stared at me.

"They want to kill me," I whispered to Crinea as they lifted dripping hands from the water, their fingers all pointing at me.

"Traitor!" one of them cried, and then the rest joined in, their words growing into thunder, rumbling like an earthquake beneath my feet.

"Traitor!" they all cried at once, in a hundred different, triumphant voices. "We see you."

FIVE

WHEN THEY MANAGED TO WAKE ME, I SHOOK SO HARD MY TEETH rattled and tears I didn't remember crying ran down my face. I lay curled into a ball against the far wall of the shed, my breath coming hard and fast, with the chief and Melia on either side of me. I must have been talking while unconscious, and as I opened my eyes, the words kept coming.

"I'm sorry...sorry, sorry, sorry."

"Calm yourself," the chief said, leaning his face in close to mine. In some back part of my brain, it registered that the centaur chief was kneeling in the dirt, with his arm supporting me. "You are safe. You have done us a great service—we will not allow you to come to harm!"

But his words brought a moan, unbidden, to my lips, and I pushed away the hands that I knew could not really help me. I tucked my head in against my chest and wrapped my hands around my knees.

"Amy?"

There were not many voices that could have broken through the hysteria of that moment, but Crinea's voice, and her hand on my shoulder, were enough to bring me to my senses. I turned in amazement, to see her standing on wobbly legs beside me.

"What are you doing, walking around?" I gasped, pushing myself up to sitting, and wiping the moisture from my cheeks. "Go lie back down, before you hurt yourself!"

She knelt on the ground beside me, and hugged me. I couldn't help it—I hid my face in her shoulder and sobbed. Crinea remained stoic and dry-eyed, too much of a warrior for weeping, but her arms around my shoulders were tight.

"Thank you," she said, when my cries had quieted and we had pulled apart enough to look at each other. "I do not know what you did, but I know it has cost you dearly. You have given me the whole world, twice over, today." Her eyes flicked to the small form Finar crooned over a few feet away.

"Crinea," I asked. "Are your eyes still clear with Truthsight?"

"It is fading," she said, touching her temple gingerly, "but not gone."

"Then go look at your baby," I said, pushing her towards him. "Go and really look."

Crinea gave me an uncertain glance, but I had earned her trust enough that she did not ask any questions before going to stand next to her baby. I leaned back, limp against the wooden wall, unmoving, and willed my heartbeat to slow. A moment later I heard Crinea gasp softly, and then she turned to me.

"But what does it mean?" she asked.

"It means he is a miracle, Crinea. There was a reason he needed so much from you. Your chief thought your people were dying out. He was wrong." Even with everything I knew was coming for me, I couldn't help but smile as I spoke. "Your people are evolving. Your little one is something new. The first step. A centaur who can change his shape at will—who can choose to walk on two legs instead of four. I don't know how his gift will work exactly, or what its limitations will be. But I know it will change everything. It will be a hard road, and he will need his mother. I'm glad he will have you by his side."

"Stay with us," Crinea said suddenly. "We owe you, and we need you. Stay with us, and let us keep you safe from whatever makes you so afraid. Amy…" and then she paused, a puzzled look on her face, and I realized the Truthsight was still strong enough in her for that name to taste wrong on her lips.

"Crinea," I said hurriedly, scrambling to my feet. "You don't owe me anything for what I have done today. I couldn't have done any less. But what you have seen…"

She nodded, understanding what I feared. "Your secrets are your own. Amy." She said the name with effort. "I will not take them from you. But there must be something we can do to help."

"No one can help me," I said, brushing dirt off my hands. "And I can't stay here. I have to go."

Crinea wrapped her arms around my neck in a quick, tight hug. "Thank you, Amy," she said. "We will bring the baby to see you at the clinic in a week or two, so you can see how he is faring."

I hesitated, wondering how much I should say. "Okay," I answered. "Bring him. And Crinea?"

"Yes?"

"You should trust Jason. He's a good doctor, too. He'll take good care of your boy."

Crinea's face hardened. "I don't want Dr. Jason. I want you."

I squeezed her arm and turned away without answering. Everyone fell silent as I gathered up my things, Melia hurrying to help me.

"Can someone lead me back to my truck?" I asked when I was ready, hoping my voice didn't sound as shaky as I felt. I adjusted the strap of my bag on my shoulder. "I'm not sure I remember the way."

"I will take you," the chief said, striding over to the door and holding it open for me.

I looked back for a moment, to where Finar and Crinea crouched beside their little one, making encouraging noises as he tried to rise for the first time onto his new, wobbly legs. Crinea's face, still a bit pale, was lit up and smiling. Finar's eyes kept going back and forth between his new child and his wife, a look of dazed happiness on his face.

They were worth it. Whatever the cost, whatever comes next, I will remember how they look right now. And I will not regret.

I walked outside and stopped in amazement. All the other centaurs were gone. The entire crowd had disappeared and, if not for the hoofprints that covered the packed dirt of the clearing, I would have doubted my own memory of the horde that had been gathered here.

"They left as soon as Crinea and the baby were out of danger," the chief said, answering my unspoken question. "Everyone is preparing and tonight there will be a great feast in celebration of what has happened. You could stay." He took a step closer, his eyes searching mine. "As my guest, and under my protection. We would honor you for what you have done, if you would let us."

I shook my head. "I have to go," I whispered, and saw the confusion in the chief's eyes as he turned and led me back into the woods. We walked in silence until we reached my truck. I was throwing my bags into the back when he broke the silence.

"You have your own affairs, and I respect that. I will not try to force you to speak when you choose to keep your silence. But we are in your debt now, for the service you have done us. You must give us some way to pay you back."

Of course. I rubbed my eyes hard, kicking myself mentally for forgetting this part. "Yes," I said, looking up at the chief steadily, so he could see that I understood. "There will be a way for you to pay me back. I just need a little time to think. I'm sorry. It is just that I am very tired now. But we will work it out. Okay?"

The chief nodded slowly, his hoof pawing the ground. I smiled at him as steadily as I could manage, then climbed up into my truck and pulled carefully back onto the road. When I looked back in my rear-view mirror, I could see him still standing there, watching as I drove away.

I drove for only a few miles before I found a quiet spot to pull over. I rolled down all the windows so the fresh air could find me, and tried to force the chaos in my mind to settle into meaningful thoughts.

I could run. I had done it before.

I could pull back out onto the road, and drive like the Devil was behind me, which was more or less the truth. Grenalda's son had said they were coming—not that I had to be here when they arrived. I could throw myself back out into the wind, and hope I could find another place to squirrel myself away where they wouldn't find me, at least not for a while. But if I ran, the Clan mages would follow my trail, which would lead them straight to the clinic. Straight to Jason. *Three days more and they're at the door,* the child had said. I shuddered. I knew exactly what they would do to everything and everyone they found behind that door, if they didn't find me.

They would destroy it. And it was perfectly possible that they would hurt or kill anyone who happened to be there. A sob bubbled up from my chest, but I clamped my teeth together and refused to let it out.

There was nothing else to think about really. I couldn't run—not this time. And simply waiting around until they came to find me wouldn't be enough. I would have to go out and meet them. Once they had me, they'd have no reason to track down where I had been living. The clinic, and Jason, would be safe.

I had known, deep down, that it would come to this eventually. At least now the guilt, the waiting, and the constant fear would end.

The only real question I had to answer was how much time I had. I looked at the clock radio on the dashboard. It was four in the afternoon. My best guess was that it had been three hours since I tapped into the Source. How long would it take the mages to find me?

Grenalda's son had said three days, but I couldn't rely on that too heavily. I had to be sure. I leaned my head back and closed my eyes, trying to calculate objectively. They had seen me clearly, but it would still take them time. They would have to make a portal. It wasn't simple magic, and it wasn't something everyone could do. It took hours, sometimes days. And when they did come, it wouldn't be just one or two; they would form a hunting party. Getting that many people together took time. I sucked in a long, hard breath between my teeth, ignoring the way it made my chest throb. It would probably take them two days, but I couldn't afford to wait too long. I stared at the clock radio. Twelve hours then. I would give myself twelve hours to go home, to put everything in order.

And there was one thing I had to do before anything else.

I threw open the car door and stepped out onto the grass. The Truthsight was still with me, and though it was fading rapidly, what I needed it for now wouldn't take much. Still, I had to hurry. Once it was gone completely, I could not afford to tap into the Source a second time. I pulled out the emergency kit I carried in the back of my truck, tossing aside the flashlights and flares, the first aid supplies and bottled water, until I came to what I wanted. The thermal emergency blanket was covered in shiny, silver material, meant to use the sun to help you keep warm if you were stranded outside in the middle of a South Dakota winter. I spread the blanket out on the ground and knelt down beside it. It was a far cry from the silver bowls or crystal balls traditional for scrying. But it would be good enough.

Eventually, I knew, emotion would come. I would feel fear, and grief for all that I was losing. But now I just felt numb. I reached down and touched the blanket's silver surface, pulling the remnants of the Truthsight's clarity to the forefront of my mind.

The silver swirled under my fingers. "Meri?" I whispered, "Can you hear me? Please. I need to speak to you."

I waited, my heart pounding, fear and hope warring in my chest. I missed her so much, but as much as I longed to see her face, I dreaded it, too. What if she was sick, and wasting away? What if the eyes that used to fill with love as she tucked me in at night looked out at me now with hatred and resentment? As the moments stretched on, my breath came in short, shallow gasps. I had only tried to scry for Meri a few times since everything had gone to hell. Each time, I had gotten through to her for only a moment. And the last time I had managed to hear her voice she had been barely coherent.

The silver began to change color, dulling to a muted, dirty gray. Then it turned to black.

"Meri?" I called again, leaning my face close, squinting into the dark. "Are you there?" But there was nothing. No familiar face gazed back up at me.

Then a small voice floated up from the darkness.

"Asa?"

"Yes, it's me."

She didn't answer.

"I'm right here!" I called desperately. "Please Meri, talk to me!"

"Asa." Her voice floated back to me, "I miss you."

I didn't deserve that. "I miss you, too," I whispered. "So much. Are you all right?" I swallowed hard, dreading the answer to the question I could not help but ask. "What are the rebels doing to you?"

"Hurts," she whispered. "Dark here. Always."

My vision clouded with tears. "It's my fault," I gasped, closing my eyes and covering my face as the wave of guilt swept through me. "My fault you were weakened—my fault you were captured. After all you did for me—all the years that you were all I had. I'm so, so sorry Meri."

"Don't cry, sweet one," she whispered back. "I could never be angry with you."

"You ought to be," I whispered.

"No." Her voice grew a little stronger. "You are my daughter Asa, in everything but blood. Nothing can change that."

"Do you know where they are holding you? Can you tell me what you see? Or a face, a name? Anything?"

There was a long pause, and when her voice floated back to me, weaker than before, she whispered, "Dark here."

I fought down another sob.

In all the years she had been held against her will, this was still all she could tell me, the only thing she knew about the prison that had somehow held the most powerful mage in history in its grasp for so long. For a moment an image of her swam up to the front of my mind; a small sprite of a woman with a lean, flat frame, a smoothness to her features that had more than once led those around her to mistake her for a teenager. But the silver eyes that gazed out from underneath her thick brown hair held an ancient power inside, and once Meri truly looked at you, her face expressionless as you felt her power diving inside of you and dredging all your worst secrets up for her to see, you could never mistake her again for anything but what she was, a mage of great power.

Most people only knew that side of her. But I knew what her silver eyes looked like when they lit up with laughter. I knew that the power she projected was partly a shield, meant to keep the others from guessing at her weakness.

"Meri," I said, speaking slowly, hoping she could understand me through all her disorientation and pain. "Something has happened."

"Is the Pearl still safe?" Her voice quivered with fear.

"Yes!" I answered eagerly, clinging to the little bit of comfort I could give her. "I have the Pearl. It is still hidden." My fingers pressed hard against my chest, and for once I was glad of the burn there. I took a deep breath, forcing myself to say the words I knew would upset her. "But soon the Pearl will come back to you."

"Asa, what are you talking about? You can't remove the Pearl yourself. It will kill you!"

"I know; it isn't that. I had to use my Truthsight, Meri. I couldn't help it."

A pause stretched out.

"Run." She sounded calm, but I could hear the fear beneath her words. "Right now. You shouldn't have taken the time to contact me. You have to go, Asa! This instant!"

"I can't." I closed my eyes, knowing my words were causing her even more pain, wishing I could think of any way to stop it. "Not this time, Meri. I'm so, so sorry. But they are coming, so I wanted to say...goodbye."

"Don't talk to me like that, Asa." Her voice had taken on the tone of command I remembered so well. But she knew as well as I did that it had never worked on me.

"I want you to know that I'm sorry for what I did. More sorry than I can ever say. When I die the Pearl will come back to you."

"Stop!" she cried. "We're going to talk about this. We're going to figure something out."

"It's your chance." I went on, "once you have the Pearl back, you'll be stronger. You can break free."

"Asa, listen. Please just listen to me. I will get stronger—strong enough to escape. Then I'll be able to protect you from them. You just have to stay alive till then. You just have to hide."

"I can't." I swallowed hard. Nothing I could say would make her understand, and I couldn't ease her pain. "Not this time. I'm sorry, Meri. And I love you. Goodbye."

"No, Asa! Wait. You have to..."

I stood up and pushed the blanket with my foot. The black solidified, then cracked like ice. A second later, only a reflective blanket lay on the grass.

No tears came as I stood there. I felt like I was filled with ice, frozen on the inside, with nothing but shock and numbness in my heart. I stumbled back to my car and fumbled around in the glove compartment until I found my cell phone.

"I need to see you," I texted to Jason. "Right away. Come to my place as soon as you can. Please."

I meant to drive quickly, but I couldn't quite manage it. I kept looking at the fields as I drove past, breathing in the air that streamed through the open windows. It was all so beautiful, and I had been a part of it. For years, this had been my place, as close to a home as a person like me could come.

A few miles from the house I stopped into the one and only Italian restaurant in well over one hundred miles. When I pulled away, the seat beside me was lost beneath a tower of tinfoil pans, and the whole truck smelled of garlic and melted cheese.

Jason's truck was parked in front of my front door when I pulled into my driveway.

Sitting on his open tailgate, with his legs dangling and his baseball cap pulled low over his eyes, Jason looked handsome and carefree. A day ago I would have rejoiced to see him so healthy and strong. Now I felt a strange sense of loss.

His head snapped up as I pulled in, and he jumped down from his truck and hurried over to me. For a second I imagined how good it would feel to rest my head on his chest, to tell him the truth, and everything that had happened. To let him wrap his arms around me and tell me that everything would be okay.

But that would be a lie. And telling Jason the truth would do nothing but put him in danger. The warmth of his arms around me was not a comfort I could allow myself to take.

"Are you all right?" he asked, squinting in the sun's glare. "I got your message and I was worried and..." His words trailed off as he got a good look at the expression on my face. "Damn." He whistled slowly. "What happened?"

"Listen, Jason," I said, my voice breaking a little. "I have this list in my head, of all the things I want to do before tomorrow morning. In a little bit, we'll talk. There are some things I need to tell you. But first, I really, really just want to sit with you, and eat something. Maybe chat about things that don't matter much at all. Just for a little while." I glanced at my watch, clearing my throat to hide the catch in my voice. "Give me one hour, okay? Just one hour of stuffing our faces and enjoying ourselves. Then we can talk about the hard stuff."

One hour, I told myself. One hour before the way he looks at me changes forever. One hour in which I can pretend that I have a future. That *we* might have a future. One hour when I can pretend we don't have to say goodbye.

Jason's eyes softened, and I knew he had seen more than I had wanted him to. "All right, Amy," he said softly. "We'll do whatever you want."

"Good. Then come sit at my kitchen table, and help me eat some of this food. I bought enough for about twenty people, so I hope you still like Italian."

Jason stood up, following me as I walked around to the other side of my truck.

"What about the clinic?"

"We're closed tonight."

"Closed?"

"Yup. I spent all day delivering a centaur baby. I'm dead on my feet and in a foul, foul mood. If I try to treat another patient tonight, I'm not sure either of us will survive." I shoved several pans into Jason's arms, picked up the rest of them, and shut the truck door with my hip.

"You're kidding—it came so soon? How are Crinea and the baby?"

"They're both fine." I turned and trudged toward the porch, Jason following close behind me.

"That's amazing, Amy! I can't believe it. What happened?"

"Lots of interesting things that I don't want to talk about now." I set the pans down on the counter and began to pull plates out of the cupboard. "Can you grab some forks? For once, I have a decent appetite, and all I want to do is sit with you and eat."

Smiling, Jason turned and pulled open one of the cupboards. "Sounds like a plan. And we'll open a bottle of wine, too. You kinda look like you could use a drink, and I sure wouldn't mind one."

An hour later, I had eaten a few bites of everything, and Jason had polished off almost an entire pan of lasagna. I couldn't eat as much as I wanted; my body just wouldn't let me. But every bite I managed tasted like heaven. When I couldn't force down another forkful, I poured myself half a glass of wine, watching as Jason drained his fourth. We ate and drank and laughed, telling each other stories we both already knew about crazy things that had happened in the clinic. Pip lay curled up by my feet, patiently waiting for the moment when one of us would drop some food on the floor, or leave a plate unattended long enough for him to help himself.

"Okay," Jason said after he had set down his fork and leaned back with a contented groan. "I can't help it, Amy. There's something I just gotta ask you."

"All right," I said, suddenly nervous. "Shoot."

"I know you." Jason's smile was lopsided, and he waved a finger in my direction. "I see your face when you're in the clinic, working. It's like you're all lit up inside. You love it. Hell, you've worked yourself half to death doin' it, building the whole damn place by yourself and working night and day."

"Yes. Okay. What's the question?"

"So how come you make them pay?" Jason's brow furrowed. "I've never understood it. You build this place—you run yourself ragged running it, then you turn around and make 'em pay through the nose—even for the work *I* do, and you know I don't care about that stuff. Those stones you make 'em bring you." He motioned to the necklace around my neck. "It isn't like they're easy for these creatures to come by. I don't get it."

I stared down at the wine in my glass, swirling it slowly around.

"I've never told you about the first patient I had here, have I?"

Jason shook his head. "Nope. Not that I remember."

"He's what got the clinic started. When I first moved to the area, I really wanted to learn my way around. I went on a lot of long drives, and longer hikes." There was no reason to mention that I had wanted to find a few good hiding places, or to figure out how I could disappear, if necessary, quickly and on foot. "One day I was out hiking, and I saw something." I hesitated, trying to think of a way to talk about what had happened that wouldn't give any of my secrets away.

"What?"

"It's hard to describe," I said. "It was almost like a rippling in the air. A disturbance, kind of like the way the air shimmers when it gets super, super hot—but it was cool out, and early morning. I went to take a closer look, and I saw there was something hidden, just under the surface of the soil. I dug down just a little...and I found him. He wasn't far from the surface—he hid when he got too sick to move. The disturbance in the air was his distress signal. He hoped one of his people would find him before it was too late."

I shrugged. "Instead I did. He was a gnome—old, but with good years left. I brought him back here, to do the best I could for him. We were never quite able to figure out what was wrong—my best guess was he'd eaten something contaminated by pesticide. Usually they're able to tell, and stay away from that stuff, but sometimes it still happens. Anyway, it was one of the most difficult cases I've ever had. I spent three weeks nursing him back to health. I was damn proud when I'd done it, too." I took a large sip of my wine. "He got better. Then he stayed."

"Stayed? Where?"

"Here. In the barn, in the house. I couldn't get rid of him. He was always hanging around. I figured maybe he was lonely, or maybe he was just still a little weak and he felt safe here. I didn't mind. I figured he'd leave when he was ready. He kept offering to do stuff around the house; mend things, build things—all kinds of stuff. 'Oh no!' I'd always say, 'Don't worry about it! I'm so happy I was able to help!' After a while I noticed he seemed weaker, listless." I brought the wine glass to my lips, and drained it. "Then he died."

"Died?" Jason cried. "What killed him?"

"I did." I set my glass down and rubbed my eyes. "I didn't understand until it was too late. I had no idea, and he didn't have the words to tell me. You have to understand, Jason. Some of these creatures need freedom like you and I need oxygen. Some of this you know already. If you took a pixie, and locked her in a cage overnight, what would you have in the morning?"

"Dust," Jason said, any trace of lightheartedness gone from his face.

"Right. There are reasons humans still don't know about most of these creatures. You can't catch them, can't hold them. They just disintegrate. They are fundamentally fragile in a way that's hard for us to really understand. And so I, even knowing what I did, never imagined that to that gnome, debt was a kind of confinement. A kind of servitude. And these creatures can't live in servitude, Jason. They are simply unable to survive. That gnome didn't want to stay here, but he couldn't go home—not until he felt his debt was paid— a debt I kept trying to tell him he didn't owe. I killed him, or at least my ignorance did. After all those long nights spent sitting beside him, after all that care."

I cleared my throat and pushed a curl that had come loose back under my bandanna. "Anyway, that's the reason I charge them. Because it's the only way to keep them alive."

"Well, shit," Jason exclaimed. "I had no idea, Amy."

"That's my fault, too. I should have explained it you—there just has been so much to talk about, and somehow that never seemed to be the most pressing thing. But it was stupid of me to leave things out, to not give you all the information you would need. And it's important you understand all this now."

"What do you mean?"

"It has to be something real, of true value." I leaned forward, anxious to be sure what I was saying was clear. "It can't just be a symbolic payment. It has to be an item, or a service, that seems to them to be of equal worth to the service you gave them."

"Okay. Sure, I understand. But you didn't answer my question." Jason tilted his head back and stuck his thumbs through his belt loops. "What do you mean it is important for me to understand all this *now*? What aren't you telling me, Amy?"

I looked down at my watch. My hour was up. It was time for the hard part.

Slowly, I reached down into my pocket and pulled out my house keys. I lay them down on the table and pushed them over to Jason. He gave me a blank look.

"For you," I explained. "This is a beautiful house, and it deserves to have somebody living in it. I was hoping you might be willing to keep an eye on Pip, too."

"Okay," Jason said slowly, his brow furrowed as he tried to understand. "When will you be back?"

I shook my head slowly. "I won't be," I said. "Not ever."

Jason leaned forward in a sudden, almost violent motion, banging his elbows against the table and leaning his face into mine.

"Jesus, Amy," he said, and I fought not to flinch away from the sudden anger in his eyes. "What the *fuck* is going on?"

"I can't tell you that."

"That's a bullshit answer, and you know it." His face flushed, and he tapped the table top between us. "We've been through too much together for you to brush me off like that. How long have I been helping you out in the night clinic? It wasn't long after we started working together in the ER that you recruited me, right?"

I sighed. "A month, maybe two. Just until I realized there was something different about you." At first he had just been another medical student I had to trip over and try very hard not to snap at. Then one day I saw him standing in the hallway, reading a medical chart with his head lowered, his face drawn and intense. And his irises had widened till there was no white left in his eyes, the blueness of them shining so much that they glowed.

"Which makes it two years I've been hauling my ass out here, staying up all hours, and working with you side by side." He turned his face away and swallowed hard. "You were the one who broke it to me that the reason I felt so sick all the time, the reason I had always felt different, was that I wasn't all human. And you were kind about it, gentle. You didn't give up on me, not even when nothing seemed to make sense, and we couldn't figure out what I was or how to make anything better. You stuck with it, Amy, even when I was ready to give up. And I feel better now than I ever have in my whole life. That's because of you. So don't you look at me and tell me you're walking off and disappearing without an explanation, and it's none of my business what's got the strongest woman I've ever met turnin' tail and running out the back door like some thief in the night."

"I'm not running." I stood up and walked to the other side of the kitchen. I needed a little space from Jason's anger—if I wasn't careful, I'd get angry too, and then we'd both say things we'd regret. "Running's what I've been doing for a long time, Jason. And I'm sick to death of it. I'm done. Now I'm going to do what I have to do, what I probably should have done a long time ago."

"All right, fine." Jason opened his hands on the table top, reaching out. "So tell me about it. Let me help you."

I stared at the floor as I answered. "There is only one way you can help me. Stay. Keep the clinic going when I'm gone."

"Goddamn it, Amy! That's not what I meant and you know it!"

"I know, but just listen to me. This clinic is the only thing in my whole life that I'm proud of. You've known me for only a few years. There are things—other things—that are a part of my story. Things I'm not proud of, that keep me up at night. I've always known that stuff would catch up with me sooner or later." I took a deep, shaky breath. "And that's what's happening now. And I can handle it—I really can. I just need to know the clinic will survive, that it will still be here. I need to know that all that work meant something, that the patients who have come to count on me will still be able to get help when they need it. I'm being honest with you, Jason, as much as I can be. I know you want to help."

I crossed the kitchen in two long strides, and took his open hands in mine. "This will help me. It would mean more to me than words can say. Please. Do this for me."

He dropped his head to his chest, and his fingers tightened around mine. For long moments no one spoke.

"All right," he said at last, and when he looked up at me, his eyes were moist. "Fine. I give up." He wiped his eyes with the back of his hand. "In the end, I don't think I'm so different from the pixies and all the rest of 'em. I owe you, and I know it. If me running the clinic is what you want, then I'll do it."

"I'm still pissed with you," he added. "Don't think that I'm not. But I'll keep the clinic going. For you." He glared at me. "I'll collect the stones they owe for the care I give 'em. And I'll save every single one of them for you. For when you come back."

"Thank you," I whispered, knowing the words were not enough. "I can't say how much that means to me."

"You are a stubborn and difficult woman," Jason said, reaching down to scratch Pip's ear. "You're just lucky I like the dog."

SIX

HE LEFT NOT LONG AFTER THAT. I WAS THANKFUL FOR THE exhaustion that crept over me as I climbed up the stairs, grateful for the sleep that swept over me as soon as I lay down, despite the aching in my chest. But I still woke long before the sun rose, and lay motionless. Thinking. When I was sure I had it figured out, I crawled out from under the covers and called Finar. The sunlight had just begun to creep through my curtains, but he answered on the second ring.

It took a while, especially since the chief refused to get on the phone, forcing Finar to act as a go-between. But eventually we worked it out.

"A guard," I explained to Finar. "That's how you can pay the debt. At night, when the clinic is open, to protect the patients, and the doctor, from anything that might try to hurt them while they're being treated. Just for a few months."

Though the chief wasn't actually on the phone, the boom of his voice carried, and I could hear his approval in his tone. This was something that made sense to him, a service they could do that would not be an insult or a burden.

"Agreed," the chief said. "Two guards every night."

"You really only need to send one," I protested. "Just for a little while."

"*Two* guards, every night," the chief insisted, talking a little louder when Finar tried to break in, "For as long as the boy lives."

For a moment I was speechless. Centaurs lived a long time, sometimes for centuries. The chief promised too much.

"You don't have to do that!" I protested, raising my voice so the chief could hear me directly. I had the impression that Finar had given up trying to repeat things, and was simply holding the phone up in the air. "That is too much. Just a few months, six at the most..."

"Do not argue with me, human!" the chief roared. "Do you think I do not know my duty? That I am not capable of paying back this debt?"

"All right!" I cried, throwing my hands up in the air and ignoring a sudden stinging in my eyes. "All right. Fine. Thank you."

I hung up, pulled on a pair of jeans, and my favorite blue sweater. I tied my bandanna back around my hair. I walked down the stairs slowly, and went and stood in the kitchen, leaning heavily against the counter as I looked around.

I loved this house so very much. Deep down, I had always known I wouldn't get to keep it.

The kitchen smelled of lemonade, and the raspberry tea I always made for myself before work in the morning. It was small, but clean and bright, the ancient iron stove gleaming black, a battered copper kettle polished and hanging on a hook above the range. A braided blue and red rug lay under the round, unvarnished kitchen table. Red and white checkered curtains hung on the window, and a line of houseplants stood in lush green procession on the sill. I took a deep breath, letting the quiet of the house sink into my bones one last time.

I'd never met the elderly widow who owned the house before me, but in the years I had lived here, I'd come to feel as though I had. She had been too old and too weak to keep up the fields that were attached to her house, and she had sold most of them off soon after her husband died, living off the money from the sale and keeping only the house, the old barn, and a few of the acres that circled the house. They had no children, and when she died the house was considered almost worthless. An old farm house and barn with no farmland attached to it, out in the middle of absolutely nowhere, with no central air, no modern appliances, not so much as a phone line to make it marketable.

It had been perfect for me.

I loved the house from the first moment I saw it, and soon after I moved in I could tell how much she had loved it, too. Everything had been cared for meticulously, no screen left unmended, no paint chipped. Instructions, written in pencil by a careful, deliberate hand, were posted on the wall in the basement, outlining what to do when the old furnace went out.

I changed almost nothing in the house. In many ways, I had always thought of it as still being hers. Her furniture, her dishes, all had been left behind and, having nothing of my own, I used them gratefully, and tried to care for them as well as she had. Her pictures still sat in silver frames along the mantle-piece—having none of my own to put up, I'd left them where they were. Sometimes on a Sunday morning when the light streamed in the windows, I wondered if she looked in on the place. I hoped she approved of the way I cared for it, saw how much I appreciated her lending me this house and allowing me to make a home here while I could. For what I had done with the barn, I could only hope for her indulgence.

I had often imagined her, wearing the old blue apron that still hung beside the kitchen door, throwing knotted, work-worn hands into the air and laughing. "My goodness," I could almost hear her exclaim. "Now that's something I never could have seen coming. Well, no harm's done, I suppose. Though I do wish they wouldn't trample so on my marigolds."

I was glad Jason would be here. Somehow I couldn't bear the thought of the house being empty, and slowly falling to ruin. And

Pip would still have the fields to run in, and his favorite spot on the couch to curl up. I knew Jason would take good care of him, too. I walked over to where Pip lay, sprawled out on the rug. He half-opened his eyes and grinned up at me when I crouched down and stroked his head, licking my hand affectionately before closing his eyes and going back to sleep. I swallowed convulsively, and quickly walked out, slamming the door behind me. I had given my house key to Jason, and didn't have a spare. The only way I could get back in now would be by climbing in the window. That made it a little easier to pull away. But it didn't stop the tears.

It wasn't until I had put a few miles between me and home, driving by instinct, that I realized where I was going. The road was familiar, and as I went the terrain outside changed until the harshness of the landscape outside my window matched the empty, aching feeling in my heart. The trees disappeared, and then the green grass. Soon it was as though I drove on the surface of some alien planet, with only red dirt and towering stones all around. I had loved the Badlands from the first time I had seen them, and it was somehow natural to come to them now. This place was half sky, the strange landscape stretching wide and open before me as I drove the twisting roads.

Eventually, I pulled up to one of the scenic overlooks and parked my car. There was nothing to stop me from just walking out into the rocky wilderness, and I left my keys on the seat and struck out. It didn't much matter where I went exactly, just that it was somewhere remote. I walked and walked, remembering legends I had read about where this land came from. Eons ago the thunderbird had defeated a great monster and thrown its body to the ground, leaving its bones to fossilize and become the multicolored rocks that now stood around me, shoulder to shoulder. I was surprised by how much I enjoyed the feeling of the sun on my face, and the touch of the breeze as it pressed, chill, against my cheeks.

When I was well out of the sight of the road, I found a large, smooth rock and climbed up to sit on it. The surface of it was a little warm from the sun, and I leaned back, spreading my palms out flat as I looked around. It was so peaceful here. Somehow it didn't seem like such a bad place to die. And, since I was sure they wouldn't do me the kindness of burying me, it wasn't a bad place to stay, either. I didn't mind resting here.

I nodded to myself, and took a deep breath. I knew what I had to do. For a second I closed my eyes, steeling myself. Then I opened them, and turned to the silver speck waiting in the corner of my vision. I reached out to it and pulled it close. A moment later I could see the Source, flowing like a brook at my feet. I leaned over, and dipped just the toe of my shoe into the silver water. *There.* I thought. *That couldn't be much clearer. They know where I am now, and they'll come right to me. All I have to do is wait.*

I tried not to think, in the hours that followed. There was no point in dredging up old regrets. I had made choices, both good and bad. They had led me here. I closed my eyes and leaned my face back, trying to feel nothing but the sun on my cheeks, trying to be as hard and unmovable as the rock beneath me.

I felt them a few hours later, moving towards me like a gathering storm. I sat, ignoring the slight tremble in my hands and the way my breath came short and jagged. The pain in my chest swelled, as though the pearl knew what was happening and was pushing against me, eager to escape. I strained my eyes, searching the horizon. I wondered how they would come.

By foot, it turned out. I didn't know how much time had passed when I first saw them on the edge of the horizon. About twenty of them. I watched the ripple of excitement spread through them as they saw me, saw their speed pick up as they began to hurry, some of them breaking into a run while others fanned out to the sides, boxing me in. As though I had not come here, announced my location, and then waited for them to arrive.

I could not help the hand that rubbed my chest as the burn flared there.

When they were close enough for me to see their faces, I slid down off the rock and leaned against it. Having the warm rock at my back helped me keep from running. I couldn't deny that the instinct to run now was powerful. No matter what you tell yourself when you are alone in the sunlight, the truth is that when a group of people, intent on killing you, array themselves around you like a noose, a powerful instinct surges in you to run. To flee. To try like hell to survive. I shoved my hands deep in my pockets, and looked down at my boots. I didn't want to look at them, to see the weapons they held in their hands, or feel the hate that radiated from their stares. I didn't want to know which of my former friends had volunteered for the hunting party.

"Traitor," a voice said, painfully familiar.

I glanced up at the man who stood at the head of the group, several feet away from me. "Paul," I answered, looking only at him, refusing to recognize the other faces, or to admit how small and frightened my voice sounded.

"You waiting for us?"

"That's right." I nodded, feeling the others move in closer, until they stood in a tight circle all around. "I'm through running."

"You sure as hell are," Paul agreed, and nodded at someone.

Pain exploded in my temple before I'd even felt the blow. My knees gave out and I was distantly aware of my body crumpling beneath me. As the ground rushed towards my face, I hoped, in a dispassionate sort of way, that they would kill me quickly.

SEVEN

I woke to the smell of woods all around me, and the intense confusion of not being dead.

A blindfold cut across my temples, the knot of it pressed hard into the back of my head. My arms were stretched over my head, hands bound above me around something that felt like a tree branch. The kind of quiet that only lives in forests surrounded me.

My chest throbbed, but for once that seemed to be the least of my troubles. I breathed in and out slowly, waiting until the worst of the disorientation swirling in my head passed, before trying to take stock of my injuries. Then I began the slow and painful work of testing my body out as best I could. Nothing seemed broken, I determined after a few moments, though I couldn't move enough to be sure the ache in my side didn't indicate one or two fractured ribs. I probably had a concussion. There weren't many places that didn't hurt. My parched mouth tasted coppery, and dried blood pulled at the skin all along the right side of my face and down my neck.

How long had I been unconscious? Where was I? They had blindfolded me so that I couldn't access my Truthsight, and between that and not being able to see, disorientation set in. I tried to sift through my memory and figure out what had happened, and where I was, but all I could remember was falling to the ground, and curling in on myself as the blows and kicks rained down, hoping that soon it would be over. And then...nothing. "Are you awake?"

I started. The woman's voice was right by my ear, but I had not heard anyone approaching. The voice was familiar, and there was kindness in it that took me by surprise.

"I've brought you something to drink."

Before I could think of how to answer, a straw pressed to my lips.

"Here," the familiar voice said, and I sipped without thinking, gulping the cool water as quickly as I could.

"Where am I?" I asked when the water was gone, my voice coming out thick as gravel.

"In the woods, not too far from where they found you."

"Shanie?" I asked, almost certain I was right, but still hardly able to believe it. "Is that you?"

Just a beat of hesitation passed before she answered, "Yes, it's me."

"Don't let them see you giving me water," I warned, leaning away from her as much as I could in my restraints. "You've got to stay away. The other mages know we were friends. It isn't safe for you to be seen with me."

"They can go to hell," she answered, and her words, which might have been considered almost mild coming from anyone else, shocked me. The Shanie I had known never cursed. "Paul didn't say we couldn't give you anything to drink. I'm not disobeying any orders."

I started to respond, but held back the words. I couldn't see anything, and there was no way for me to know we were alone. Then I felt slight, soft fingers on the side of my face, and she pulled the blindfold away. I blinked until the blurriness in my eyes cleared, and I could look over into the eyes of my oldest friend.

"W...well," I stammered. "I guess you're disobeying orders now."

Shanie shrugged and wrapped her arms around her waist. "Yeah," she said. "I guess I am."

We were alone, although I could see movement in the trees behind her. I glanced around quickly. It looked like we were somewhere in the black hills. Pine trees towered overhead, and a thick layer of needles covered the ground beneath my feet. Daylight still lit the forest, so I couldn't have been out for that long. I didn't spend much time looking around, though. I was too busy staring at Shanie. The last time I had seen her, she had been just a little over seventeen, but it wasn't the changes the years had brought that made my heart hurt as I looked at her. The young woman I remembered had a soft, glowing face, and auburn hair that swung down to the small of her back. Now Shanie had chopped the hair off just below her chin, and it was dyed black, a black that matched her clothes and the dark makeup she wore around her eyes. The only thing that broke all that black up was a thick pendant that hung from her neck. It was a silver fish wrapped round and round with wire. More than anything, her face had changed. Where there had once been softness, there were now only angles and bones. Her brown eyes were wide and haunted, and she looked as though she was about to cry.

"I've missed you," I said softly, the words spilling out before I had time to consider them. Her lips trembled.

"Really?" she challenged. "That's interesting. Because you're the one that deserted me. I needed you. You have no idea..." She bit her lip, tears welling in her eyes as she looked away, as though she couldn't stand the sight of me. "They were killed, Asa," she whispered. "Both of them, in the fighting. Just two days after you ran."

"Oh, Shanie," I whispered, hanging my head as pain coursed through me. I hadn't realized there was any part of my heart still whole enough to break. "I am so, so sorry."

My fault. My fault, a voice inside my head whispered, and suddenly I wished I had the blindfold back on. Looking at the lost despair on Shanie's face was almost too much to bear. I didn't have to ask who she meant. Shanie's mother had died a few years after I had lost my parents. Her father had never been in the picture. She was left parentless, just as I had been—but unlike me, she had had two older brothers. They had raised her and loved her, and been her whole world.

"Just a week after that we lost Meri," she was still not looking at me, her voice climbing in octaves as she recalled all the losses she had suffered. "And all this time I've been all alone. Why did you go? How could you just leave me like that?"

"I didn't have a choice." I gritted my teeth and stared at the ground, shifting a little against the bindings that were beginning to cut off my circulation. "You know what I had done."

"I know the what." Shanie said, taking a step closer to me. "But not the why. And all these years later, Asa, I still can't understand it. What the hell were you thinking?"

"I was stupid." God, I wished they had killed me when they first found me. There wasn't much I wouldn't give to avoid the pain of this moment. "When I came back home after finishing medical school, Meri asked me to help her. She was in pain, she said. She wanted me to see if I could lessen it. She said she had been waiting to ask me for years, until I came fully into my abilities, to see if I could make it better."

I hesitated, swallowing hard, half-willing her to stop me. But she didn't. "I had always known she carried a terrible burden—everyone in the clan knew that. But it was only that day that I realized the reality of it—the amount of pain she was in. It was so much worse than anything I had imagined—she was in agony, Shanie. Terrible, constant, agony. You know what Meri was to me—she practically raised me after my parents died. She was all the family I had. I *loved* her." My voice shook, and I closed my eyes against the memory. "I couldn't just leave her like that. I couldn't. I had put her under while I was working on her, and I just ...."

"You're making it sound like you didn't plan it, Asa. But that's not what people say." She shook her head, angry now, and I was glad of it. Her anger was easier for me to bear than her misery. "People say you went away to school, and met rebel mages. They say they recruited you for their cause. That you joined up with them, and came back from your schooling as a traitor and a spy."

"That isn't true." Shanie had been my one real friend in childhood. We had both been through so much loss. Suddenly, I wanted so badly for her to understand. "I owed Meri everything. I would have done anything for her. I never meant to betray her. In the moment, when I was doing it, it felt like I was helping. That's all I wanted to do." I hesitated. "It's true I met some of the non-clan mages while I was away…"

"I knew it!" Shanie said, her expression savage.

"Wait," I cried. "You don't understand. They came to me for help, for healing. What Meri was doing was causing them pain, too. She had been denying access to the Source to everyone outside the clan for generations! And a mage who has no access to magic suffers."

Shanie's face hardened, but I wasn't going to let this go.

"It is true, Shanie, whether you want to admit it or not. Mages are human—but they are like humans with a hormone deficiency. They need magic in their veins in order to flourish and grow—they can survive without it, but never be really healthy. Meri was damming the Source and only giving access to those of us who were in the clan. It meant the rebel mages were sick, all of the time. They suffered all kinds of disorders. With Meri denying them access to magic, they were all anemic or brittle-boned by the time they were teenagers."

"And they convinced you that things had to change?"

"No! They heard about what I could do. They came to me and asked for healing. And I don't turn patients away." I spit the words out, daring her to argue with me. I had made mistakes, and I knew I would pay for them soon enough. But I would never apologize for helping those people. "They never asked me to do anything more than to patch them up as best I could. At first, I thought that there had to be a way I could fix them—something I could do that would let them live comfortably, even without access to magic. But I can only heal people—I can't change what they are. The best I could do was relieve the worst of their symptoms."

I had to swallow hard so I could speak past the rising lump in my throat. "I decided I had to talk to Meri, to convince her that she had to stop damming the Source. I know why she did what she did—I understand that, a long time ago, she sincerely felt it was necessary to harness all the magic, pulling it through herself to control where and to whom it flowed. When she made that decision, there were mages doing terrible things, and that was the only way that she had to stop them. And insisting that mages had to join the clan to get access to magic was a way to control what mages did and how they used their power. She made a great sacrifice."

"Don't talk to me about sacrifice, Asa!" Shanie cried. "I know what sacrifice is."

"I know you do," I answered quickly. "I'm just saying that what Meri did saved a lot of lives. But that doesn't mean it could go on forever. Innocent people were suffering."

"The rebels are *not* innocents!"

"Meri refused access to magic to so many, to anyone she didn't deem worthy, or who refused to swear fealty to her. What crime were all those people guilty of? And she was suffering, too. She hid the pain so well that most of us never guessed it. But filtering the Source through her own body was torturing her, every day. It is a miracle she kept her sanity. She couldn't have kept doing it forever."

"So you ended it."

"Yes," I whispered hoarsely.

"You released the flow, took down all the barriers she had built. Flooded the whole world with magic."

"I *healed* her," I said, blinking back the tears that rose in my eyes. "She had contorted herself, made her own body into a dam to stem the flow of magic to the world. I undid that. Yes. I made her whole again. I didn't plan it—all I wanted was to take away some of her pain. But I felt her body knitting together under my fingers and I...I couldn't stop. She was sleeping, but I saw her face ease, saw when the burden was gone from her shoulders after so long spent suffering in silence. I did that."

There was a long silence.

"And then," Shanie said. "They came."

"I swear," I said through the tears I couldn't hold back any longer. "I swear to God, and on my mother's soul, Shanie, I had no idea the rebel mages would attack."

"But they did." There was no forgiveness in her eyes, only building anger. "What did you think would happen? *Of course* they would attack, Asa! If they had left Meri alone, she just would have put the barriers back up, once she was strong enough."

"That isn't true," I protested. "She told me she wouldn't. She was angry with me when she woke up, but she wouldn't have lied to me. She said she was finished with that, and it was the truth."

"Even if what you're saying is true, it made no difference to the rebels. They wouldn't have believed her, no matter what she said."

We fell silent, not meeting each other's eyes.

"When they attacked, Meri told me to leave," I said, trying to explain, though I wasn't sure Shanie was really listening to me anymore. "She was weak, and she felt she was losing control of the Clan. Everyone was so angry with me. She said she wasn't sure she could protect me, and that the best thing was for me to just disappear until things calmed down. She said the fighting wouldn't last—it would just be a day or two. I could come back in a couple of weeks."

Shanie let out a humorless bark of laughter. "That part, at least, was more or less true. It was just a couple of weeks before it was all over."

"What happened?" I whispered. The few times I had managed to communicate with Meri, she hadn't been able to give me any clear answers. Her own memories of those days were too clouded with confusion and pain. "After I left? How did the rebel mages get to her? I don't understand how it could have happened."

"We aren't really sure." Shanie's eyes fixed on her silver pendant as she fiddled with it. "The fighting had been pretty intense. We were winning. I mean, the losses had been bad, but it seemed like it was almost over. There was a truce, and one of the rebel mages came to talk to her. They met alone—Meri refused to let any of us come. To this day, we aren't sure what they said, but after the meeting, the rebels started to pack up. It seemed like they were leaving, going home, acting as though the fighting was over and there was nothing else to say. I went into Meri's room, and asked her what was going on. All she said was that she was tired and needed to rest. She said we'd have a meeting after she was up again. I left her to sleep. A few hours later she was gone."

"Just like that?" I tried not to sound skeptical. But I knew what Shanie could not; Meri was sure one of the mages from the Clan had betrayed her to the rebels.

"Just like that." Shanie kicked a rock away from her foot. "It had all been a show to throw us off our guard. And we're almost certain that during that 'meeting' the rebel mage that met with her drugged her somehow. She seemed so out of it—so sleepy. Anyway, we searched and searched." Shanie shrugged. "We can only hope they killed her quickly."

I bit my lip to stop myself from correcting her, and telling her Meri was still alive. Even before she had been captured, Meri had felt dissension simmering in the Clan. When she sent me away, she gave me the Pearl to keep hidden for her, because she feared someone in the Clan might try to take it from her by force. When I had finally managed to get her to speak to me, after she had been captured, she had forbidden me to tell anyone in the Clan anything. She said she did not know who she could trust. But it was hard not to give Shanie the little bit of comfort I could.

"What is it?" Shanie asked, studying my expression, her brow furrowed. "What's wrong, Asa?"

I hesitated, struggling to decide whether or not I should tell her. Out of the corner of my eye, I saw two figures approaching.

"Paul is coming," I gasped, my heart sinking. "Quick. Put the blindfold back on."

Shanie's eyes widened and she stumbled forward, pulling the blindfold back up with hurried, clumsy fingers.

"One more thing, Asa," she whispered, her mouth close to my ear. "Why did you tap into the Source? After all this time, I thought they'd never catch you. I thought you'd been too smart for all of us."

"I couldn't help it, in the end," I stammered. "I had to…"

"She was stupid, that's all!" Paul's booming voice cut through our whispers. "Of course, we knew that already. Only an idiot would betray the clan."

He left his sentence hanging, expectant, as though waiting for me to contradict him, to launch into some heartfelt defense of all the mistakes I had made. I just dangled, blind and silent. The moment came and went.

"So now you can see for yourself, Alice," Paul said. "I told Alice here that we'd got you, but she couldn't quite believe me. Do you feel better?" he asked her. "Now that you see it is true?"

"I feel better than I have for years," a woman's voice answered. Then she addressed me, "Do you remember me, Asa?"

"Yes," I answered, my voice little more than a croak.

"Good." I felt something cold and sharp pressed against my neck. "And can you guess what this is?"

"A knife?" I grunted. I wanted to shrink away, but my back was already flush against the tree trunk, and it was impossible to pull away.

"Leave her alone!" Shanie cried out. "She'll be executed tomorrow. Isn't that enough for you?"

But Alice ignored her. "It's my son's knife. My Daniel's. My own boy, who is dead because of you."

I focused on my breathing, and said nothing.

"We'll each get a turn. That's what they say. Tomorrow morning. For you, they are bringing back the old ways."

I gasped with dismay. I couldn't help it. A ritual death sentence, with each mage proving their loyalty by taking a turn with the knife. Nothing like that had been done in living memory. I had heard the stories, everyone had, but I had thought them myth. I'd known that they would kill me, but they were much more imaginative than I had given them credit for.

"I've been carrying it around with me for years, waiting till the day we found you," Alice went on. "I knew it would come." She leaned in closer, whispering, "I'd kill you right now, if I could."

She pressed the blade up against my skin, until I could just feel the bite of it on my flesh. I shuddered and bit down on my lip to keep from crying out.

"I've imagined it so many times, I half feel like I've done it already. But they say it has to be done in public, with everybody there. They say that anyone who jumps the gun will take your place at the execution. Things have gotten a lot more brutal, since the Meridian is gone. That's another thing we have to thank you for." She sighed, and pulled the knife away from my skin. "I just wanted you to know what was going to happen. That way you can fear it. That will make it sweeter, I think."

"It's sick." Suppressed tears clouded Shanie's voice. "Meri would never have allowed you to do something like this, Paul, and you know it."

Paul laughed. "Meri is too soft-hearted for her own good. Always has been. I'm in charge now, and tomorrow everyone, even you, is going to participate. Unless you'd like a spot at her side? We could always do a double execution, if that would make you happier."

"No," Shanie said softly, after a long pause. "I'll do it."

I didn't blame her. I would never have wanted Shanie to suffer for my sake. Still, fresh tears rose in my eyes, making me grateful for the blindfold.

"Enough of this," Paul said. "Come on, Alice. Leave her alone for now. You won't have to wait much longer. Let's go. There's no need for us to hang around here. And you." He snapped his fingers at

Shanie. "You stay away from her from now on. No more water, no more whispering. Execution is in the morning. She gets nothing and talks to no one till then."

I was so grateful when they were gone and I could be alone in the darkness and the silence. I tried to force myself to think of happy things, to imagine myself back safely at the barn, but remembering what I was losing just made the pain harder to bear. Instead I ended up going over and over everything Shanie and I had said to each other. And then the conversation with Paul began to replay itself in my head.

Suddenly my heart stuttered. What had he said, exactly? "Meri is too soft-hearted for her own good." He had spoken about her in the present tense. As though he knew she was still alive. My heart rate started to accelerate and my chest began to ache. What if Paul had known that, with Meri gone, he would be the one leadership would fall to? What if he was the one who had betrayed Meri to the rebels? It might mean he would know where she was being held.

Bitter regret swelled inside me. Even if I was right, there was nothing I could do about it now. I was helpless. And soon I would be dead.

The grass rustled with the sound of many feet. My eyes were still blinded, but I knew that a small crowd was forming all around me. I could hear them breathing, could feel the pressure of their eyes. I was bound and helpless, and the small cut Alice had made on my neck throbbed, but I held my head up and waited for them to start to yell, to hurl insults, maybe to start kicking me again. I almost wanted them to. I knew I deserved it, and the physical pain seemed somehow easier to bear if it distracted me from the painful thoughts that just wouldn't stop coming. But nothing happened. I just hung there with my heart racing, while they looked at me. The gathering was pervaded by the grim silence of a funeral, one where the body just happened to still be alive.

Time stretched on and on, and the coolness on my skin told me the light had faded and the dark was beginning to build around us.

Slowly I heard the rustling sound of the crowd fading away. I heard a low babble of voices from a distance, where I imagined the mages must have set up some sort of camp. I tried to imagine faces I had grown up with, changed now from time and hardship, putting up tents and pulling out sleeping bags. Sitting around a fire, and talking with excitement about what they would do to me tomorrow.

There was nothing for me to do but wait.

It was impossible to sleep the night before being executed, but a sort of dazed stupor did come over me deep in the night. The cicadas hummed in the trees, and when the breeze picked up, the leaves and branches rustled. I let the sounds wash over me, the coolness of the wind like a soothing hand against my face.

EIGHT

I'M NOT SURE EXACTLY WHEN I BECAME AWARE THAT SOMETHING WAS watching me. My arms ached, and my wrists had gone numb. I had long since lost sensation in my hands. Then, quite suddenly, I realized I couldn't hear the wind in the trees anymore. Or the cicadas.

"Hello?" I whispered, wondering if Shanie had come back again.

No response came.

Fear bubbled inside of me, but I pushed it away, forcing myself to breathe and straining my ears to pick up some clue about what was happening. But I couldn't hear anything at all. The night had fallen inexplicably silent all around me. I was aware of a distinct pressure, the kind of pressure you feel against your skin when someone is staring and staring at you.

There is no reason to be frightened, I told myself, even as my heart rate picked up and sweat broke out on my forehead.

You're tied to a tree, and condemned to die a slow death by multiple stab wounds in the morning. As far as hitting bottom goes, you're pretty much there already. So stop panicking; that doesn't make any sense.

"Who's there?" I called out, keeping my voice as calm and steady as I could. "I *know* someone's there. What do you want?" I tried to keep my mind from imagining what could have crept in from the forest under the cover of dark, lured to the edge of camp by the sight of someone who could not possibly defend herself. Maybe I had been too confident in thinking that I had already hit bottom. Being eaten alive while trussed to a tree might be an even worse fate than the one that waited for me tomorrow.

The voice, when it came, was such a shock I gasped and tried to pull away, though my hands were tied firmly in place. Someone stood inches from me, his breath hot on my cheek.

"Who are you?" he asked, his voice a deep, rumbling bass, along with something distinctly *other* in his accent. This was no voice I had ever heard before, and I knew with a deep, intuitive surety, that the voice did not belong to a human.

"*What* are you?" the voice continued.

With no warning, I felt his face pressed up against my stomach. I cried out and tried to jerk away, but there was nowhere to go as he made inhuman sniffing sounds, his movement rucking up my shirt and exposing my flesh as he moved upward slowly, smelling the length of my body. I tilted my head back, away from him, and he stopped with his nose just below my chin, his lips dry and rough as they brushed against my neck.

"You smell like mage, and magic," he growled. "But you are not one of them."

Rough, calloused fingers scraped against my forehead and yanked the blindfold away. Dazed and blinking, I stared up at a creature the likes of which I had never seen before.

He stood so close that his bare chest brushed up against me. Wider than a human's, his eyes were blue and ringed with yellow, with hostility flashing in them. He towered over me, at least a foot taller than I. He looked almost like a man, only more thickly muscled, his chest covered in thick hair that was the same ashen gray color as the hair that hung down to his shoulders. Thick horns, like those of a ram, pushed through his hair to curl into sharp points around both sides of his head. Leather straps held a sheathed knife to his left forearm. On his right arm a complicated pattern drawn in black ink wrapped around his arms like vines. His cheeks were smooth, clear of any sign of hair. His nostrils flared.

Why had he come here? What was he? My mind stuttered as I tried to think.

"What do the mages want from you that they have brought you here to die?" he demanded.

I shook my head, whispering back to him urgently, "You've got to get out of here. Quickly. I don't know who, or what you are, but the mages won't care. If they see you talking to me, you'll be killed. Please—just go."

He snorted, a distinctly animal sound. "The mages are blind. They will only see what I want them to see. But you ... you are different. Is it true, what I hear them saying?"

"I don't know what you're talking about," I answered. "But you've got to believe me. You're in danger here."

"I hear them say you are a healer of great power," he said, ignoring my warning, and folding his arms as he leaned back to study me. "I have been listening to them gossip inside their tents. They hate you, but when they speak of you, they speak in whispers. I do not understand. They are gathered here, to watch you suffer and die—but when they come to look at you, a prisoner bound and helpless—no one calls out insults, or jeers. I have heard them murmuring that you can work wonders that no one else can do."

"It isn't true." I shook my head. Bitterness crept into my voice. "They're just talking. Just telling tales."

"I do not believe you." His voice dropped to a whisper, and I got the feeling he was speaking more to himself than to me. "It can't be a coincidence. To find her now. Left hanging on a branch, like fruit ripe for picking,"

"Look, I don't know who you are, or what you want from me," I said, welcoming the anger that had sparked inside my chest. It burned the fear away, and gave me something I could cling to. "Some of those things you heard might have been true, a very long time ago. But they aren't true now. I've been running for a long time, but all of that is over now. It's through. I'm going to die in the morning, and if you don't feel like joining me, you had better get the hell out of here. Now."

Silence fell heavy between us, and for a second I half hoped, half feared he would listen. But then he shook his head.

"No," he said, and I was surprised to hear a twinge of anger in his voice to match my own. "I do not think you will get off that easy."

"What the fuck are you talking about?" I cried in a furious whisper. "I'm tied up, hanging here, waiting to be executed in the morning by people I used to count as friends. Look at me!" I shook my bound hands as well as I was able. "Does this look easy to you?"

"Yes," he answered, his voice a slow, threatening whisper. He moved a fraction of an inch closer to me, and I could feel the heat pouring off his body. "It looks like total surrender. You've given up. You are letting them strip you of everything. But I need you." And suddenly arms, hot and hard as iron, had wrapped around my waist, and my hands fell free to my sides. "I'm sorry," he said, as he held me. "But if you want to curl up in the dirt and die, you'll have to do it on another day."

And then we were moving. He carried me pressed hard against his chest, and I felt the absurd instinct to call out for rescue from those gathered all around to kill me.

"What are you doing?" I moaned, trying to push away the arms of my captor, but my limbs were limp and useless, the return of blood-flow like fire in my veins.

"The earth lays claim to you, healer. I lay claim to you. I have need of what only you can do."

Night wind and blackness whipped against my face as he hoisted me in his arms and sprinted away. My eyes were still adjusting after the long darkness of the blindfold, but I could see a mass of black, the thickness of trees, not far off in the distance.

"The mages will come after you," I warned him, my words catching in my throat.

How was it possible that we had traveled these few steps without being challenged? I tried to see through the thick darkness that surrounded me. There was no way they would have left me unguarded. We should have been stopped by now. We should have been dead.

"Even if they haven't seen you yet—they'll just hunt you down and kill us both!"

He laughed at that, his breath coming evenly and his voice serene, though he ran at an incredible speed. "I have nothing to fear from them, and neither do you, for as long as you are with me. But they have much to fear from *me*."

And then I felt something like a breeze, except it stung lightly against my skin, a tugging, as though something had just been pulled away from my flesh. In that instant the night grew lighter, as though a thick veil of darkness had been thrown from our shoulders. Suddenly shouts erupted all around us, shrill screams and the pounding of feet. He laughed, a deep, wild sound that was nearly a howl.

"Cling close," he whispered, and then his muscles tensed.

He jumped—a great leap that lifted us both up into the air. We hurtled back down toward the ground, but a small fracture in the surface of the earth widened as we got closer, opening like the gaping mouth of some dark beast, eager to swallow us up. And then we were falling, falling, falling—not over the earth, but into it.

NINE

I COULDN'T PULL AIR INTO MY LUNGS, AND ON EVERY SIDE OF ME LAY stone, packed earth, and crushing pressure. An all-encompassing darkness blinded me more effectively than the clan's blindfold ever could. I wanted to scream, but I could not fill my lungs. The unbearable feeling of being closed in on every side filled me with a blind, unrelenting terror. We moved, sliding deeper and deeper into darkness and a sudden, searing cold. My skin ached as though I had plunged into frigid water, and I convulsed and struggled blindly.

"It will be all right," his deep voice told me. "We are nearly there."

His thick arm wrapped tightly against my chest. It anchored me, and I clung to him despite myself, instinctively pressing closer to the heat of his skin, the protection of his embrace.

Then, suddenly, came a terrible lurch, and we fell on to ground thickly covered in moss. Trees stood wide and silent on every side. My captor released me, and I managed to turn and crawl a bit away before I retched up the meager contents of my stomach.

A large, warm hand came to lie against the small of my back. "You will be fine in a minute," his deep voice promised. "The sickness passes quickly."

I wiped my mouth with the back of my hand and stood to face him, moving away so that his hand fell away from my back.

"Where are we?" I demanded, trying not to let him see how my arms and legs shook, or how close I was to fainting. "What did you do?"

"Did you think the magic you mages wield was the only magic in the world, healer?" he asked, his voice mocking. "Does it frighten you to know you were wrong?"

"You haven't answered my question. Where have you taken me?"

He shrugged. "My home."

"Did we travel far when you did...whatever it is that you did to us?"

"I believe humans call this land the Yukon. I haven't paid much attention."

My vision swam, and I gave up trying to conceal my weakness, rocking back until I had landed gracelessly on my backside. I pressed the heels of my hands against my temples.

"Canada?" I gasped raggedly.

It was impossible, or should have been. Mages can travel great distances quite quickly, but it takes time to prepare, and great skill to conduct. To simply jump and hit the ground, sink down into it, and then come up again in another country, as it seemed we had done—it defied belief. And how was I going to get back? If the mages couldn't follow me here, they would search the area. They would find the clinic. Jason would be there, with the two centaur guards I had thought I was so clever for arranging. I had thought I was leading danger away, and leaving them all well-protected. But what if the mages found them, and it led to a fight? The bloodshed that would surely follow would be all my fault.

"Are you all right?" he asked, taking a step forward, his wide eyes creasing in concern.

I held out a hand, motioning him away. He stilled, giving me a good few feet of space, and I stared up at him, trying to grasp some part of what had just happened to me. What was he? My eyes ran over his frame, trying to understand. His chest was wide and I could see how muscular he was even through the short gray fur that covered his chest. Could he be some kind of giant satyr? No. I looked down quickly, and could clearly see human legs through the tattered pants he wore belted loosely around his waist.

"Are you all right?" he asked again, and for the first time I heard something almost gentle in his voice.

"What are you?" I struggled to my feet, and leaned heavily against a tree.

"What does it matter?"

"You aren't a satyr," I persisted, and the corners of his mouth curled up slightly.

"No," he agreed. "Not a satyr. My name is Rowan."

He was avoiding my question, but I had to know, had to get my bearings somehow. If I knew what he was, I might be able to piece together what he wanted from me, or, at the very least, the rules he operated by. Right now I was flying blind, and I had had quite enough of that already. I folded my arms over my chest and raised my chin.

"Some kind of fae, then?"

"I asked you if you are all right. Are you hurt? Did the mages injure you?"

"I've seen a lot of species," I replied, refusing to be distracted, pushing my hair out of my eyes and trying to stand a little taller. "But never one like you."

He just stared back at me, motionless in the moonlight.

"Why did you bring me here?" I asked, deciding to try a different tactic. I remembered what he had said to me back at the mage camp. He had asked me if it was true that I was a healer, if I could cure patients no one else could help. "Are you sick?"

"No," he answered, and his eyes darkened. "Not me."

"But someone is?"

He gave me the barest of nods.

"Look." I unfolded my arms and tried to speak calmly. "You're a lot stronger than me and, obviously, if you want to you can just pick me up and carry me away. Again. I'm in no condition to fight you off. But if you really want me to treat someone, to *help* you, then you're going to have to help me understand, at least a little." I took a shaky step closer to him, staring up at him with as much wonder as fear. "What are you?"

He looked at me for a long, hard moment, and then, unsmiling, motioned toward himself. "I am a leshy."

"A leshy?" I blinked up at him, confounded. "No. That isn't possible. There aren't any left. The leshies have been gone for centuries."

His nostrils flared, and he stiffened to his full, impressive height. I took an automatic half-step back, away from him.

"Don't call me a liar. We aren't gone. There are few of us, God knows, much less than there used to be. But we haven't died out, at least not yet. We've just fled to the deep, wild places. We are still here."

"A leshy!" I whispered, and for the barest second, all the fear and terror of the last hours were lost in wonder. "A spirit king of the forest! So you...you rule here?" I asked, gesturing to the trees around me. "This is your land?"

"My father rules here," he answered. "But we have no time for talking. He is desperately ill." The anger that had filled his eyes melted away. "Believe me," he said. "I have no wish to take you against your will. But what can I do? My father is dying. I have no choice, and I will force you if I must. Will you come with me willingly?" He stretched out a hand. "Or must I carry you?"

I glanced around me, not sure what I was looking for: escape, guidance, anything. But the trees were dark and silent all around me, and the light the moon shed was weak and offered no comfort.

"I can walk," I said, pushing myself away from the tree, but ignoring his hand. "You haven't left me much of a choice. But know that the mages will come looking for me. They hate me, and they won't give up. The instant I use my Truthsight to heal your father, they'll find us. And then we will all die."

He shook his head, and the moonlight glinted off the semi-circle horns that curled around his ears. "Here in the heart of my home, we have no reason to fear the mages." He laid a heavy hand on my shoulder. "You don't need to be afraid. Come."

"Is it far?" I asked as we started through the trees.

"Not far now. Our jump brought us most of the way."

There was no path here, but the trees did not get in our way. Soon I could not help getting the strangest feeling that the trees were moving aside to let us pass.

I walked behind him, keeping my eyes on my feet, concentrating on not tripping over the branches and vines that twisted thickly across the forest floor. I did not realize we had come to the edge of a cliff until Rowan stopped suddenly in front of me.

"Here," he said, wrapping his arms around me and jerking me off my feet. "Hold on."

And with no more warning than that he had sprung up into the air. I did not have time to protest, or to scream, or to feel afraid. One moment we were sailing through the gray, early morning air, and the next we had landed softly on the ground below.

"Are you insane? What the hell are you doing?" I pushed his hands away from me, and he released me readily enough. Turning, I looked behind us—to where bone-white rock jutted out danger-ously into the darkness. "We should be dead," I whispered in shock. "There's no way we should have survived a fall like that."

"This land is my father's," Rowan said, pulling my arm impa-tiently. "As long as he lives, it will never harm me. Now come."

Just a few minutes later, Rowan pushed through some trees and pulled me behind him into a small clearing. The ground underfoot was smooth, soft dirt that was carefully swept and cared for, like the sand in a Japanese garden. High above, huge leaves that seemed more white than green spread out into a ceiling. In the center of the clearing rose a gnarled tree trunk that twisted, thick and graceful, up past where my eyes could see. Someone sat leaning against the tree trunk, his eyes closed and face slack, with moss and leaves layered over him like blankets. Three other forms knelt in a cluster around him, but they stood and turned to face us as we approached.

"Brothers," Rowan called softly. "I have found a healer for Father. There may be something she can do."

Two of the brothers came closer, their long thin faces hard, their lips creeping up slightly from their teeth in hostility. I shuddered, forcing myself not to back away. The two looked so much alike that I decided they must be twins. They both looked very different from Rowan. Where he was dark, they were pale. Their sun-blond hair was thick and curly, while Rowan's thick gray hair hung down, lank and straight, to his shoulders. While Rowan was built like a football player, they were like triathletes, with long slender limbs and slim forms. But mostly I was fascinated by their horns. Rowan's horns were thick half-crescents that curled, like ram's horns, up and under his ears. His brothers' had thin white horns that extended straight back and into the air, like an antelope's.

The last brother did not move, but looked at me intently from his place at his father's side. He was much smaller and younger, with a smooth, well rounded face, and curly black hair that accented the pearl-white of the two small nubs of horns just starting to push out from underneath his hair. He smiled at me, his expression friendly yet uncertain, and I gave a weak smile in return.

Rowan, I noticed, was the only one who carried a weapon. And none of the others bore tattoos, at least none I could see.

"Where did you find it?" one of twins asked, leaning in to stare at me, his head tilted slightly to the side.

"I found *her* at the mage camp," Rowan replied. "They were going to execute her. They had her hanging from a tree so they could carve her up in the morning."

I was surprised to see both the twins relax, their near-snarls disappearing, replaced by looks of open fascination.

"What had she done to anger them?" he asked.

"I don't know, Neven. I've had no time to ask her," Rowan replied, his eyes narrowing slightly. "And we still do not."

The one Rowan had called Neven turned to his twin, his eyebrows raised. "What do you think, Yasen? Should we let the healer do what she can?"

"We do not have much to lose," Yasen said, sighing heavily as he looked over his shoulder at his father's crumpled form.

Rowan turned his attention to the younger brother who still knelt by his father's side. "What say you, Elias?"

"All right," the youngest brother said, his voice high and wavering slightly, as he stood up and took a few steps away from his father, motioning for me to take his place.

Rowan let go of my arm, and suddenly they all looked at me expectantly.

I walked toward their father, feeling the weight of their regard as I moved. I knelt in front of him and looked, not touching him or attempting to wake him, but giving myself a moment to try to get a sense of who he was. With his barrel chest and thickly muscled arms, he looked more like Rowan than any of the others. But his girth seemed hollow. His chest moved up and down slowly, and the effort of it made the muscles of his neck stand out, as though each time his chest expanded, he had to lift some terrible weight. His hands, motionless on his lap, were gnarled and work worn, black dirt thick under his nails. His eyes were closed, but I could tell he was conscious, could feel his attention centering on me. We studied each other, and I found suddenly that I wanted to help him. He looked so tired.

I turned to Rowan. "I'll have to use Truthsight to treat him, and once I tap into the Source all the Clan mages will know where I am. They will come for me, and when they do, it will put your whole family in danger."

Rowan shook his head. "I can shield you," he said. "They will know that you have accessed your abilities, but nothing more than that. They will not know what you are doing, or be able to trace you back here."

"I've never heard of anyone being able to do that," I said.

The corner of his mouth quirked up into a small smile. "You had never heard of a living leshy, till just an hour ago," he pointed out. "You will be safe, and you will not endanger me or mine. You can trust me."

I stared at him for a second, unsure. But he did not seem the type for idle boasting, and it wasn't as though I had much of a choice.

I looked at the old leshy's face, and in the farthest corner of my vision, silver flashed. I pulled it toward myself, feeling it reciprocate and reach out to draw me in. The silver came quickly, dripping down over the old leshy's body, beading on his skin like dew. I closed my eyes, letting a giddy feeling of dizziness and a flash of bitter cold tremble through me.

Then I opened my eyes, and looked up.

We were alone in the clearing. I rose slowly to my feet, body tense as I glanced all around. But Rowan had been true to his word. We were far from the silver stream, and thick thorn bushes stood all around us, shielding us. For the moment, at least, I seemed safe. I turned my attention to Rowan's father and then froze, staring at him, trying to take in what the Truthsight showed me.

In my Truthsight the old leshy stood with his back against the great, gnarled tree. His whole body was made, not of flesh, but of thick, gray clay. Coal black eyes with a red center that burned gazed at me.

Thick vines, like ropes, stretched up from the ground and clung to every inch of his body, binding him to the tree behind him. They wrapped around his shoulders, encased his legs. His arms and hands were completely covered, lost under the brown and green mass. He stared at me silently, his eyes dark and fierce, his mouth set in a hard, tight line. He looked, I realized, tensed for an attack, facing bravely someone he did not trust while he stood helpless.

I walked toward him slowly and reached out, and with one finger touched a thick length of green that ran over his shoulder.

"This looks so heavy," I murmured, not able to keep the

sympathy from my voice. And just like that, the wariness melted from his eyes.

"It is," he said. He sighed deeply, and the exhaustion he had been trying to conceal was suddenly painfully obvious in his face. "I am a foolish old man. I clung to life and to the forest so tightly that I refused to let it leave me. Perhaps I loved my sons too well. And now the forest will not let me go."

"Would you like..." I hesitated, not quite knowing what to say. "Would you like me to try to pull this off?"

He nodded, the movement somewhat obscured by the thick foliage that extended up even to the back of his head.

"Yes, I think I would. I am too old for this, it seems."

"Tell me if this hurts you," I said, and reached up and began to pull a tendril of ivy from his shoulder.

He closed his eyes as I worked, and he groaned deeply when they began to fall, but I recognized it for the sound of relief it was. I worked carefully, tugging the vines from him as gently as I could. Some were thick and heavy as rope, and some were thin and sharp as wire. My palms were soon raw and my arms sore and aching, as I tugged at layer after layer.

The labor was so difficult, and I was so focused on my task, I didn't realize that Rowan was coming until he was pounding up behind me, his words a roar of fury at my back.

TEN

"WHAT ARE YOU DOING?" HE BELLOWED. "I BROUGHT YOU HERE TO help him! Not to make him worse!"

"Rowan, wait!" I cried.

I turned to him, my hands held palm up in front of me as I tried to find words to calm him. But I couldn't. My mind stuttered in shock at his very presence.

He shouldn't be able to do that.

No one could simply walk into the Truthsight vision of another. Not the most powerful mage. Not even Meri. When mages use their Truthsight, they use the most intimate, most honest part of themselves. Rowan should never have been able to simply stride into mine. I fought for calm, and I tried very hard not to think about the fact that he did not seem the slightest bit out of place here, in a place that should have been utterly my own. What's more, the Truthsight had no effect on him whatsoever. He stood before me, looking exactly as he did in real life, utterly untouched by the magic that should have been prying him open like a book before me.

But I couldn't think about that now. His chest heaved, his nostrils flared, and his eyes flashed as they darted between me and the place where his father stood just a few feet away.

"When you came, he was breathing steadily," Rowan snarled, his face pressed close into mine and his lips pulled back from gleaming teeth. "Now he is gasping for air. His skin is growing cooler." His voice broke, and something desperate peered out from behind the mask of anger in his eyes. "I thought you would help him," he whispered.

I found that I couldn't fear someone who had so much sorrow in his eyes.

"I *am* helping him, Rowan," I answered gently. "Look at him. Really look."

Rowan turned to his father, and I saw when understanding came, and grief. His lips parted, and he moaned, slow and soft.

"Oh, Father," he whispered.

"You just stay here," I said, taking a step back from him, my hands held up. "Don't come any closer. Just wait."

The work was easier after that.

The old leshy stood and stared into Rowan's eyes, and somehow the vines were looser and fell away with less effort on my part.

"I am sorry, Father," Rowan said after a bit, his voice choking.

I did not turn and look round at him, but kept my head bent over my work, giving them as much privacy as I could.

"I know I've been a disappointment to you. I never meant to cause you pain, but I know I have. I'm so sorry."

"No, Rowan," the old leshy said, shaking his head. "You are your mother's son. Can you really think that grieves me?"

"I have disobeyed you time and again."

"Well, that much *is* true. And in that, too, you take after your mother. So much of who she was lives on in you. Her passion, her joy in living." The old leshy's eyes crinkled in a faint smile. "Her temper. Your path is a difficult one, Rowan, I have known it ever since you were a boy. I would have picked an easier way for you, if I could, and there was a time when I thought I could force you to it. That was my mistake, Son, not yours. And truth be told, even if you were what I once tried to make you, there still could be but one chosen in my stead. You will make your own way."

He laughed softly. "You are too stubborn to fail. And never doubt that I have loved you, and taken pride in that strength of yours, even when you used it against my wishes."

I had managed to get the old leshy's right arm free. He sighed with relief, rolling his shoulder and stretching his arm out gingerly before him. With the ivy gone I could now really see his body for the first time. The gray clay of his arm was wrinkled and tinted green from the moss that had started to grow up and over him. He reached over with his newly freed hand and began to push at the mass of green that still encased the other side of his body. I hurried to help him, pushing the thick fingers of the vines away one by one, until finally a great mass of leaves fell away. He was free, and now I could see that in his left hand he held a long, thick wooden staff.

I took a step back, and all three of us stared at the staff in his hand. It looked like nothing more than a tree branch long ago cut down and worn from use. But in my Truthsight I could see the way it pulsed with life and power.

"This is yours," I said, gesturing toward the staff. "And no one will take it from you. But when you *want* to lay it down ... you can."

The old leshy smiled at me, the edges of his eyes folding into deep wrinkles.

"Yours is a kind soul," he said. "I thank you for your help." He looked down at his staff, and shook his head. "I admit," he said, "it has grown very heavy."

He looked up over my shoulder to Rowan, and his smile faded.

"I am sorry, child. It is not mine to give you,"

"I understand, Father. Please don't worry about that now."

"You will find your own burdens to carry."

"Yes, Father."

"Wander well, Rowan. Find what you are seeking."

"Father, wait..."

But the old king closed his eyes, and let the staff fall from his fingers. It thudded softly onto the dirt, and in an instant the king was gone, carried to a place where not even Truthsight could see him.

For a moment silence hung, perfect and aching, over the spot where Rowan's father had stood.

Then Rowan threw his head back and howled, a roaring, heart-broken sound of loss.

All around the sky seemed to darken and flash. My Truthsight flickered, and suddenly I was back in the forest, under the wide ceiling of leaves spreading out from the strange, old tree. I gasped for breath and glanced around me.

What was happening? The Truthsight had never ended like that for me before. I always chose when to leave it, or fell asleep, or passed out and woke when it was gone. But Rowan had carried me back into the real world with him. In the spot where his father had been lying there was nothing left but dirt and leaves.

"He is gone," Yasen cried, but there was no real surprise in his voice, only sorrow.

"He had already stayed too long," Rowan said, his voice choked with grief. "The healer could do nothing but ease his way."

The youngest brother, Elias, walked slowly over to where his father had lain. He picked up the staff and leaned it gently up against the tree trunk. "There isn't even a body to bury," he whispered. "With Mother we at least had that. But he is just…gone. And what will happen to us now?" His lips trembled. "We will be separated. Scattered," he sniffled, a child's sound. "I thought he would get better. I can't believe he left us so alone." A sob broke from him.

Suddenly, he threw his head back and keened, the howl that rose from his lips a sweeter, softer version of Rowan's roar. Rowan clamped both his hands to his brother's shoulders, supporting him as though afraid that grief would knock him down. The twins came to stand beside them, and I, feeling like an intruder, stood and backed away, trying to give space to their grief.

Rowan turned his face towards the sky, his eyes squeezed shut. He shuddered, and then his own howl rose up again, deeper and more savage than his brother's. The twins joined in, their voices higher and more melodic than Rowan's raw cry. They all stood, the sound of their separate grief coiling together, making the leaves on the trees that edged the clearing shake. The forest had gone utterly silent, as though every creature that lived in the shadows of those trees had frozen, listening to their lament, waiting to see what would happen next.

Like a dirge, the wordless cry went on and on, deep and ragged and shockingly loud. I stared at the four of them, awestruck by the ferocity of their mourning. Tears leaked from Rowan's closed eyes, and dripped down the face of his black-haired younger brother. Then, in the same instant, they all fell silent. The quiet felt heavy, coming so soon after the intensity of their wails. It was like a physical presence, like the taut feeling in the wind right before a storm begins to blow.

And then the wind became real, blowing roughly through the branches of the great trees overhead, running its fingers through my hair and throwing errant curls into my face. Leaves that had been lying, dormant and peaceful and partially decomposed, launched themselves skyward and shot through the clearing, plastering themselves to my ankles, flying past my eyes.

"So soon?" Elias cried, staring around in horror. "Will we not have a single day to grieve together?"

Rowan leaned forward and wrapped his arm around his brother's shoulders. "We cannot hold it at bay," he whispered roughly. "And it is better that we know its decision quickly." He straightened up, and dropped his hands to his side. "And now, Brother, I think it would be better if you did not stand too close to me."

Elias looked at Rowan, his face screwed up as though about to protest. But Rowan jerked his head to the side, motioning for his brother to leave him. Fresh tears beaded in Elias's eyes, but he obeyed.

"Healer," Rowan called out, turning to me.

Following some silent cue I could not see, all of his brothers began backing away from each other. Rowan held out his hand toward me, his eyes anxious. "Quickly. It is beginning—you must come and stand behind me."

I hurried over to him. He pulled me back, to the edge of the clearing, and placed his body in front of mine, his eyes wary and moving from one brother to the next.

"What's going on?" I whispered.

"Now that my father has died, the land will pick a new ruler," Rowan replied without looking at me. His voice sounded calm, but his jaw was clenched, and his eyes flashed with tension.

The wind continued to build until I had to put up my hands and try to shield my face from it. I would have run for cover, except that the leshies stood silent and still as statues, staring up and into the trees. The trees began to wave their branches violently back and forth, as though the whole forest were convulsing in some sort of epileptic seizure. Rain appeared, though the sky had been clear moments ago, and I did not see it falling—the air misted, and water lay like tears on my face. Suddenly a deafening crack sounded, and one of the limbs on a frantically swaying tree broke away. Then came the sound of thuds and a rushing of leaves, as a branch hurtled down through the understory.

Rowan's brother, the one he had called Neven, stepped forward. He looked up, reached his hand skyward, and caught the staff easily as it fell.

For an instant the wind moved faster, but now Neven became the center of the storm. The wind twisted around him, swirling leaves and dirt at his feet, making his hair fly up wildly behind him.

And then it was over. The wind died as suddenly as it had come, and the silence returned as Rowan's brother stood in front of the tree, in the same spot where his father had been lying, and held his staff up for all to see. Inches away from me Rowan shuddered, and his whole body convulsed. He grunted, one short hard sound, as though he had been punched savagely in the gut. He reached behind him and grabbed my arm, as though for support.

"What is it? What's happening?" I whispered, but he held out his hand to silence me, and never turned his eyes from his brother.

For a minute Neven stood perfectly still, his eyes closed. Then he opened them and looked around at his brothers. Nostrils flared and chest heaving, he turned toward Yasen, the brother who was closest to him, with a glint in his eyes that promised violence. Neven took several strides in Yasen's direction.

Yasen retreated. He lowered his hands, palms open, to his sides, and turned his body so that he faced away from his twin. He dropped his eyes to the ground.

Neven stopped and snorted, and stood motionless for a moment, watching Yasen closely to make sure he did not move or offer challenge. Then he turned to the youngest, black-haired leshy, and beckoned. His younger brother hurried to him, stooping over slightly as he approached, and at his brother's gesture, went to sit with his back against the great tree.

Then Neven turned to Rowan.

Rowan met Neven's glare without flinching or looking away, his eyes narrowing as Neven stalked toward us. Every muscle in Rowan's body was tense, his chest heaving with short, rapid breaths as Neven moved closer to us slowly with small, measured steps.

His lips pulled back from his teeth, and a snarl—so quiet it was almost silent—bubbled from between his clenched teeth. Rowan held his ground, only the rapid rise and fall of his shoulders giving away the agitation he felt. Suddenly Neven rushed forward, and he brought his shoulder up to crash into Rowan's chest, throwing his full weight against him. Rowan grunted at the impact, but did not fall back. He reached up and pushed his brother away savagely. Neven stumbled a few feet, then caught himself, and turned to face us again. I gasped at the fury in his eyes, at the sudden violence that had sprung up between them, watching in horror as Neven pawed the ground, snarling in earnest now as he lowered his horns toward Rowan and prepared for another charge. This one would draw blood.

Rowan stared back at his brother steadily for a long moment and then let out a long, deep, shuddering breath. He turned his head to the side, and for a moment, his eyes met mine. I could see his heart breaking, could see loss layered on top of unbearable loss. Then his shoulders fell. He took two long, slow steps back and lowered his eyes.

I fell back, too, having no desire to be left standing alone between Rowan and his brother, who still seethed with anger, and was coming forward again. Shaking his sharp, thin horns like blades before him, he danced closer, forcing Rowan to give way again. Following quickly, I realized that Neven had forced us all the way out of the clearing, but still, he did not seem satisfied. Silence rang all around us. The trees, so still after the sudden storm, seemed to be holding their breath. Neven took a long step forward, and raised his staff as though to strike. Suddenly, Rowan dropped to one knee in a graceful, fluid movement. Bowing his head, he placed both of his hands in the moist, black dirt, and then moved them forward, so that he pushed tiny mounds of soil toward his brother's feet.

"It is yours, Neven," he said, his voice hoarse. "It has chosen you. I would not fight you for it, or go against its will." He looked up, his face still wet from the tears he had shed for his father. "I would not spill your blood, Brother."

Neven stared at Rowan for a long moment, his chest still heaving. Then his breathing slowed, and the fury melted from his eyes. He straightened up and looked around him, as though not quite sure what had been happening, or where he was.

"May we stay the night?" Rowan continued, his eyes still lowered. He nodded over his shoulder in my direction. "The human woman needs rest, and I am weary from our vigil."

"Stay till you have strength for traveling," Neven replied, the anger completely gone from him now. His voice was filled with what sounded almost like pity, and regret filled his eyes. "And grace go with you when you leave, Brother. I am sorry that it cannot be different."

Rowan rose to his feet, and looked up to meet his brother's eyes. He smiled, but the expression was bitter and sad. "We cannot change what we are," he whispered. "Father shielded us for as long as he could, but now we must face it." He turned to Yasen. "You will go east, Brother?"

Yasen nodded. "I will. I feel the pull more, now that Father is gone. Maybe I should have gone earlier—but I did not want to leave him. It calls me, now."

"That is good." Rowan nodded. "Your bond with that land is strong. You will be fine." He turned back to Neven. "Thank you for keeping Elias with you."

Neven shrugged, somehow making the movement graceful. "He is too young to challenge me, so I feel no urge to drive him out, at least not for now." He shook his head, eyes downcast for a moment. "Goodbye, Rowan," he said. "May you find what you are seeking before your strength is gone."

"Thank you, Neven. Be happy here." Rowan looked around the clearing slowly. "Take care of it for me."

Without a word, Rowan locked eyes with Yasen, and with Elias. Then he turned and, wrapping his hand around my wrist, pulled me with him as he walked away.

"Rowan," I asked, glancing behind me to where his brothers still stood, watching our retreat. "What just happened?"

He grunted and stumbled. I grabbed his arm and tried to support his weight, though he was so much larger than me that I knew I had no hope of holding him up alone. "Are you in pain?"

"We have to hurry," was all he said in response. "This way." And he crashed through the undergrowth, leaving me to pick my way through after him as best I could.

A few minutes later I caught up to him just as he lowered himself to the ground on the banks of a small creek. Almost as soon as he sat down, a convulsion racked through him. He fell over on his side, his teeth clenched, as every muscle in his body suddenly tightened and his back arched. It was over after just a few seconds. I dropped to the ground beside him, pushing the hair out of his face so I could see his eyes.

"Rowan," I said, forcing myself to speak slowly, so my words would be clear. "I need you to tell me what's going on."

He locked eyes with me, and I could see him taking my measure, deciding how much he would say.

"You can trust me," I said, my voice softening. "I don't know if I can help you, but anything I can do—I will. Please. What's happening to you?"

"The land is leaving me," he grunted, and his eyes fluttered shut. I gripped his forearm, shaking him to wake him up.

"What does that mean?" I called. "Rowan! You have to stay awake, and explain this to me."

His eyes stayed closed. Grabbing him by both shoulders, I shook him again, harder this time.

A snarl rumbled deep in his chest, and I froze.

Shit.

He looked so human, I had almost forgotten how careful I had to be. He was a wounded creature, in pain, who didn't know me. And here I was, manhandling him like an idiot, shaking his shoulder when that probably hurt him. *Stupid, stupid, stupid.* I stilled, not daring to remove my hands from his shoulders, and holding my breath.

His eyes opened, and I could see panic there, and aggression. But then his eyes focused on my face, and the anger disappeared.

"Sorry," he muttered.

"No," I said, easing my hand away and leaning back to give him some space. "That was absolutely my fault."

We were silent for a minute, me watching him for any signs of new aggression, him drawing in deep, wheezing breaths.

"Explain this to me," I said, when I felt sure he had calmed down. I motioned toward his body, but didn't touch him. "You said the land is leaving you. What does that mean?"

He closed his eyes, and I was afraid he had passed out, but then he started speaking.

"It means my connection to the land is broken, now that my father is dead. I am a leshy. Everything we are, we get from the land. It is the source of our strength, our power. It is the anchor of our lives. It has been this way for me ever since I was born." He stopped and took a deep, heaving breath. "But my father is dead, and the land can have only one ruler. It chose Neven." There was no mistaking the bitterness in his voice. "It is no great surprise—I think we all knew, deep down, what would happen." He squeezed his eyes shut and lay his hands against his chest as he fought for air. "I am cut off."

"But what does that mean?" I lifted my hands into the air, poised to do...something, though I had no idea what. I wished with desperate fervor for my clinic and all its supplies. "What happens to you now?" He did not answer, and did not open his eyes, and sudden horror stabbed my heart. "Rowan?" I cried. "Are you dying?"

"No," he grunted. "I hope not. At least not yet."

"Oh, stop being so cryptic, goddamn it!" I cried, my voice rising to a yell. "I want to help you! You have got to tell me what the hell is going on!"

He jerked his eyes open with a look of profound surprise.

"What?" I cried, "Are you in pain?" I raised my hands again, trying to think of what I could possibly do to help him. Could I do CPR on a leshy?

"Do you always yell at your patients if you fear they are dying?" he asked, and I rolled back on my heels and stared at him. Relief and irritation flooded me in equal measure. If he was well enough to be a smart ass, then he definitely wasn't at death's door.

"If there is the slightest possibility that it will keep them alive, then yes," I answered. "And I'm still waiting for you to fill me in."

Despite his still pained breathing, a hint of amusement lit his eyes. "The separation is painful and dangerous," he answered. "But it is unlikely to kill me. It is like an umbilical cord being cut. You understand? The pain will pass. It is after that that the real danger begins. I will no longer be able to draw on the earth. I will weaken. Gradually...but it will happen."

As a doctor I had learned long ago how to keep my face impassive. "What happens then?"

"Then I will die," Rowan said, and closed his eyes again. "Unless I can find another land that will accept me, before my strength runs out. But there are not so many places left that are wild enough to house a leshy. The humans have taken over almost everywhere, and our kind does not have so long left before we have nowhere left to go. Then we will be truly gone, as you thought we already were. I will search, because I have no other choice. But I do not like my chances. Even if I can find another place that is wild enough to be my home, the land will most likely reject me."

I fell silent for a minute, trying to process that information.

"And how long do you have, then? To find a new home?"

He shrugged and opened his eyes, looking up at the sky. "I cannot know for sure. A month, if I am unlucky. Two, if fate is kind."

"Rowan..." I searched for words, aching for all he had lost. I reached out and put my hand on his, then gasped as I stared at his fingers. "Rowan?" I asked, and he pulled his hand from mine, holding it up in front of his eyes. On each of his fingers, a thin pink line stretched from fingernail to knuckle. "What is that?"

He grunted. "I have never seen it. But I have heard the stories." He dropped his hand and I quickly leaned closer to examine it. "The longer I am separated from the land, the more the markings will spread."

"It looks almost like blood poisoning," I whispered, running my fingertips lightly over the markings. "It doesn't pain you, does it?"

He shook his head. "It is the weakness that will kill me. The markings are just a warning of what is to come."

"I am sorry, Rowan," I said, covering one of his big hands with both of mine. "So very, very sorry."

His fingers closed around mine. "Me, too," he murmured.

ELEVEN

WE SAT FOR SEVERAL MINUTES. HE RESTED, WAITING FOR THE PAIN TO pass, and I had no idea what to say. Then, suddenly, his body tensed. He started to push himself up onto his elbows, grimacing in pain at the movement.

"What?" I started to ask, but he shook his head and gave me a look that silenced me.

Soon I heard what he was hearing—a rustling in the leaves just off the bank of the creek, and the sharp sound of angry voices. I knew from the expression on his face that he could make sense of the faint babble of sounds that, to me, were little more than a buzz of voices. Anger hardened his features, and he forced himself up onto his feet. The effort drained him of color, and his lips had pressed tight with suppressed grunts of pain by the time he stood. I darted to his side, but he ignored my outstretched hands and stood alone, folding his arms across his chest as he turned to face whatever came toward us from the trees. Though I kept my face impassive, I couldn't help the thrill of delight I felt when the leaves parted and I could see the creature pushing its way out into the light.

I had always wanted to see a satyr.

None had ever come to the clinic. I studied the short form in front of me with sharp curiosity. I had read many descriptions of satyrs—but now that I was looking at one in the flesh, none of those descriptions seemed to have been especially accurate. I had the impression that satyrs were supposed to be graceful, mischievous, sometimes sly. The creature standing before me looked downright dangerous. About four and a half feet tall, his goat legs and human torso melded together in a thick cascade of curly brown fur that matched exactly the twisting locks that fell to his shoulders. He was dressed for battle, a shining shield strapped to one arm, and a short, gold-tinted dagger naked in his right hand. He bared pointed, interlocking teeth with serrated edges, and his eyes flashed. His short bare arms were thick with muscle. All in all, he seemed much more threatening than I ever would have expected a satyr to be. He came to stand in front of Rowan and pulled himself up to his full height, which suddenly seemed surprisingly impressive. Then he bowed deeply.

"Hail, Lord!" he cried, just as a dozen more satyrs broke through the bushes and formed up ranks behind him. They were all dressed identically aside from the fact that a few wore soft leather vests. I wondered if those were the females. They all bowed deeply and repeated their leader's cry.

Rowan stood silently for a moment, studying them. Then he replied, "Greeting, friends. Though I think the news must have reached you that I am your Lord no longer."

Many of the satyrs muttered and stamped their feet, and their leader nodded.

"We have heard, and wept for your father. He is the only ruler any of us have ever known." Those behind him nodded. "Even our parents knew only him as king here. But that was only part of the reason we wept. Our tears turned to tears of outrage when we heard that your brother took the kingship for himself, rather than passing it you."

"Neven did not take anything," Rowan explained evenly. "The land chose him as its leader."

"But you were the firstborn son of your father!" the satyr exclaimed.

"That has nothing to do with it, and you know it, Tany," he said in a strained voice.

The muscles in his neck stood out as he clenched his teeth. He seemed steady on his feet, but based on the pain he had been in only moments ago, that steadiness had to be a show, a front he put on for the benefit of others.

"The land picks the son that it feels the deepest connection to. Yasen is already linked to a new land that will be his home, and Elias is too young for ruling. In a choice between me and Neven, the land chose him. There is nothing else to say."

"Yet we have said nothing at all!" The other satyrs nodded, calling out their agreement in short, deep bleating sounds. "You are the one we want," he said. "You are the one who has earned our trust, who stood beside us when we most needed it, and led us into battle against the Yono tribe."

"That was folly." Rowan's voice was harsh.

"It was not, and you know it," Tany said, and he stomped a hoofed foot on the ground. "You parrot the words of your father, but you know better than anyone the good we did. How many lives did we save by that action? And with our people's numbers dwindled to so few, each of those lives is so precious."

Rowan looked at him, his eyes narrowing, and gave the slightest nod of his head. "Folly or not, it makes no difference," he muttered. "Not when it comes to ruling the land."

"How can you say that?" Tany asked.

His eyes had no irises. They were a full, deep black.

He lifted his chin. "We know who we want to rule us. We have not forgotten, nor will we ever. Your brother may understand the land, but he does not understand us. The land may have chosen him, but we do not!"

Rowan snorted. "What are you thinking of, Tany? That we are humans, and will take a vote? That all the creatures who are sheltered in these woods will step forward and say which of the leshy brothers they prefer? That is not how it works! These things are determined by the deepest, most primitive magic there is. I assure you, it does not care what you think any more than it cares what I desire! It has chosen Neven, and that is the end of it."

"It is the end of it for as long as Neven is in the forest," Tany corrected him. "If he were to leave, if he were to choose to forgo his rulership, and go out and seek a new home elsewhere, then the land would have no choice but to make a new selection. His bond with this land is only hours old, and not fully formed. He is not yet so strong that he cannot be challenged."

Shocked silence hung in the air. The other satyrs gazed intently at Tany, their hands tight around the hilts of the weapons that hung from their belts. Standing slightly behind Rowan, I could see the muscles in his back tense and gather, could feel anger swelling in the air around him like a storm.

"You would threaten my brother?" he asked, his voice quiet.

I heard the warning that lay just beneath the surface of those words. But Tany didn't. With his face turned to address the rest of the satyrs, he spoke more to them than to Rowan, heedless of the mounting danger.

"I do not believe threatening him will be necessary." His voice was brash now. "Once he understands he is not *wanted* here—" He laid thick emphasis on each word. "I hope he will do the right thing. I believe once we help him understand his true position, he will be happy to seek his fortune somewhere else. Do not worry, Lord Rowan." His words were full of gallantry, but he did not look up to see the fury in Rowan's eyes. "You may be too noble to rise up in your own defense, but you are not without friends in this forest. We are loyal to you. We will do for you what your own heart is too tender to allow."

"I. Forbid. It." Rowan bit out each word.

I wanted to cry out, to grab Tany by his shoulders and shake him until he understood how much Rowan had been through, how much pain he was in at this moment, and how far he was pushing his control.

But Tany just smiled, as though he was being clever. "You yourself just reminded us that, at the moment, you do not rule here. Once you are back in your rightful place, we hope you will forgive the friends who acted on your behalf. But if you do not, it is a risk we will take upon ourselves. Rest yourself, Lord. We will take care of everything. You will be in your rightful place soon."

Tany turned and began to lead his small troop back into the trees.

With an ear-splitting roar, Rowan crouched low and then launched himself into the air. He pivoted to land in front of Tany, his face a mask of fury. He leaned down and grabbed Tany with both hands. He lifted him high into the air and then threw him bodily to the ground.

"Do you think I would allow you to threaten my brother? To spill his blood?" he bellowed, stalking closer to Tany who lay, dazed, in the dirt, staring up at Rowan. Behind them the rest of the satyrs stood frozen, their shock a mirror of my own.

"You would have me lose more today than I already have? Losing my father and my home was not enough for you. Now you would also take my brother from me, and make me a usurper against my will?" His hands balled up into fists, and he roared, a deep howl of fury.

I have to do something, I thought to myself. *He's going to kill someone.*

Moving before I had a clear idea of what exactly my plan was, I ran forward and crouched over Tany, covering as much of his body with my own as I could. I said nothing, only looked up at Rowan, and waited.

Rowan's howl cut off suddenly, and he stared down at me. The fury disappeared from his eyes, replaced with sudden and absolute surprise.

"What are you doing?" he asked, his voice strangled.

"Calm down," I said softly. "You don't want to hurt your friend. You are in a hundred different kinds of pain right now, but if you hurt him, you'll hate yourself later. Tany is going to listen to you. Right, Tany?" I prompted.

Tany pulled himself out from under me onto his knees. He stared up at Rowan and, suddenly, the war-like expression on his face crumpled. His mouth quivered, and his wide, dark eyes, which suddenly seemed doe-like, filled with tears. He threw his knife away from him and burst into the unrestrained sobs of a child.

Rowan took a stumbling step back. His shoulders slumped, and he rubbed his hands roughly over his face.

"Go home, Tany," he said at last.

Tany quieted. He stood, stumbling over to Rowan and looking up at him with a lost expression. Rowan put his hand on his shoulder.

"We can't change it," Rowan said, his voice gentling. "You mustn't grieve. We've made our choices. We knew the land would not accept me. Not after..." and his words petered out. He shook his head. "Anyway. We knew this day would come."

"I hoped not," Tany whispered, his voice still thick with tears. "We hoped you would stay with us always." He turned toward Rowan, and suddenly a new light took hold in his face.

"Take us with you," Tany said, his eyes glittering. "We will come along!"

Rowan sighed and glanced in my direction, but I couldn't read his expression.

"Friend," he whispered. "You know I have no place to go."

"We will help you!" the satyr protested, and it was only now that I realized how young he was, how childlike. "We can assist you in your search!"

"Ah, Tany." Rowan shook his head. "You are a better friend than I deserve. I can't do that to you. I have nothing to offer you, no way to provide for your needs."

"But..."

Rowan's sharp look cut him off. "I have lost so much today," he said gently. "My father and my home. Let me at least keep my honor. Spare me sentencing others who might have good futures from sharing in my fate. You are right that I can no longer command you. But grant me this, as the request of a friend."

Tears welled up in Tany's eyes, and he nodded, too overcome to speak.

Rowan patted him on the shoulder. "Go home. Drink and dance together. Sing songs by the fireside. Soon you will forget me."

"We will not forget," Tany bleated. "But we will do as you say. It is the only way we have left of honoring you." He turned, and led his sad band of followers back toward the woods.

"Rowan?" he called, turning back.

"Yes?"

"If you survive..." Here he had to stop to swallow down unruly emotion. "If you find a home, I mean. Send for us. We will join you there. I understand if you cannot take us with you now, but, please, do that much for us."

"All right." Rowan nodded, after a moment's hesitation. "I will. Be well, Tany."

"Good travels, Rowan," Tany said. "And be careful in the woods. The king and his protection have barely left us, and already there are strangers in these trees."

"Strangers?" I asked, my breath catching in my throat. Tany turned his black eyes to me and nodded.

"I do not know who or what they are. But I heard their voices in the wind," he answered, and turned away. A moment later he and his people were gone.

For a moment we both stood, staring at the spot where they had disappeared into the forest.

"Rowan," I asked, trying to keep my voice steady, "do you think the strangers that he is talking about are the mages coming for me?"

He shook his head slowly, his eyes drawn with worry. "I do not know. I would not have thought it possible." He sighed heavily, then pointed to the creek that flowed nearby. "Quickly," he grunted. "We will not wait here to find out. Drink as much as you can. The water is clean, and it will be some time before we have water again. We cannot stay here any longer."

"You are not well enough for traveling," I protested, even as my eyes probed the trees, straining to see through the shadows that suddenly seemed threatening. "Your brother said we could stay the night. You have to let yourself rest."

"We have no choice," Rowan answered, and strode down to the river bank. He leaned down to the surface and drank long and deep. When he finally lifted his face, his hair was wet from trailing in the water. "My presence here is calling Neven's leadership into question. If there is one group running around, talking about running him out of the forest and setting me up in his place, then there could be more."

"That isn't your fault," I exclaimed. "And you stopped them from challenging him!"

"It makes no difference. If Neven hears of it, he'll have no choice. His instincts will take over, and he will come after me. We can't let it come to that. And whoever the strangers are, neither of us is in any condition to confront them. We must leave this place. Quickly."

TWELVE

"WHERE ARE WE GOING, EXACTLY?" I ASKED ABOUT A HALF HOUR later. "Not that tramping through the wilderness with you isn't everything I ever dreamt of and more."

I tripped over another root. There were so many of them, extending up and out of the ground like gnarled, knobby fingers to grab at my heels. If I kept my eyes on the ground, making sure to watch my step, then I couldn't see the low-hanging branches that seemed to spring out of nowhere to scrape against my face. Strange sounds periodically erupted from somewhere behind us, continually making me halt and turn to look behind us. My mind kept playing tricks on me, and every few minutes my breath froze in my chest as I thought for a second that I saw a glimpse of Paul's face through the trees. If not for the ache in my chest, which built and burned more painfully with every step, I might have broken into a run. As it was, I struggled behind Rowan, trying to believe it was physical exhaustion, rather than fear, that made my legs unsteady. I had told myself I was done with running but, somehow, I was back to doing exactly that. I hated the fear that churned inside me, and hated the weakness that allowed fear to bloom.

"You know," I grumbled, "I've read legends about leshies. How they used to amuse themselves by leading people they didn't like astray in the forest and then leaving them to starve. Are you sure that isn't what's going on now?"

Rowan had been silent since we started out, his face set in grim lines and his lips pressed together. Now he paused and turned back to look at me, his expression unreadable.

"I know a sheltered place a few hours' walk from here," he said at last. "It is far enough from my brother's land" his eyes tightened at the phrase but his voice didn't falter, "that our staying there will give no offense."

"A few hours?" I stopped walking and pushed the hair back behind my ears.

Sweat streamed thickly down my neck and tickled as it trickled down my back. Though the sun was close to setting, the trees seemed to hold the warmth in, and the air here hung thick and heavy. "We won't make it before dark, then."

Rowan didn't respond, but his answer was plain on his face.

"You can't do what you did before?" I asked. "Jump into the ground and pop up someplace else?" It was a sign of how desperately tired I was, and how uncomfortable with the idea of still being out when darkness fell, that I suggested that mode of transport.

"Not so soon after being separated from the land," Rowan said, and grimaced. "I am not strong enough. A day, maybe two from now, after I have rested, I will be able to again." He hesitated. "And when I am able, I will of course take you to wherever you need to go."

I nodded, wiping my sweaty palms on my pants leg to hide the sudden tightness in my chest. "Thank you. I need to get back as soon as I can."

Rowan stared. "Back? What do you mean?"

"Back to the mage camp." I peered up, trying to see through the overhanging branches to where the sun hung low in the sky. It was hard to be sure how long I had been gone, but I didn't think it had been more than twelve hours.

"Healer," he said, stepping closer and touching my hand. "I meant I will take you someplace where you'll be safe. You know what the mages intended to do to you. Is there any doubt what will happen if you return?"

I stepped to the side so his fingers were no longer touching mine.

"Thank you," I said. "But I have to go back."

"Why?"

I looked at the ground, digging a little hole in the dirt with the toe of my shoe as I tried to find words to explain. "I don't have a choice. Someone I care about is being held against her will. While I was a prisoner in the mage camp someone said something that seemed…suspicious. I think he may have had something to do with her disappearance. I have to go back—to try to find out whatever I can. If I can figure out where she is being held, then maybe I can help her get free. It's the only hope I've had of saving her in years." I shrugged. "I have to try."

Rowan rocked back on his heels, studying me. For a long moment he said nothing, then he nodded as though to himself.

"Very well. Then I will go with you, and help you find your friend."

"You don't have to do that, and it isn't a very good idea. If the mages find us, they won't care who you are or why you took me from them. They'll just kill you. Besides, you don't have much time. You have to focus on finding a new home."

He shook his head so that his hair swung back and forth. "I will help you. I am in your debt, and honor-bound to repay you for what you have done for me and mine."

"You brought me here to heal your father, Rowan," I said as gently as I could. "Which I wasn't able to do."

"You did save him, though." His voice was rough, and he looked away as he spoke. "You freed him from his burden, and from the pain he was enduring for my sake."

"You don't owe me anything for that."

"After that," he went on, speaking louder as he cut off my words, "you put yourself in danger to bring me to my senses, when grief and rage had stolen my reason away. And now you are allowing me to drag you through the forest in order to avoid a confrontation with my brother, though you are suffering from a pain so great that it hurts you to move."

I gasped. No one had ever guessed the pain I was living with.

"How do you..." I stuttered as I searched for words. My eyes widened as Rowan took a slow step forward, as though he was afraid if he moved too suddenly I would startle, and flee. Then, with gentle fingers, he touched me just below my collarbone, in exactly the spot where the pain was the worst.

"You see things, healer, that others do not." He smiled faintly, something conspiratorial in his expression. "And you are not the only one." He turned his head then, hearing some sound off in the distance that was too faint for my ears. "We must continue now. If you can?"

I nodded, feeling dazed.

He reached out and took my hand in his large, calloused palm. "We will walk together. It is not as far as you think. If you get too tired, tell me. I can carry you."

"I had quite enough of that the first time, thanks," I snapped. "I can manage."

But I didn't pull my hand away.

It might have been an hour later that my vision started doing funny things, and the dark that descended seemed to twist and curl around me. The moon rose, and the shadows reached out for us as we hurried past. I could no longer feel my toes, and my calves and thighs had gone numb. I stopped thinking, stopped doing anything but putting one foot in front of the other. That, at least, was something I knew how to do, and there was some comfort in the mechanical movement. I lowered my chin to my chest, and just kept going.

"We are nearly there," Rowan murmured at last, but I was too tired to do more than nod silently.

Soon he guided me into a space where the ground felt rocky underfoot, then through the entrance of a small cave. I reached out in the darkness, stumbling forward until I could feel the cave's wall at my fingertips. Then I half-sat, half-fell to the floor, turning so I could lean my burning forehead against the soothing cool of the stone.

"Is there any sign of someone following us?" I asked, my voice rough with exhaustion.

"None," Rowan answered. "We are safe, at least for now. There is a river very near to here. Would you like to go and drink?"

I shook my head, my eyes already closing.

"Healer?" Rowan crouched close to me. "Are you well?"

"I'm sleeping," I said faintly, waving him away with my hand, too tired to produce full sentences. "Or will be once you quiet down. Rest first. Hydration later."

He laughed softly and said something I was too far gone to understand. And then I was dreaming.

THIRTEEN

"ASA?" A VOICE CALLED.

A wonderful, deep darkness cocooned me. Distantly, I was aware that my body lay on cold, hard stone. I knew in a vague, disinterested way, that waking would bring pain and worry, and my mind burrowed deeper into the black.

"Asa, wake up!" A hand came to rest on my shoulder, shaking me. Fear uncurled deep inside my chest, chilling and insistent.

The only people who know my real name wanted me dead.

My eyes flew open and my body stiffened as I pushed away the hands that held me, trying to crawl away from the touch that could only mean me harm.

"What's wrong? Healer?"

"Get away from me. Let me go!"

Large, warm hands released me. I scrambled away, retreating until my back was up against the wall of the cave. Rowan crouched next to the spot where I had been lying, his hand still stretched out in my direction.

"You're safe here," he said slowly, confusion plain on his face. "Everything's all right."

Heart still pounding, I scanned the cave, searching for danger, expecting to see mages with weapons drawn closing in on me.

All I found was Rowan. I sat down heavily and gasped for breath.

"You scared me, Rowan!"

His brow furrowed. "I didn't mean to frighten you. You were moaning in your sleep."

"How long have I been out?" I asked, rubbing my eyes. My voice was little better than a croak.

"A few hours."

"And how in the *hell* do you know my real name?"

Rowan's eyebrows climbed. "I hid outside the mage camp for hours yesterday. Listening. I heard the name the other mages called you. I'm sorry."

"No. No need to apologize. I shouldn't have cursed at you. You just took me by surprise." I tried to take a deep breath to calm myself, and an involuntary gasp of pain slipped through my lips.

"You're hurt," he exclaimed, leaping to his feet and taking a step toward me. Even though his voice was filled with nothing but concern, I shied away, flinching and raising an arm to shield myself.

He stopped short, and his brows gathered as he looked down at me.

"You fear me," he said. It was not a question.

"Sorry," I muttered, forcing myself to lower my arm and try to relax. "I'm still waking up and you seem kind of ... tall, right now."

He snorted and crouched down, hunching his shoulders in an apparent attempt to make himself seem smaller. It gave him the appearance of a large, uncomfortable boulder of muscle with brooding eyes, but I appreciated the effort.

"I have been trying to wake you for some time. I feared you had been injured. I looked for a wound, thinking perhaps you had been bitten by a snake, but I couldn't find anything."

I blinked my eyes rapidly, trying to dispel the image that rose unbidden in my mind of Rowan, running his hands up and down my body, and the unwelcome flash of heat that followed it. *You may not be attracted to the leshy,* I told myself, sternly. *That isn't even legal.*

"I have some food, if you are hungry," he went on. "Do you eat fish? My mother always liked it."

He held out a wide strip of bark with a large piece of fish on it. It still steamed from the fire, and smelled amazing.

"Where did you get this?" I asked, as I took it from him and hurried to pull a piece off with my fingers and pop it in my mouth.

It was so hot that it burned my tongue, but I didn't care. I was starving—and the fish was delicious.

"There is a river there." Rowan pointed behind him. "There is more food if you want it. I built a fire outside, just beside the entrance to the cave. Once you've eaten you can go outside and take a drink."

"This is so good," I told him honestly. "Thank you."

I ate, and he watched me for some minutes in a comfortable silence. Then he folded his hands in front of him, and looked at me, his expression almost guilty.

"I heard more than just your name that day."

"Oh." I shifted my body, trying to get comfortable on the hard ground. "What did you hear?"

"I heard that you were the one who pulled down the dam, and let the Source flow out to mages who are not of the clan."

"Hmm." I kept my eyes on my fish, picking a bit of flesh from a bone. "And what do leshies know of the Source, or the concerns of mages?" I had not forgotten the way he had walked right into my Truthsight vision when I was healing his father.

"I know the clan has long held back access to magic to anyone who would not bend the knee to them. And I know that several years ago—suddenly—everything changed."

"Wow," I said, trying not to push too hard, remembering his temper. I lifted another piece of fish to my lips. "You must have heard a lot."

"I heard your conversation with your friend," he said, hesitating. "And, also, my mother was a mage."

I choked on my fish, coughing until it worked its way down. "What are you talking about?" I sputtered, but he didn't answer. "Rowan? What do you mean, your mother was a mage? Mages are human. You're a leshy."

"Yes," he said, sighing and still not looking at me. His eyes were trained steadily to the side. "And all leshies are male. We mate with human women, who bear fully leshy sons."

What? I thought, but almost immediately it began to make sense. In all my study of ancient folklore, and the accounts of leshies I had seen, I had never heard of a female leshy. And it would explain how very close to human he appeared. I felt a rush of heat in my cheeks.

Don't blush! I thought to myself, chanting it like a mantra in my head. *Don't blush, don't blush.* But I could feel the crimson creeping, warm, up my cheeks, and suddenly the cave felt smaller, more intimate than it had just a moment before.

Luckily Rowan was still looking away, talking in a hushed voice. "My mother was born a mage, though her whole life she was denied access to her birthright by the Clan."

"And that's why you can access Truthsight?"

He nodded, and looked back at me, watching me closely for my response.

"Can your brothers?"

He shook his head slowly. "With Elias it is still too early to know. But Yasen and Neven—no."

"So are you..." I tried to get a handle on what he was telling me. "Are you a mage, Rowan?"

"No." He shook his head so vigorously that his hair swung back and forth a little. He stared down at knotted fingers. "The truth is I've never been really sure of what I am. A leshy, yes. But not only that. And not even that, in a way that was pleasing to my father. I am resistant to mage magic. My mother knew it from the day I was born—it is why she named me Rowan, because rowan trees are proof against Truthsight, and against the kind of magic you can do. I can see the Source, can walk through your visions, but I cannot wield them. My magic is leshy magic." His chest swelled a little, and I could see the pride in his eyes. "Leshy magic is different. It runs deeper, and is wilder, than what mages can do."

As suddenly as it had come, the pride disappeared from his face. He ran a hand over his eyes, as though trying to hide the sudden pain that shined there. "With no access to magic, my mother's body wouldn't work the way it was meant to. Until the day she became my father's mate and the land gave her its fealty, she suffered."

His voice caught, and it was a second before he could continue. "Once she could access leshy magic, the pain left her. She always said it was like seeing the sun for the first time in her life, the day she woke up and her body didn't hurt. But she never forgot, and she made sure we knew everything. That she had been labeled a "rebel" because she dared to be born to parents who refused to bend their knees to the clan. If it is true, what those mages were saying—if you really are the one who changed all that—then many would call you a hero. And they would be right."

"You don't understand, Rowan," I said softly. "I am sorry, so very sorry, for what your mother suffered. But people died because of what I did. There was fighting, terrible fighting and people I knew— people I cared about and thought of as family—were killed. The Clan mages are right to hate me. The fate you saved me from is one I've had coming for a long time."

He recoiled as though I had struck him.

"You can't believe that," he spat. "You undid a great injustice. They hate you because they loved the power they lost."

"It isn't their fault that they hate me Rowan," I whispered. "My motivations were good, but I acted rashly, and alone. The result was bloodshed and ruin. You can't possibly understand the cost of what I did. I tore their world apart."

Rowan's eyes flashed.

"The Clan had been hoarding power for years," he growled.

"They didn't care what it did to people, didn't give a damn about the price others paid. Believe me, a fight was coming—it had been coming, for years and years. Did the clan really believe the other mages would suffer in silence forever? They were angry, and in pain. The blood that was spilled was the price they paid for that—it is what happens when one group of people oppresses another for so long."

He fell silent, his teeth clenched, staring at me as he waited for me to respond. I just stared back at him. I felt shaken, as though he had taken me by the shoulders and slammed me side to side. I simply had no words.

He reached out, and lay his hand lightly on my knee. "Think of the people who aren't suffering anymore, because of what you did," he whispered. "I wish my mother had lived long enough to see it. But people like her—people you've never met—think of what you've done for them."

When had I started crying? Saltwater on my lips startled me, and I automatically ran my fingers across my cheeks, covering my eyes for a moment to escape the heat of his stare. Could he be right? For years I had carried guilt heavy inside me. I wasn't sure I knew how to put it down. And I remembered Shanie, and the pain in her eyes. The loss of her brothers, and so many others, triggered by a choice that I had made. I looked up, and Rowan was watching me intently.

"I appreciate all that you've said," I told him. "But you realize it doesn't change anything? I still have to go back. For Meri's sake."

"Who's Meri?"

"She was the head of the Clan."

Rowan's face hardened, and I knew what he was thinking.

"I understand your mother must have hated Meri for denying her access to the Source," I said hurriedly. "I get that. I really do. But Meri had reasons for what she did, and she meant well. And for many years, she was like a mother to me."

I looked down, feeling my throat tighten. "My parents died when I was nine. I stayed with my friend Shanie for a while after it happened, and her family tried to be kind. But I missed my parents in way that felt like physical pain."

I closed my eyes, shaking my head to try to force away the memories. "Some days I couldn't get out of bed, and Shanie's mother didn't know how to help me. So Meri took me in. She's so ancient that she's watched all her friends and family die around her. She understood my grief, and she stayed beside me while I felt it through. We were always a team after that. She had been alone for a long time. She was happier, once I was with her. I know she isn't perfect—she's made mistakes, and because she is so powerful, her mistakes cost that much more. But Meri is my only family. There isn't much I wouldn't do for her."

Rowan gazed at me for a long moment, then nodded curtly. I had put it in terms he could understand—the loyalty due to a parent.

"Before I left, Meri asked me to carry something for her. She called it her pearl. You see, all those years that she was channeling magic, there was magic that was withheld. It had to be kept somewhere."

"Because she would only allow it to flow to mages she approved of," Rowan said, his face contorting.

"That's right. So she held onto that magic, hiding it inside of herself."

"She hoarded excess magic inside her own body?"

"She stored it away, to keep it from being used in the wrong way."

"Or by someone she did not approve of."

"I suppose you're right." I rubbed my hands together and avoided his eyes. "Anyway, after I healed her, she was weak. She couldn't bear to carry it, but needed someplace to keep it that was absolutely safe. Just until she got her strength back. She asked me to carry it for her for a while."

"Why was carrying it so difficult for her?"

I shrugged. "She was weak, and very tired. It is not an easy burden to carry. Pearls are very beautiful—but they are born out of the pain of the oyster that carries them.'"

"So she asked you to keep the Pearl inside your own body?" Rowan gestured toward my chest, his eyes wide. "Did she know the pain it would cause you?"

"It was only supposed to be for a week or so, until things calmed down," I explained, anxious for him to understand. "I can't remove it safely myself—the magic is too complicated, and I think Meri is the only one who could really do it without harming me. Neither of us could have dreamed she would be captured."

His eyes widened in surprise. "*She* is the friend you spoke of? Is it possible to imprison such a powerful mage?"

"It shouldn't be. But when I speak to her, she always sounds confused. As though they are drugging her, or something. I've hardly ever been able to hear her clearly, and even when I have, she's never been able to tell me where she is being held. All this time, and I haven't known how to help her. But then, the other day, when I was in the mage camp..." I shook my head, still stunned. "I think I might know who betrayed her." I spread out my hands. "Maybe there is some way I could help her. Maybe I could find out where the rebel mages are holding her, and set her free."

For the first time, Rowan seemed eager. "If she were free, would she tell the clan to let you be?"

I nodded. "She was angry with me for what I did, but she also understood." I shrugged. "And she loves me." I hesitated.

An idea had formed in my mind, sometime while I had been sleeping. But I wasn't sure what Rowan's reaction would be. "There is something else," I said, watching his face carefully. "Meri is incredibly powerful. Or, she will be—once she has the pearl back again. I'm almost positive she could help you, Rowan. Not provide you with a new home, but keep your strength from running out while you search. Give you all the time you need to find a new land."

Rowan stiffened, and his nostrils flared. "No," he said, his voice cold and suddenly distant. "I have no desire to be in debt to one such as her."

"Oh, don't be an idiot," I snapped, and Rowan's sudden iciness disappeared as quickly as it had come.

He turned to stare at me, his eyes wide. I thought I saw a flicker of amusement there.

"If you help me save Meri from imprisonment, you won't be in her debt. *She* will be in *yours*."

He said nothing, but his expression changed. I had handled it right—he was considering it. The idea of holding the mage who had denied his mother access to magic in his debt appealed to him.

"Here's my idea," I said hurriedly, hoping if I spoke fast enough he wouldn't have time to argue. "We'll go back to the mage camp together, just like you said. I think that the new head of the Clan, Paul, might have been the one who betrayed Meri. I want to look at him with my Truthsight. Could you shield me again while I use it, the way you did yesterday?"

Rowan nodded.

"Good. I just need to get a good look at him. Treachery like that leaves a mark—if he was the one who turned on Meri, I think I'll be able to see it. That would at least give us a place to start."

For a moment Rowan sat quietly, not meeting my eyes. I could feel him weighing my words, and forced myself to stay still and silent while he decided what he would do.

"All right." Rowan nodded sharply, and sprung to his feet with a sudden movement that surprised me. "I will take you back, so you can try to free this woman, who will protect you from harm, and who may be able to give me more time to find a home. Once she removes her pearl from your body, then the pain will no longer flower in your chest?" And he pointed again to the spot where the pearl was nestled.

I nodded.

"Good. Then we will go. But understand this, healer." And he leaned down over me, his blue-gray eyes pressing into mine. "I can hear the words you do not say out loud. Before, when I found you in their power—you had surrendered yourself to the mages, hadn't you?" His eyes burned into mine, and I couldn't breathe or look away. I nodded.

"I thought so." His lips pressed together into a hard line. "You plan to look at this Paul, and see if he is the traitor. But in the back of your mind, you are resolved that, if you cannot free your Meri, you will give yourself over to the mages once again." He shook his head slowly. "Know now that I will not allow it. While I am with you, I will not allow you to come to harm. Not by someone else's hand, and not by your own. Do you understand?"

"Yes," I answered, a little breathlessly.

"Good," he said, holding his hand to me. "Then let us go."

FOURTEEN

"Are you sure you're strong enough? I thought you would need a day or two to rest."

The lines that marred his skin had turned from a faint pink to an angry, painful red, and had stretched up farther, spreading past his wrist. Rowan glanced down at them, and shrugged. "I have strength enough for this," he said. "And you are suffering. We must not wait."

I followed him outside, where a narrow river flowed peaceably by, just a few steps from the entrance to the cave. Kneeling down by the water, I cupped my hands and took drink after drink. Rowan dunked his whole head under the water and drank deeply, coming up with his hair and face streaming. The muscles in his back flexed as he straightened up, the water dripping down his chest. The sun glinted on his horns and in his eyes and, for a second, I couldn't pull my gaze away from him.

"This trip will not be as difficult for you as the last time," Rowan told me.

I blinked and looked away.

He stood and shook his head vigorously, spraying water through the air. "The last time we traveled in this way, you were trying to breathe. There is no need for that when we are under. Rocks don't breathe. Soil doesn't breathe. When we are together, inside the earth, we become a part of it—you don't need air. If you try to get it, you'll just strain your body and make yourself sick."

"Okay." I could hold my breath, right? That didn't sound so hard.

"But you should know that the trip back to where I found you will take longer."

My heart sank. "Why?"

"Because I don't have any connection to where we're going now. Before, I was coming home—I know this land. I know what it tastes like, how it feels. It was simple for me to reach out, find it, and pull us back here. But I don't have a feel for the place you come from—I was only there for a few hours. It will take me longer to find our way back."

"I can help with that." A woman's voice, low and threatening, made my heart stutter.

I spun around. Alice stepped out from behind the outcropping of rock that had concealed her.

Her upper lip curled up as if the very sight of me disgusted her. "I'll save you the trip, traitor, and send you straight to hell. Right where you belong."

She clutched a naked knife in her hand, but that wasn't the real threat. Her eyes sparkled, flecked with silver, full of the magical power that coursed through her body. I stumbled back a step.

"How did you find me?" I gasped.

Alice laughed. "Did you think you had gotten away from us clean? That staying away from the Source would keep us from finding you again?" she asked, taking a long step closer, her lips stretching in a grotesque smile. "Did you forget this?" And she held the knife up in the sunlight, so I could see the dried blood that stained the blade.

My hand darted to my neck, to the long, shallow cut Alice had left there the night before. And I understood.

"Fresh blood," Alice confirmed, seeing the understanding in my eyes. "More than enough on the blade to feed the tracking spell that led me straight to you."

I knew a curse was coming. I could feel it building inside her, mounting in the air like a building storm.

"Listen, Alice—" I stammered, but she kept on talking as though I hadn't spoken at all. "I could have told the others," Alice went on. "But then they all would have wanted a piece of you, and what would have been the fun in that? I told you before, all these long years I have been dreaming of killing you. And now I get to have this moment all to myself."

I took another stumbling step back, slipping a little when my foot landed in the creek. My mind spun. I could try to use magic to defend myself, but I was a healer, and had never been especially good at defensive magic. And to use it I would have to tap into the Source. All the other mages would immediately know where I was.

But then there was no more time to think.

Alice took in a long, hissing breath between her teeth, and her left hand flew out toward me. I threw myself to the ground, hoping to escape the worst of the curse she had hurled in my direction. Rowan stepped in front of me, and batted the spell away.

It was like nothing I had ever seen before. He stood directly in the path of the magic, and simply pushed it aside, a look of mere irritation on his face. There was a sound like glass shattering, and for a split second the air in front of him pulsed with silver light.

And then, nothing.

The curse was simply gone. It did not even seem to cost him any effort to do it.

Alice and I both stared at him, dumbfounded, as his lips curled back from his teeth and a deep snarl rumbled from his chest.

"You trespass in these woods, mage," he growled. "You are not welcome here."

Alice's eyes flashed, and she threw a second, nastier curse, this one aimed directly at Rowan.

With a growl, Rowan reached up and caught the spell in his

hands. For a second I could see it, glowing faintly; an amorphous, silver bubble undulating in his hands. Then, with a flick of his wrist, he hurled it back into Alice's face. Her eyes widened with shock right before the curse hit her, and she had time for a half strangled cry of surprised pain.

Her body spasmed when it hit the ground.

"*No!* Wait!" I cried, as I scrambled toward her, knowing that, no matter how quickly I moved, Rowan would get there first.

He stood over her, his fist pulled back high into the air, ready for the killing blow, when I reached them. I knelt down next to Alice, and held my hands out, shielding her.

"Leave her alone!" I cried, and Rowan stared at me in wonder.

"She came here to kill you, healer. And the death she planned to give you was no clean one."

I barely heard his words. I was busy checking Alice's pulse and breathing. She would suffer no real harm—the curse had been meant to incapacitate, not to kill. I was not really surprised. I had a feeling she had planned to take her time, and use her knife for the rest.

"We aren't going to hurt her," I explained from between teeth that would not quite unclench.

"And do you think she will abandon her search for you, or give up her blood thirst, now that you have spared her?"

Face set with grim determination, I told him, "No."

I pried the knife from her hands, and carefully wiped the last traces of my blood from the blade before placing it in the sheath that hung from her belt. "Her son is dead because of me. She isn't going to stop. But we aren't going to hurt her."

I straightened Alice's legs, checked to make sure she was breathing evenly. I folded her hands on her chest. Rowan just stood, watching me with narrowed eyes.

"You wouldn't have fought her," he said when I stood and brushed my hands off. "If I had not been here. You would not have hurt her—not even in defense of your own life."

I studied my shoes, refusing to meet his angry gaze. "I already caused her to lose her son. I don't think I could bring myself to hurt her even more."

"Asa," Rowan whispered. "You are not the one who killed her son. Your hands are clean."

"That's not the way I see it."

"So you would throw your own life away? When you have such awesome abilities, when there is so much good you can do? You would lie down to die before this woman, who is little more than a husk of pain and hate and anger?"

I rounded on Rowan, my own anger finally rising. "And if she is that way, whose fault is that?"

He just stared back at me, his eyes suddenly sad rather than angry.

I rubbed my hands across my eyes. "Anyway, this is over. At least for the moment."

"Then what shall we do now?"

"Exactly what we were going to do before. This changes nothing. We'll go back to the mage camp, and get within sight of Paul. I will find out what I can, and we will do whatever it takes to free Meri. Here." I straightened up and turned toward him, pulling my necklace out from underneath my shirt and holding it out so he could see the stones. "Would this help you find your way back there? All these stones are from the land near my home."

Rowan looked up, and his eyes widened. "Where did you get that?" he gasped, and in one long stride he closed the distance between us and fingered the necklace, his long fingers brushing against my collarbone.

"I run a clinic from the barn next to my home, for creatures who need healing. This is how they pay me—with stones like this." I undid the clasp and poured the necklace into his hand, taking a quick step away and trying to pretend that the warmth spreading from my neck up to my cheeks wasn't because of the feeling of his fingers against my skin.

"Yes," Rowan murmured, his eyes narrow as he concentrated on the stones. "This is perfect. Give me a moment."

I stood back, and watched Rowan work. He stood perfectly still. The only thing that moved were his fingers as he ran them back and forth over the stones. After a moment I could feel potential welling up around our feet, and the air felt taut, like the tension of a bow string as it pulls back and back. The air filled with the smell of lavender and smoke. A minute passed, and Rowan began whistling, a low sound as his fingers continued to move steadily up and down the length of the necklace. The color of his skin began changing to match the color of the rocks he made contact with. Blue, magenta, shiny brown, the change came and went so quickly that I could hardly convince myself that what I thought I saw was real. But then he looked up at me, and smiled.

"I've got it now." And he held out a hand.

I reached out, and the touch of his fingers sent a flash of heat coursing through me. I avoided his eyes, hoping that he couldn't sense the effect his touch was having on me. I walked over to him, and he turned me so that I was standing with my back to him. He draped one arm over my shoulder, and wrapped his other arm around my waist, pulling me tight against him. I could feel the coarse hair on his chest against the bare skin of my arms, and the brush of his breath on my temple. He smelled of wood smoke and dried leaves. He still had my necklace clasped firmly in one of his hands.

"Ready?" he asked. "Don't fight it, and you'll be fine."

I braced myself, expecting for him to jump up and then fall down into the ground as he had last time.

Instead, the ground beneath us suddenly opened, and we just fell through.

I closed my eyes, and tried not to feel the pressure. But still my chest ached and begged for air.

What if Rowan was wrong? I thought frantically, as time, impossible to keep track of, ticked by.

I tried to feel Rowan's arms around me, and willed myself to believe that his protection was enough.

What if he doesn't need to breathe, because he's a leshy—but I do? What if he doesn't realize that, and we're underground too long, and I suffocate?

Even though I kept my eyes resolutely shut, I could feel the darkness, thick, around me.

I was so cold.

I felt trapped, closed in, and utterly helpless.

What if Rowan really isn't strong enough to be doing this yet? It suddenly occurred to me. *If he runs out of strength, there's nothing I can do to help him. We'll be trapped down here, buried alive.*

The panic that swelled in me then had a mind and a will of its own. It was a feral animal, trapped in my chest, clawing at my insides. The need to be above ground, to be in the open, overwhelmed me. Rowan's arms tightened around my chest, and I realized I was fighting him, writhing in his grasp, but the realization wasn't enough to stop me. Reason and my body had parted company, and I fought with a mindless desperation to break free.

Suddenly we broke the surface. Instantly Rowan released me, backing away several paces before I could push him away. He crouched nearby. I collapsed on the grass, shaking and gasping for air. My clothes clung to me, damp with sweat. My breathing eventually slowed. I sat up, wrapping my arms around my sides. After some careful consideration I decided I did not absolutely need to throw up.

That's good, I thought. *I really enjoyed that fish. I'd like to hold onto it for a little longer.*

"Asa?" Rowan asked, his eyes wide. "Are you all right?"

I shook my head. "Never again, Rowan," I rasped. "Never, ever again am I traveling that way with you. Ever."

"It does not seem to agree with you," he agreed in hushed tones.

I let out a half-hysterical bubble of laughter. "That's one way to put it."

I ran my hands over my face briskly, then looked around. "Where are we?"

"Not far from where I found you. I came up to the surface a little earlier than I had planned since you were in distress."

"Thank you for that," I said, and stood up.

Thick woods surrounded us. It felt like home, and there was comfort in that. The trees stood close together, but they were no longer the strange and towering giants of Rowan's home. In their place stood pines and ash-wood trees, tall and slender, clustered tight around us. Green and brown pine needles lay like carpet over the red-dirt floor. The blue of sky and long, thin streams of pale cloud stretched above. A breeze slid between the trees. I closed my eyes, and took a deep breath of familiar air. When I opened my eyes again, Rowan was looking at me, an intensity in his eyes that made me blush. I cleared my throat.

"Is that where the mages are camping?" I asked, pointing up the hill a bit to where I could see flashes of color that did not belong to the forest.

"Yes."

"I need to be able to see them."

Rowan nodded. "I will show you where I hid to watch them yesterday."

Rowan stood and beckoned for me to follow him. The pine needles and leaves that covered the ground muffled my footfalls. Still, I heard the sound of my movements. His feet must have touched the ground, but I never heard him make the slightest sound. As we got closer I bent over, creeping through the under-brush until I could peer through the veil of leaves and see what was going on.

"Careful," Rowan breathed, and I crouched beside him in a cluster of bushes. "We cannot get much closer than this."

Several tents were set up in a semi-circle around a burnt-out fire. A number of people stood in a loose cluster around Paul, who lay propped up on the ground. I squinted through the leaves and inched a little closer, trying to see what was going on.

"Dammit!" Paul's voice rose above the low murmur of voices as he cursed at a woman who had been dabbing at his face. "That stings!"

I wasn't close enough to see his injuries, but I recognized the sound of a complaining patient easily enough.

"Sorry," Shanie's voice answered, though she did not sound very apologetic. "But I have to clean these cuts so they won't get infected." Paul hissed with pain as she kept working, and I could see Shanie's black hair swing as she shook her head. "Really, Paul. I don't know what you were thinking."

The crowd moved, and Paul leaned his head back with his eyes squeezed tightly shut as Shanie tended to his injuries. "I was bored," he said, his tone slightly too belligerent to count as a whine. "I came here for retribution. Not to sit in some backwoods wasteland for days and days, twiddling my thumbs. And where the hell is Greg?"

"You sent Greg and Mark out to search again."

"I know that," Paul snapped. "They're the trackers; it's their fucking job. But I sent them over an hour ago. It shouldn't take so long."

"Next time, don't get injured and you can go with them and make sure they do it right. You could have gotten yourself killed." She finished what she was doing and stood up. "People can say what they like, but at least you're holding the Clan together. I don't like to think what would happen if you were gone."

Paul began to reply, but his words were cut off by Greg pounding his way into camp. "We're back," he announced, mopping his forehead with the back of his hand.

Greg had always been the biggest man in the clan, but now he was even rounder. The years since I had last seen him had added a solid fifty pounds to his weight. With his curly brown hair falling to his shoulders, he was a small white mountain that sweated and panted as it moved. Several feet behind him, almost lost in the big man's shadow, Mark followed. Hands shoved deep in his pockets, his sharp brown eyes took in everything around him through his thick, black-rimmed glasses. Where Greg was ponderous action, Mark was all wiry muscle and barely contained anxious movement. Somehow they had always worked together as a perfect team.

"The next time you want a sweeping spell, someone else can make the damn thing," Greg said. "That's the third one we've done in the last twenty-four hours, and each one has been a royal pain in the ass."

"Was there any sign of her?" Paul demanded.

"No," Mark said quietly as he came to stand next to Paul. "Not a trace."

"Just like last time, and the time before that." Greg settled himself heavily onto a folding camp chair next to the fire. "I keep telling you, man. She's gone. She may be a traitor, but the bitch knows how to disappear. We'll just have to wait till she gets desperate, and taps in again. She's long gone from here. Really." He looked around at the small knot of mages gathered round. "There's no reason for us to stay. Seriously, let's go home. I need my sleep number bed, and a decent meal. Sleeping on the ground is murdering my back. I was never the Boy Scout type and this, "he motioned at the campsite, "this is just ridiculous."

"We're staying." Paul grunted, and I could hear a few people call out weak protests. "End of story!" he yelled, and the complaining instantly died down. "She hasn't tapped in, so she can't have gotten far. She's got no friends, no resources—she's hurt and she's scared, and cowering in some hole. We stay until we find her, drag her out, and gut her. And that's it."

"If she was nearby, I would have sensed her," Mark said, hardly bothering to keep his tone civil. He took his glasses off and polished the lenses with the corner of his shirt. "She isn't here, and hanging out around the campfire isn't going to somehow make her appear. We need to flush her out. Track her backwards by finding where she came from. Figure where she was living before. She's been somewhere all these years. We need to know what connections she might have to go back to."

"What about that thing that carried her off?" Greg countered. "What if it's helping her? Or maybe it finished her off for us."

Paul scoffed. "I didn't see anything that night except for a lot of darkness, somebody running, and a bunch of mages acting like idiots. We had her, and we let down our guard. She slipped free and made a run for it. That's all that happened. People who say different are just trying to cover their asses, making up stories to explain why they couldn't hold onto a single, tied-up woman for one damn night."

"You're wrong," Alice said, appearing from between the tents.

I gasped, and Rowan's hand tightened on my shoulder. I had expected Alice to come back, but I had never suspected she could recover so quickly. "She's got some kind of creature helping her."

"How would you know that?" Paul asked, propping himself up on one elbow to glare at her. "And where the hell have you been all day?"

"I tracked her down. Nearly had her, too."

Mark rounded on her, his face turning scarlet with sudden outrage. "If you had a way of tracking her, you should have told us!"

"I work better on my own," Alice grunted. "I was just going to grab her and bring her back. But she's got some kind of pet now— something I've never seen before. Like a gladiator, with horns. And it can deflect magic."

"Bullshit," Paul said softly. "You screwed up, and now you're lying about it. Nothing can do what you're describing."

"It batted my binding spell away like it was nothing more than a fly," Alice said, and she walked over to glare down at Paul. "And you can call me all kinds of names if you want to, but don't dare to call me a liar. You know me. You know how badly I want her caught. Do you think anything normal could have kept me from taking her down?"

Paul stared at her for a second before shaking his head slowly. "No," he admitted. "I don't."

"I'm telling you, I know what I saw this thing do. And it's helping her. As long as she's got it with her, we have a real problem. That creature—whatever it is—is a threat to us. And they're coming back here. Both of them."

There was a moment of stunned silence.

"You're sure?" Shanie asked.

Alice nodded sharply. "I heard them talking about it."

"But why would they do that?"

"Doesn't matter," Paul cut in, and he climbed unsteadily to his feet. "If we know they're coming, we can find them. And from now on, killing this creature that's with her is priority number one. Got that, people?" He looked around, and there was a general nodding of heads.

"Asa?" Rowan breathed, and I started. I had been so engrossed in watching the mages that I had forgotten what we had come here to do. "We can't get any closer than this, and at any moment they may sense us. Hurry, I will shield you. Use your Truthsight now."

I nodded silently, sucked in a deep breath, and closed my eyes for a second as I reached out in my mind and pulled the silver toward me.

When I looked back up, I was staring at the mages, but through a thick hedge of thorn bushes. Rowan's shield obscured their faces and made the sounds of their speech oddly muted. I could no longer make out their words clearly, and I had to inch closer to the bushes, angling my head dangerously close to the thorns as I peered through, trying to get a clear look at Paul.

At first I couldn't see him at all. A woman stood directly in my line of sight, blocking my view. Blackness wrapped thickly around her, encasing her like layer after layer of gauzy black veils. She turned, and I could see Shanie's face peeking out of the darkness. Her wrinkled skin was the stark, sickly white of one who has gone for far too long without being in the sun. A chain hung around her neck. At the end of it, instead of a pendant, hung a small circle of emptiness, like a hole, or a tunnel that led to nowhere at all. It swung back and forth slightly as she moved. My heart stuttered as I stared at her. Was this really what the grief had done to her?

"Asa?" Rowan breathed, and I started. "I do not like this. We are too close."

"I need more time," I managed to whisper, forcing the words out past the painful tightness in my chest. Then Shanie stepped away, and I could see Paul clearly.

We always hope, I think, that for someone to hate us, there must be something fundamentally wrong with them. It would be easier to understand the world if everyone who was our enemy was somehow twisted deep inside. It hurt me, a little, to see that Paul was beautiful.

His Truthsight-self stood with legs braced apart and ears perked forward. I had seen Great Danes in reality, and they were huge, intimidating dogs. Paul's Great Dane form was bigger still. Short, white fur with large black spots covered his ears and sides. He held his tail up straight behind him, his whole body quivering slightly as he took long, searching, breaths of air. Then he tilted his head and suddenly, he stared straight at me.

"Healer!" Rowan's voice was still soft as dew, but his hand tightened insistently on my shoulder. "We must go. Now."

I shook, but the thorn bushes still stood in front of me. Paul's eyes moved away.

"I can't," I whispered back. "I need longer."

Rowan glanced to the side.

"That one, there," he said. "The thin one with the glasses. He knows something is going on. He isn't sure where we are, yet. But we can't stay here any longer." He leaned in closer to me, so that our faces were only inches apart. "Weak as I am, if they find us now, my strength probably won't be enough to save you. Still, I will try." He shrugged, and looked away from me, flinching a little. "The world will not much mourn me. But you will die, too—and then who will help your Meri?"

I stared at him dumbly for a second, then nodded my assent. "All right," I murmured. "You're right. I'm sorry. Let's go." I shivered as I let the Truthsight fall away from me, and Rowan took my hand and pulled me back down the hill the way we had come.

The tree limbs wrapped like arms around us and the shade fell thick on our faces. Rowan didn't quite run. There were too many trees for that. Instead he danced between the tree trunks, graceful and sinuous, pulling me behind him as he went. I found my movements mirroring his own. My own steps grew swifter and surer as I followed his lead. He moved on the balls of his feet, sliding over the ground as though it was ice. We covered ground quickly and had gone a very long way before he pulled us to a stop. I leaned my back against a thick tree, bracing my hands against my knees and breathing hard.

"Are they coming after us?" I gasped.

"No." He shook his head. His eyes narrowed as he scanned the trees behind us. "I don't think so."

"We can go back later," I said, still gasping. "We'll find a better place to watch from, and—"

"Look out!" Rowan shouted suddenly, and he lurched toward me.

He grabbed me by both shoulders, slamming my back against a nearby tree. Before I could say anything he had placed himself directly in front of me. His back pressed up against me as he shielded me with his body and he drew his dagger.

A bare instant of silence stretched out. Then the leaves parted and a savage war cry rent the air. Colors swirled, hooves pounded, and sunlight flashed on metal.

"Who are you?" I heard Rowan cry, but then came a clang as his dagger barely turned away the deadly, falling arc of a blade.

A centaur was attacking us.

FIFTEEN

"WHAT ARE YOU DOING?" I SCREAMED AS THE CENTAUR RAISED HIS
sword to strike again.

His black hair swung behind him and his face contorted
with rage.

"Leave us alone! We've done you no harm!"

He charged and Rowan raised his dagger, the only weapon he
had against the centaur's full length blade. If he had been in his own
home, with the strength of his land running through him, I knew
the centaur would have been no true threat. But he was weakened,
with none of his usual sources of strength to call on, and he grunted
with effort as he blocked the centaur's swing and pushed him back.
The centaur stumbled farther backwards, then straightened and
paced in front of us. The muscles in Rowan's back rippled as he
moved to mirror the centaur, always keeping his body in front
of mine.

Suddenly, the centaur lunged. He reared up on his back legs, his
arm raised for a killing blow. Rowan leapt forward and caught the
centaur's wrist in his grip. There was a low, sickening crunch, and
the centaur bellowed in agony. His sword fell to the ground. Rowan
brought his right leg up, delivering a swift, fierce kick to the

centaur's chest. All four of his hooves left the ground as he flew backward and crashed into the red dirt, his legs moving feebly and his ruined wrist held limp against his chest.

Instinctively, I took a step toward the wounded creature, to see what I could do for him now that the danger had passed. But Rowan put an arm out to hold me back, and I stilled.

"What is it?" I whispered.

"More of them," he replied, and then I, too, could hear them.

Hooves pounded against the soft ground. Rowan dropped down into a defensive crouch in front of me as we heard their voices.

"Arvid?" a deep voice called.

The crumpled centaur in the dirt groaned loudly in response.

"Arvid is down!" another voice called, and then the leaves all around us rustled as a dozen centaurs came into sight, all with swords drawn and fury in their eyes.

A twig snapped behind us, drawing my gaze back. Four more centaurs approached from behind.

"No, no, no," I intoned to myself.

This was about to be a bloodbath. Rowan crouched down, his eyes wild, his dagger in one hand, while he spread the other hand out on the ground in front of him. Not for balance, but so he could draw strength and power from the earth. Except that this earth was not his own, and it would offer him no protection. His whole body vibrated with tension, and sweat poured off his skin. The centaurs slowed when they saw him, but kept moving forward.

A deep sound of warning rumbled in Rowan's chest, as he pulled his lips back from his teeth in a wide snarl.

"Stop this!" I yelled, craning my body to the side so that they could see me behind Rowan's protective form. "That centaur attacked us, and we defended ourselves, but we are not your enemies! I'm Dr. Amy. Stop this right now!"

The centaurs kept moving, their eyes still trained on Rowan, but I thought I saw a flicker of uncertainty in some of their faces.

"Where is your chief?" I hollered, as I struggled to remember every conversation I had ever had with a centaur, and mimic their speech. "How dare you attack us unannounced, and without provocation? Ambushing us as though you were thieves! For shame! Where is your honor? I demand to speak to the chief immediately!"

They paused, and I let myself hope that I had succeeded in getting their attention. A few of them glanced at each other from the corners of their eyes. There were about twenty of them, and no familiar faces among them.

"I am Dr. Amy, who delivered Crinea's son last week!" I called out, and felt a fierce pang of satisfaction as shock ran over their features. Out of my peripheral vision I saw one of them lower his sword. "This is my friend, Rowan." I didn't say what kind of creature he was—I had no idea if there was animosity between their species. "And we are no threat to you or yours."

"Steady," said the centaur in the lead. He held out his hand, palm up, to still the movement of the others. I could tell from the way all eyes turned to him that he was the leader of the group. "We will wait till we know what is going on. Someone go and tell the chief that we need his guidance."

"There's no need," called out the young centaur who had lowered his sword. "He is coming, and nearly here already."

"Then we wait," the leader announced. No one seemed to be paying any attention to the injured centaur, whose sword still lay on the ground, and who was now back on his feet despite the pained noises coming from him.

I leaned forward. Was I imagining it, or had the stress of the fight made the red lines on Rowan's arms spread further? Tendrils of red crept up his forearms now, reaching up almost past his elbows. Slowly, so as not to startle him, I laid a light hand on his shoulder. "These are friends," I whispered. "Once they know for sure who I am, I don't think they will hurt us."

He turned to look back at me, his eyes wide and wild.

"There is a centaur herd in this forest?" he asked, his voice strained.

"Well…yes."

"Why didn't you tell me?" he spat through clenched teeth. He still held his blade out, in front of him, ready to attack.

"I had no idea you needed to know," I stammered back.

"How many?" he whispered, turning back to face the centaurs, who now watched us closely.

"What?"

"How many centaurs are living here?"

"I'm not sure. Two hundred? Maybe more?"

Rowan swung his head back around to stare at me.

"No," he muttered. "Not in such numbers. That's impossible."

"Says the leshy," I responded under my breath.

The centaurs that surrounded us parted. Intense relief flooded through me when the chief came into view. He stalked slowly through the trees, his thickly braided hair bouncing against his back as he moved. He was so huge that he made the other centaurs seem small just by standing beside them. His eyes found mine, and he gave a nod of greeting. I bit down the urge to call out and ask him how Crinea and the baby were doing. The danger here had not yet passed. But as we looked at each other, an instant of understanding flashed between us. That look told me he realized just how precarious this moment was and that, like me, he would do all he could to keep it from coming to violence.

"You can trust the chief," I whispered into Rowan's ear, realizing as I spoke the words just how sincerely I meant them. "He won't do us any harm."

For a second, Rowan stayed just as he was. Then, with his eyes still locked on the chief's face, he gave me a small, sharp nod. In one fluid movement he rose smoothly out of his defensive crouch and lowered his blade, though he did not slide it back into its sheath.

The chief stopped directly in front of him, and they studied each other in utter silence for long minutes. The other centaurs stood still, all watching intently. I shifted my weight from one foot to the other, twisting my hands together in an effort to hold still. My heart still pounded, the blood beating in my ears.

"Welcome back, Dr. Amy," the chief said, finally turning his eyes to mine. "We have been worried. There have been some disturbing rumors about your disappearance."

"I don't know what you've heard," I answered. "But if it is disturbing, and about me, then it is almost certainly true."

The chief's lips curled up in a slight smile, and he turned his eyes to back to Rowan.

"Dr. Amy says my herdsman attacked you?" the chief asked.

"Yes." Rowan's voice was grating and rough.

Beneath the hand I had resting on his shoulder I felt how tense his body was, how hard it was for him to stand and talk calmly while surrounded by warriors with weapons drawn.

"We gave no cause," I added. "And he struck without warning."

The chief did not take his eyes off Rowan, but studied him coolly for another long moment before turning his head slightly to the side. "Arvid?" he called out. "Does the stranger speak the truth?"

A long pause stretched out, and I could feel all the centaurs gathered around us holding their breath.

For a second, I became terribly afraid the wounded centaur would lie. But then I looked at the chief's flashing eyes, and realized it might be no simple thing to lie to him.

"Yes," Arvid's answer finally came. "But—"

"Silence!" The chief's voice cut through his words like thunder. "You have shamed me."

He turned back to us. "A few of our herd were attacked yesterday. One was killed. As a result, we are more wary of strangers than usual. I gave orders for all intruders who were found to be detained —not hurt. You were attacked unfairly, in a way not in keeping with our laws. Dr. Amy, we owe you a debt, and you have my apologies." He nodded to Rowan. "And you as well." He held out a hand to him.

For a fraction of a second, Rowan hesitated. Then he sheathed his blade, and grasped the chief's forearm. It was as though the whole woods heaved a sigh of relief. Instantly each centaur sheathed their swords and the ferocity in their eyes melted into guarded curiosity. Rowan's shoulders relaxed, and the straining muscles in his neck smoothed down.

Still shaking his hand, the chief pulled Rowan's arm up so he could examine his tattoo.

"Those are satyr warrior markings, are they not?" he said as he released Rowan's arm.

"They are," Rowan conceded, his voice deep and cautious.

"A warrior leshy," the chief exclaimed, pawing the ground. "If I had not seen it with my own eyes, I would never have believed it. And those are the markings given to a commander. You led them in battle?"

Rowan did not answer, but spread his hands and inclined his head very slightly.

"Impressive," the chief murmured, and Rowan started.

"I am surprised to hear that you think so."

"Why is that?"

"It is unusual for one of my kind to participate in violence. Many would call it...unnatural."

The chief grunted. "Nature is wider and more vast than most are willing to realize. It has a place, and a need, for all kinds."

He glanced down at the ground. The centaur who had attacked us had dropped his sword, and it still lay in the dirt before us. The chief nodded toward it. "The one who raised that sword against you did so without my leave, and without cause or warning. By our laws, the blade is yours by right, if you wish to keep it."

Rowan reached down and picked the sword up. Holding it blade down, by its pommel, he offered it back to the chief.

"We came to no harm through his actions," he said. "And I have a blade of my own. No blood was spilled, and no answer is required. Take it, and let there be good will between us."

The chief took the sword from Rowan, but his brow furrowed.

"You know of the centaur law that requires that blood be answered with blood?"

Rowan shrugged. "I suspected it. Satyrs have a similar custom."

"And when you were attacked, you thought of that, and acted to prevent the need for further bloodshed?"

"I hoped to prevent it, yes."

"Again, impressive," the chief said, almost to himself.

"And what of me?" The wounded centaur shouldered his way to the front. "I have been injured. What answer will be given me?"

"None." The chief bit out the word, his face hard and cold. "This is not the first time you have failed to heed my orders, nor the first time you have been warned of the consequences of such a misstep. You should thank the prince leshy, Arvid. We are in debt to this doctor. If she had come to harm from your actions, it would have been the worst kind of dishonor. You would have received far worse from my hands than a broken wrist."

Arvid flushed an angry red. "Then I demand that my sword be returned to me!" he growled, and reached out as though to take his sword back from the chief's hands.

The chief stiffened. "You struck without warning or provocation," he said. His voice fell to a deadly whisper with the next words. "And you have once again disobeyed the words of my mouth. You have disgraced yourself. Did not I warn you, the last time, that your temper would be the death of you if you did not learn to keep it in check?" The chief hung the weapon from his own belt. "I do not trust you to wield this sword with honor, and I will hold onto it until I feel sure that you can."

Arvid recoiled as though he had been struck. "But without my sword, I am dishonored. Shunned. I-I can't go home."

"I am not casting you out." The chief paused. "Not yet. Wait until your wrist is healed. You can survive on your own for that long."

"But my p-parents," Arvid stammered. "They are old, and rely on me for food…"

"Your parents will eat at my own fire for as long as you are away." The chief's eyes softened. "You need time to reflect, and to find a way to master yourself. Wait until you are healed, Arvid. Then come to me. If I see a true difference in you, I will give you back your weapon, and with it your place among us. You have no need of a blade now, anyway. With your injury you could not even hold a sword."

Arvid glared around him, murderous fury in his eyes. His gaze came to rest on Rowan. "Do not think me crippled," he snarled. "You may find that, even with my injury, I can do more than you might think with a blade." And then he brushed past the other centaurs and crashed back into the cover of the trees.

"I am sorry for his behavior," the chief said, when he was gone. "The one the mages killed yesterday was his friend. His anger will cool as his grief loses its sharpness."

"Mages?" I gasped. "It was mages that fought with you yesterday?"

"It was no fight." The chief's voice was suddenly raw. "It was an ambush. A hunting party. The mages took a few of our number by surprise and set upon them...for sport. As though my herdsman were a prize, an animal who might be stuffed and displayed before the fireplace. My men fought bravely, and gave hurt to their attackers. The one who died of his wounds now walks unashamed in the land of our fathers."

"I'm so sorry." I felt suddenly dizzy. "The mages were looking for me. They were here because of me. It's my fault."

The chief looked at me sharply. "I know where the blood-guilt for my people lies, healer, and it is not with you. It was the mages who took life needlessly. It is they who must pay a heavy price."

"You plan to go after them, then?" Rowan broke in.

The chief spread his hands out. "I am no fool," he said. "I know what they are, and what such an action will cost us. But what can I do? They have killed a member of my herd without provocation or warning. They are infesting our land, scrambling through the forest like fleas on the back of a dog. We must defend ourselves, but I will do nothing tonight. We will wait, and watch. And for now we will return home. Will you return to camp with us?" he asked, turning to me. "You have every right to our hospitality and we would gladly welcome your," he hesitated for an instant, his eyes flashing between me and Rowan, pausing at where my hand still lay on Rowan's shoulder, "companion, as well."

I glanced at Rowan. His face was carefully impassive, but his jaw clenched tight, and by his side, his hands were tight fists. Somehow he felt my eyes on him, and without looking at me, he gave a minuscule shake of his head.

"No, thank you," I answered. "I appreciate your asking, but I have no desire to bring my troubles to your doorstep any more than I already have. We'll be all right."

The chief nodded, and I could tell my answer did not surprise him.

"As you wish. Be well, Dr. Amy." He nodded to Rowan, then turned and led his people away into the trees.

SIXTEEN

When it was clear that they were really gone, Rowan's shoulders dropped. He moved away from me and leaned heavily against a nearby tree trunk.

"Thank you," he said. "I was afraid you would accept his offer."

I shook my head. "I don't want to put them in any more danger than I already have. And I could tell you didn't want to go with them."

Rowan nodded. "Weakened as I am, it would be... uncomfortable...for me to be surrounded by them, to accept food and shelter from their hands. I have no wish to be in their debt." His eyes narrowed as he looked at me. "You did not have time to tell me before; what did you learn when you gazed at the mages?"

I shook my head. "Not what I expected to. I'm not sure what it meant. I don't think it brings us any closer to finding Meri." I wrapped my arms together, and looked up at the sky. "So what do we do now? The sun is nearly down."

"We find water," Rowan said, straightening up. "And food. We will settle in for the night, and then make plans for tomorrow."

Before long we found a small river. Lined on either side with thick rows of pines, the water was clean, but shallow. I picked my way over the rocks carefully until I could lean down and drink my fill.

"Do you know how to start a fire?" Rowan asked after he too, had taken a long drink.

"Of course," I answered, slightly offended. I was no leshy, but I knew a thing or two about surviving in the woods.

"Then do so. I will find us some food." He crouched down close to the ground and ran his fingertips slowly back and forth over the dirt for a moment. Then he grunted and stood back up again. "The land here will not speak to me," he commented, his expression thoughtful. "It isn't that it dislikes me—it is just not answering. Like a turtle with its head pulled deep within its shell, hiding, and watching." He shrugged. "It will not tell me where food can be found, but I will still find something for us. It will just take me a little longer. Get that fire started—I will be back before too long."

Rowan turned and slid back into the trees, and I fell to work collecting wood and clearing a space for a small cooking fire on the edge of the river bank. Despite my earlier insistence that I knew how to start a fire, it took me longer than I would have liked. I had barely managed to coax the flames into a respectable blaze when Rowan re-appeared, his arms full of large, pale yellow tubers.

"They do not taste like much of anything, I will admit," he said before I had a chance to comment. He squatted down by the water and began to wash the dirt off them one by one. "But roasted is better than raw. And something is better than nothing."

"I'm not complaining," I replied, and crouched down beside him at the water's edge to help, trying not to notice when his hand brushed against my knee as he reached for the water.

When they were cleaned, we tucked them into the ashes. Some were bigger than others, and the smallest of the lot cooked quickly. We pulled them out, singeing our fingers, and peeled away the burnt outer part so that we could eat the fibrous, slightly sweet flesh underneath. I had expected not to like them much, but I found myself enjoying them as we finished the first ones and pulled more out to devour. I also relished the silence. Rowan sat beside me, and neither of us made any attempt to make conversation. There was just the fire snapping and smoking, the stream trickling by, and the low buzzing of forest life around us, growing louder as the sun sank down. I ate the last bite of the tuber I held, and wordlessly Rowan handed me another. He had wrapped the bottom in a wide, flat leaf, so that when I took it from him I would not burn my fingers.

"Rowan, can I ask you something?" I said when all the food was gone.

He sat beside me with his legs pulled up in front of him, his elbows resting on his knees. The fading light made the shadows grow around us, but the firelight lit his face, and his eyes were warm and bright.

"Of course."

"Before, when I was trying to heal your father. You walked right into my vision, but my Truthsight did not seem to affect you at all. Do you know why?"

He smiled a little. "I only know what my mother told me. Since I am not a mage, I do not understand exactly how your kind of magic is supposed to work. But she told me I was resistant to mage magic. She took a kind of pleasure in that, I think. To know that her son was able to defy the power of the Clan that had rejected her. Why do you ask?"

I looked into the fire, at the red and yellow and blue that swayed and snapped in the flames. "I just wondered. In Truthsight our truest selves are brought to light. Recently, when I used it, the person who was with me told me what she saw when she looked at me." I shrugged, remembering Crinea's vision of a silver fish, floundering out of the water. "She couldn't even recognize me. It bothered me, I guess. I wondered if the Truthsight worked on you but that you are just...you. No matter what."

"You mean that you thought I have nothing to hide? Nothing beneath the surface that I would rather not have others see? No, healer. Like you, like anyone, I have parts of myself that I hold back from others, rooms with doors that I keep closed to all but a few. And I would not wish to be any different. If we had no secrets, then we could not have the joy that comes with choosing who to tell them to." He smiled as he spoke, and there was a sparkle in his eye that made a thrill run through me that I tried to hide.

I smiled back at him a little. "That's a nice way of thinking of it. And I can see why your mother would be happy that you could stand up to the power of the mages. Like when you shielded me, so that they couldn't tell I was using the Source. I'd never even heard of someone being able to do that ...." My words trailed off, as sudden realization filled me. "Rowan. Could you shield while I use my Truthsight one more time? Would it be dangerous for you? Drain your strength?"

Rowan frowned, and he thought for a long moment before answering. "I am no longer on land that gives me its fealty, and I am not as strong as I was then. I could shield you, yes. But only for a few moments. Why? What magic is it that you wish to perform?"

"I just want to talk to Meri," I gasped, suddenly breathless. "Just for a second. She must be so worried about me—the last time I spoke to her, I told her I was about to die. And if I could just ask her a few questions, tell her my suspicions about Paul—are you sure, Rowan? I don't want you to use up your strength."

Rowan half laughed and rose smoothly to his feet. "Do not worry about me, healer. Do you wish to contact her now?"

"Yes," I cried. "Thank you so much. I can use the surface of the water to scry with."

"Very well," Rowan said, and he turned his back to me as he crouched low to the ground and spread his fingers out wide against the earth. When he spoke a moment later, his voice was tight from the effort. "You should be safe, now," he said with a grunt. "But be quick!"

The moon shone on the face of the water. I leaned down and stroked the river's surface, imagining Meri's face, reaching out to her with my mind and all my senses. A longing filled me for the silver eyes that used to watch over me while I was sleeping. The surface of the water began to morph to inky black.

"Meri?" I called out softly. "Are you there?"

"Asa!" Her voice was weak and wavering. She sounded as though she was half-asleep, or nearly crying. "What's happened? Are you all right?"

"I'm all right, Meri. Please, don't worry about me. I got away from the mages, and I have a friend helping me now. We don't have long to talk, though, and I have to ask you something." I took a deep breath, and the words tumbled out. "Do you think Paul could have been the one to lead the rebel mages to you? He said something, while they were holding me. It made me think that he knows you are still alive. Do you think he could have been the one? If it's him, he might know where they're holding you."

There was a pause, and for a second I was afraid the connection was too weak, and I had lost her.

"I'm not sure," she said, her voice thin and wavering. "Paul never had any love for me. But I can't imagine him working with the rebels. He always hated them so much."

"Okay," I said, fighting to keep the disappointment out of my voice. "But there has to be something you can tell me, something that will help me find you. Think, Meri. Tell me anything you can."

"I don't know," she wailed, her voice filled with despair. "I haven't seen a face, heard a voice—and it's dark here. Always."

"What about sounds?" I prodded. "Or even smells?"

A long moment of silence fell, and I knew she was thinking. "Mold…I smell mold, and dust. And it's cool, too. All the time. The air is old."

"That's great," I told her, hope sparking in my chest. At least she was telling me something. "That's a good start. Maybe you're underground?"

"Sometimes there's a sound. Dripping water, maybe."

"Like a water source?" I prompted.

"Yes," she whispered. "Maybe."

A sudden memory flooded me. Grenalda's son staring at me with glassy black eyes. The first part of his prediction had already come true. But there had been more. "*A hundred mouths, a million teeth*," he had said. "*Stone and bone deep underneath.*"

"Meri," I gasped. "Do you think you could be in a mage-haven?"

"Healer!" Rowan's voice was like a thunderclap, and I snapped my head around. He still crouched close to the ground, but sweat covered his bare back and his muscles strained as if under a great weight. "I cannot shield you any longer," he cried. "You must stop before the mages sense your presence."

"I have to go, Meri!" I cried. "I'll keep looking for you, I promise!" Not even waiting for a response, I dashed my fingers over the surface of the water, dispelling the black that had pooled there and letting the connection between us fade away. Then I rushed over to Rowan's side.

"Are you all right?" I asked. "I didn't mean to tire you."

"I am winded, but otherwise fine," he answered, and sat down hard enough to stir up dust. "You were able to contact your friend?"

"Yes," I replied, sighing as I sat down beside him. "And I think I have an idea of where she may be imprisoned."

"Where?"

"I think she is being held in a mage-haven. That would explain why she never sees or hears anything."

"What is a mage-haven?" Rowan asked.

The fire had begun to burn low. He leaned forward to poke it with a long stick, his eyes upon me.

"It is a mage's personal bolt-hole, created by magic. Kind of like a panic room. It is old magic, and creating one takes a great deal of precision, and a tremendous amount of time. Years, sometimes. What the mage will do is carve out an area that is completely inaccessible by any mundane means. Like, they'll hollow out the tip of a mountain, or make themselves a cavern under two hundred feet of rock. It is incredibly painstaking work. I never made one—I never had the time, or the expertise. But when it is finished, the mage has a place that only they can access—a completely isolated area where they know they will always be absolutely safe."

"How can they be sure that no one else can get in?"

"The only way to get in is with the one key they make, which they always keep with them, like a bracelet, or a bead they weave into their hair. That way they can always get away, no matter what. The trouble is, if she really is in a mage haven, then I have to find the mage who is holding her in order to get to her. I don't know any of the rebel mages, Rowan. I don't know how to find them. And I have no idea why they are still holding her after all of this time. What could they be hoping to gain?"

"I don't know..." Rowan started to say. His eyebrows pulled together, but then he spun to his feet, firelight glinting on the blade of his dagger as it sprang out of its sheath.

"Peace," a deep voice said, as the chief stepped into the ring of firelight. "I mean you no harm. I have come to say things that others must not hear."

I didn't remember scrambling to my feet, but I was standing by Rowan's side when he slowly put his dagger away. If he was as surprised as I was, he hid it better than I did. His face was smooth, but troubled as he looked up at the chief.

"Say what you must."

The chief spread his hands. "My tribe is in danger, though many of those in my herd are too young to know the difference between how things are today, and how they ought to be. They do not know what it feels like to live on a land that is aware, that cares for the creatures that live upon it like a mother for her young, shielding them, guiding them, providing for their needs. But you are a leshy. You have only been on this land for a few hours, but already you must have begun to guess."

Rowan said nothing.

"The land slumbers," the chief continued. "And I do not know how to wake it. We live off the land, and we are meant to be a part of it. I have reached out to it in every way I know how. But there is nothing, no trace of a response. The land does not know us, does not shelter us from harm. The young of my herd are so young that they do not sense the lack, and they cannot understand the danger, but those who are older remember, and they are afraid. What happened today should have been impossible."

For a second the chief's face hardened. "The mages are strangers here. If the land were awake, it would have hidden my people from them. The land I grew up in is far from here, a place that was long ago claimed by humans and razed. But when I was a boy and the trees were thick, it was a live thing that inhabited the woods by our side. A human could walk within five feet of a centaur, and see nothing. The land held us to its bosom like its own children—and we were safe. And now, what can I do for my tribe?" The chief dropped his head into his hand, falling silent.

When he looked back up, he was the picture of composure once again. "Dr. Amy has given us new hope, a living child. A treasure. I cannot let this new hope be squandered. Unless something changes, we will be forced to flee, and seek a new home, though there are not many wild places left that we could run to."

"And what would you have of me?" Rowan asked.

The chief stared at him for a long moment before answering. "You know what I want."

Rowan looked away, toward the stream. His face creased with a pain I did not understand.

"Do you have any idea the risk you are asking me to take?" he asked quietly after a moment.

The chief raised his chin. "Of course I know it. But do not pretend that you do not share the same problem we do." He motioned to Rowan's arms.

I had been trying not to look, but now I could not help but stare. The red lines wove all the way from his fingers, up and around his bicep. On his right arm, the black lines of his tattoo and the red lines of his exile wove in and out of each other in a dizzying pattern.

"How long have you been without a home?"

Rowan stiffened. "A few days," he said, shrugging, as though it hardly mattered.

"I fear finding a new home for my people," the chief pressed. "But you must hold the same fear for yourself. What I ask is dangerous, that is true. But it is also dangerous to be a leshy without a home." He took a step closer to Rowan. "Your separation is recent. You are still strong. You have the strength to try this thing."

"Wait a minute," I broke in. "What are you asking Rowan to do?"

The chief did not answer, and when Rowan spoke, he would not meet my eyes.

"He wants me to offer myself to this land. He hopes that doing so might wake it from its slumber. Bring it back to life, and make it a safe place for his people to stay."

"Okay," I said slowly, looking from the chief's stony expression to Rowan's agonized eyes. There was still something I was missing. "Why is that dangerous? What would happen if it didn't wake up?"

"Usually a leshy forms a bond with a land before trying to connect with it. He feels a pull. The land calls out to him, and he answers. When he knows he has found a home, he opens himself up, and the connection forms—he and the land join. But this land has shown no interest in me. If I tried what the chief is asking, and the land did not wake up, or woke but then rejected me," Rowan shook his head, "I would die. To try to wake it, I would have to offer myself to it completely. If I opened myself in such a way and the land turned me away..." He shrugged. "You saw what it did to me when my homeland left me. It was a close thing even then."

"No," I said softly, shaking my head. "Don't do it, then. Don't risk it. It isn't worth it, Rowan."

Rowan looked at me long and hard, then turned his gaze to the chief.

"How many centaurs are in your herd?" he asked.

The chief's eyes hardened, and he crossed his arms as he stayed silent. In an instant Rowan stood chest to chest with him, eyes blazing.

"Do not think you can ask what you have asked of me, and then not answer every one of my questions! How strong is your number?"

The chief bared his teeth, but he answered. "Three hundred and twenty-seven."

"And satyrs? Are there any in these woods?"

The chief shook his head. "No. But there are others."

"I saw a gnome hole earlier."

"Yes. And pixies."

"What does any of this matter?" I broke in.

"It gives me an idea of the strength of the land," Rowan explained, his eyes still locked with the chief. "The stronger the land, the more preternatural creatures it can support. That was why I was so shocked when I found centaurs here. The land may not be active, but it must have been mighty once, to have so many living in it."

He turned suddenly from the chief and went to stand beside the stream. The moon had come out, and somewhere a night-bird sang a deep, grating song. I stood paralyzed, not knowing what to say, or how to keep Rowan safe.

"I will do it," Rowan said at last.

"No!" I cried again, rushing to his side. "Listen to me, Rowan." I took both his hands in mine. "Leave. I understand if you can't wait to see if Meri can help you. I know it was a long shot, and this is not your fight. Just leave. Right now—tonight. Don't worry about me. I will fight my own battles, and I will be all right. You go and search for a land that's awake. A place that calls to you. One you can be sure will accept you before you offer yourself to it. There's no reason for you to take such a risk."

Rowan's warm hands tightened around my fingers. "I have made my decision," he said, leaning his head down to me, his voice soft. "I will stay, and take this chance."

"Why?" I demanded. "Why put yourself in danger?"

"I am in danger already, Asa. The chief is right. I don't have much time. Even if your friend could give me more time, there are not so many of the deep, wild places left. My father knew the risk I would face. It is why he clung to life for so long—to shield me from exactly this situation. But it is more than that. I will stay, and try this thing." He looked down at the earth beneath his feet. "Because the chief is wrong about this land. It isn't sleeping—it is waiting. I can feel it—an awareness— watching me. I cannot be sure what it is waiting for, but I can tell that it is frightened. Maybe if it sees that I will stand by it, then it will be willing to come into its own once again. I have to try. You can see that, can't you?"

His eyes pleaded with me, asking me to understand. And suddenly I knew that, in his place, I would have made exactly the same decision. "Yes," I said, wishing I could tell him a lie that would keep him safe, but not able to bring myself to do it. "Yes, I understand. Of course I do."

He turned to the chief. "How many can you gather? Not only of your own kind, but all who dwell here. The stronger our call to the land, the more chance there is that it will answer."

"I do not know," the chief answered. "But we will begin the summoning tonight."

"We cannot wait long," Rowan responded. "I will come to you at sunrise, and then we must begin. I cannot afford to let my strength run out any further."

"Then rest while you may," the chief said, turning. "And I will see you both in the morning."

When he was gone, Rowan pulled me with him to some flat boulders by the side of the stream. We sat silently, side by side, and dangled our feet in the water.

"What will happen tomorrow?" I asked after a while.

"I'm not sure. The centaurs will gather as many creatures as they can. Together, we will call out to the land. If it emerges enough, it will test me."

"How does that work?"

"That I am also not sure of. I know only that I will open myself to it. My father said it is different for every leshy—and he inherited his land from his father, so he could not really tell me much. He had only heard stories. He said the land searches the leshy. Inside. To see if it trusts him enough to accept him as its champion."

"How will you know if it has accepted you?"

"If I am alive when it is over, then you will know that the land has taken me for its own."

My heart began beating uncomfortably fast. "And if not?"

"Then the centaurs will bury me with honor."

"No," I said, suddenly angry. "You don't get to say that so calmly, as though it's all right, as though the possibility of you dying is something I'm just supposed to nod and accept quietly. I can't do that, Rowan, and I won't. If you feel you need to try this, then fine. I can respect that. But I'm going to be with you, and if it doesn't work out, I'll be right there, next to you. I'll heal you. I'll make you well enough that you can go out there and try again somewhere else."

"Asa, you cannot. That is not how these things work."

"I don't give a damn about how these things work, and don't pretend for a second that you know the extent of what I'm capable of doing. You don't. I care about you. And I don't stand around and just watch people I care about die."

"Little healer," he said softly. "Thank you. Thank you for the kindness of you heart, the fierceness of your spirit. I am glad we are friends. If I live, then I will do all I can so that someday we can be more. But if the land rejects me, you will be no more able to save me than you were able to save my father."

"Wait," I said. "Back up a moment. What did you just say?"

Rowan didn't answer, but in the darkness he reached out and took both my hands, enclosing them in his own.

"You said something," I said faintly, suddenly feeling light-headed. "Back on that night when you first found me, something that I didn't understand. You said, 'I lay claim to you.' What did you mean by that?"

"Can you not guess?

I shook my head slowly. "No. I don't really think I can."

"When I spoke then, I spoke out of instinct. Now that I know you better, I am more sure." He stopped himself, drawing a deep breath. "We ought not speak of these things too much now, when I have nothing that I can offer you but uncertainty and the risk of heartbreak. I have no desire to be the cause of harm to you. But it is good that at least this much is now said between us."

"But what are you saying?" I whispered.

"I am saying that I want you," he said simply.

I made a sound that was half-laugh, half-sob. "You can't," I answered back, closing my eyes. His eyes were glinting in the moonlight, and I couldn't bear to look at him. "I'm all messed up, and ruined, and you can't possibly mean that, Rowan."

I opened my eyes when he ran a finger down my cheek.

"I want you," he said again.

"God damn it," I cursed quietly, hating the tears that ran down my cheeks, hating myself for being broken, wishing that some part of this was simple, and that I was good enough. "You shouldn't feel that way. I'm a bad person."

"You are not. You are a good person, with a beautiful soul."

"How can you say that? You know where I come from, Rowan. You know what I've done." I pulled my hands away from his and rubbed my cheeks dry with my palms. "I'm a mess. Two seconds ago I was screaming at you."

Rowan shrugged. "You get angry when you are frightened. I know what it is to have a temper."

"But you don't know what you're saying," I said, still not able to look him in the eye. "Not really. You've lost your father, and your home, and you're trying to find something to hold on to. What you think you're feeling—it isn't real."

He leaned in closer, until his face was just inches from mine, his eyes glowing with warmth, his breath hot on my cheek. "And you, Asa. You are tired, and in pain. You are being hunted, and blamed for crimes that are not your own. You no longer know that you are worthy of love—that it is all right for good things to happen to you. But I will help you remember."

And then he kissed me. Without warning, his lips were suddenly pressing against mine, his rough hand coming up to lie against my cheek. I meant to push him away, but his lips were so warm, and the heat pushed through me. For a split second, I couldn't move. I could only feel the warmth as it spread through me. For so long my body had felt brittle and nearly breaking. But now, suddenly, it felt soft and alive instead. Without meaning to, I leaned forward. My fingers caught in his hair, and I pressed against him, wanting the heat to swallow me up, to burn away the ache in my chest and, for at least a little while, let me forget. After a time he pulled away, and wrapped his arm around me.

"Will you sit with me, Asa, until the sun comes up?" he asked. "I do not think that I will sleep tonight."

I let myself snuggle against him, marveling at how perfectly my head fit against the smooth contour of his chest. "Yes," I whispered, and closed my eyes. The past didn't matter. The future, in all its dark uncertainty, was hours away. Here and now I was warm and wanted. I was comforted, and I could give comfort in return. It was enough. I was content. For now.

SEVENTEEN

I HAD NOT MEANT TO SLEEP, BUT AT SOME POINT I MUST HAVE DRIFTED off. When Rowan gently shook my shoulder, the sun had started to glint on the surface of the water, and birds sang greetings to each other in the trees.

"Thank you," he said.

"For what?" I asked, my voice still thick with sleep.

"I would have thought that the night before a trial like the one that I will meet today would have been full of worry and pain. Instead I spent it by your side, and happy. I would not have thought it possible."

I straightened up and stretched my arms, hoping I had not drooled on his chest or otherwise embarrassed myself while sleeping.

"I know. I can't believe I slept at all."

"We should go. I'm sorry that I have nothing for breakfast."

"That's all right. I don't think I could eat anything, anyway."

Tension began settling back into my bones. My chest thrummed with the beginnings of the pain that worry always brought flaring to the surface.

I looked around, suddenly realizing I had no idea where we were going. "You said the chief was going to gather everybody together?"

"Yes. I felt the summoning start soon after he left us last night. I can take us there, if you are ready?"

I rubbed my hands up and down my arms, trying to throw off the early morning chill, and the cold that seeped through my heart when I thought of where we were going. But Rowan had chosen his battle. It wouldn't help him to see how badly it frightened me. So I smiled as well as I could, and stood up.

"Yes," I said. "Let me just go take a drink."

After we both drank our fill he took my hand and we started out. We didn't talk much as the land slowly grew wilder and harsher around us. Soon we had left the forest behind, and trees were few and far between. The ground under my feet changed. Instead of dark black dirt and thickly piled pine needles, the earth was red, hard, and strewn with rocks. Above, the sky seemed to grow bigger as it brightened, until the soft early morning blue seemed to be a separate, brighter world that hung just out of reach above us. When I saw the stones, I knew we were heading for the Badlands.

At first, it was just a few of them. Small boulders, coming up just to my thigh, that poked their heads up from under the soil like dolphins breaking the surface of the water. Each rock was multicolored, a rainbow of reds and browns, layer upon layer of different shades of magenta and gray. As we went on, the stones became more frequent, and larger, growing so that they surpassed my height and I had to look up to see the stripes. After a while the stones towered above us, and it almost seemed we were walking on the surface of a strange planet, where there had never been, and never would be, anything but hard stone and blue sky.

It was still early morning and the air was soft, but I knew that by the time the sun had fully risen there would be no trace of dew, no moisture or cool breeze. These lands were full of strange beauty, but the heat of the summer was almost as brutal as the cold when winter came. A small orange lizard scuttled past my feet, leaving a faint trail of dust in its wake. Tiny yellow flowers peeked out of the crevices of the rocks, and popped up in deeply shadowed places on the ground, clinging stubbornly to life in any corner where a little moisture could be found. I looked down, needing to pick my way carefully over the uneven terrain, knowing that if I fell here I was likely to cut myself on the stony, ragged surface.

"Can you feel it?" Rowan asked after a while.

I looked up, shaking my head. He pointed. A mass of color and movement flashed just on the edge of my vision. And a noise rose, too faint to be anything but a slight buzz.

"The centaurs have done well," Rowan said, pausing for a minute to study what I now realized was the largest crowd of preternatural creatures I had ever seen. "I did not expect so many."

"Amy!"

I barely had time to turn to see Jason coming before he had caught me up in a hug that lifted me right up off the ground.

"I can't believe you're here!" he exclaimed, grinning down at me after he had set me back on my feet. "Did you feel it too? Is that why you came back?"

"Jason!" I cried. "It is so good to see you. Are you okay? How is everything at the clinic? Have you been all right without me?"

Jason nodded, opened his mouth to respond, then his eyes flicked upward. His face suddenly hardened, and his eyes went cold.

"Who is that, Amy?" he asked.

I followed his gaze to where Rowan stood behind me, and I knew how Rowan must appear to him. Rowan towered over us, his eyes watching us impassively, his thickly muscled shoulders thrown back and the sunlight glinting on his horns. His dagger was in plain view, and his face was stony, his hands covered in dirt.

"Is this him?" Jason breathed. "Is that the reason that you had to run?"

He didn't wait for an answer, but strode over to Rowan, his eyes flashing and fists balling up at his sides. Jason was tall, but Rowan was taller, and had at least three times his bulk. Jason didn't seem to care.

"Who the hell are you?" he demanded, pushing himself up on the balls of his feet and glaring up at Rowan. "And what did you do to frighten my friend halfway out of her mind?"

"Jason!" I called out, trying to stop him.

Rowan didn't answer, but looked at me and cocked an eyebrow, which seemed to infuriate Jason more.

"What, I'm not worth an answer to you?" he asked, his voice rising as he shifted his weight from one foot to the other, as though preparing to throw himself at Rowan. "You think that 'cause I'm smaller, that means you don't have to worry about me? That I won't stand up to you for my friend?"

My momentary shock wore off enough that I found my voice. "Shit, Jason! Stop it!" I hurried to his side and grabbed his arm to yank him away from Rowan. "This is a friend of mine. He isn't the reason I had to leave."

Jason took a step back, his chest heaving, his eyes still flashing and locked into Rowan's cool gaze.

"Rowan has been helping me," I insisted, stepping in between them and pushing against Jason's chest with both hands and all of my weight, until he was forced to step back a little further. "Calm down, will you? What's the matter with you?"

Jason blinked. "Sorry," he muttered, and he ran his hand over his face. "I don't know what's wrong with me. I've been feeling all weird and out of sorts, ever since last night."

"Are you all right? Did something happen to you?"

"I'm not sure exactly." He angled his face away from Rowan as he spoke, as though afraid he would lose his temper and start yelling again if he looked back at him.

"It started right after I locked up the clinic. I had turned out the lights and was heading for my truck when suddenly, I started to feel strange. I don't know how to describe it exactly. I was shaking a little, and I felt restless, you know? I felt like I needed fresh air, and to walk around a bit, which was weird because I was already outside and I don't usually decide to go for long walks alone in the middle of the night. But at the time it seemed to make perfect sense."

He swallowed hard and ran a hand through his hair before going on. "I went out to the woods, started walking, but it just got worse. I felt so agitated, but I couldn't figure out what was wrong. I just kept walking, not really having an idea of where I was going. After a while I realized I couldn't stop. I literally couldn't stop moving my feet. It was like I was being pulled over the ground."

His eyes flicked to Rowan and for a moment I didn't think he was going to go on. "And I wasn't the only one; there are others. I couldn't see them, but I heard them, moving through the trees." He looked around with wide, bloodshot eyes. "I don't think they were human. I don't know what's happening to me."

"It is the summoning," Rowan's deep voice made Jason start.

"What does that mean?" Jason asked, his eyes fixed on me.

"The centaur chief is calling everyone together," I explained gently. "All the preternatural who live in this area." I rubbed his shoulder, not sure how he would feel about the next piece of information. "And, Jason—you're one of them."

"The centaur chief?" Jason swallowed hard, his eyes growing wider. "Why? What does he want from me? I can't do anything special—I don't even know what I am."

"No one means you harm," Rowan said. "We need your voice to join with ours this day. There is no time now to explain, but once the ritual begins, you will know what to do."

"It really is okay, Jason," I said. "This is a good thing. It means it's been working. This is what you've wanted, for a long time. To start to find a place where you belong."

Rowan looked over his shoulder at the still-growing crowd. Then, to me, he said, "We must go."

"Don't worry," I called to Jason as I hurried away. "You'll be all right."

He nodded in reply, but the eyes that watched me leave were round and full of hurt and worry. Guilt surged inside me. I hated leaving him like that, hated the hurt in his eyes. I wanted to stop, to explain. But I couldn't waste another moment, not even for an explanation to him.

The crowd parted like curtains before us, forming a rough aisle right down its center. The chief stood with arms folded, waiting for us in the front. He suddenly seemed impossibly distant because, as we started walking, the force of all those eyes fell on us, their weight a physical thing, running over me, probing me, making me tremble. I glanced at Rowan, to see if it had fazed him, too, but he stared straight ahead, shoulders thrown back and head held high, something almost regal in his stride. As we moved forward he ran his eyes calmly over the crowd, seeming to take its measure and count its strength. I hurried my steps to keep up with him, but could feel none of his surety. I stared around us, too shocked for words. The centaurs had come, but not only them.

Groups of pixies hovered above the crowd like small, brightly colored clouds keeping careful distance from the clump of harpies who stood with their heads together, laughing and talking in shrill, angry voices. Wolves, taller and more thickly muscled than any normal wolf had a right to be, stood still as statues and watched us pass with intelligent eyes. Humanoid forms, bent over with strange, distended faces, stood with mouths gaping, staring at us. I could not decide if they were ogres or trolls. There were a few tall, graceful figures, whose species I could only guess at. The gnomes were too short to be easily visible, but I saw a few of them watching us closely from the corners of the crowd.

The chief stepped forward. "Greetings, doctor, and prince leshy. We have drawn together as many as we could."

"It is a far greater number than I imagined," Rowan said, turning to look out over the crowd again. "You have done well. If they are ready, we must not delay."

The chief turned to me. "Doctor, if you are willing, you can stand here at the front." And he motioned to a spot off to the side.

I took a step closer to Rowan, dropping my voice as low as I could.

"I don't want you to go through this alone," I whispered. "I want to help."

"Your presence here helps me," Rowan answered, putting his mouth next to my ear and whispering softly. "The hope of you, and of what we might become, helps me—and will help me endure when my time of testing comes."

I stared at him, not sure of what to do, unwilling to abandon him to this strange struggle.

"Amy." A soft hand fell on my shoulder, and I turned.

Crinea looked so healthy that for a minute I didn't even recognize her. In my mind I still saw her as she had been just a few short days ago, her skin pale and her eyes wide as she fought for her life and the life of her child. But now she was reaching out to hug me, strong and healthy, her skin glowing and her light hair blowing wild in the breeze.

"You're here!" I cried in shock, marveling at how solid she felt when she embraced me. "Where is the baby?"

"Home, with Finar," she said, pulling away enough to look at me but keeping my hands clasped firmly in her own. "Healthy, strong, and already getting into trouble, thanks to you!" Her eyes shone with sharp pride when she spoke of her child. "I had to come. My brother said you would be here this morning. I thought you might have need of a friend." She nodded to the spot that the chief had indicated a moment ago. "Will you come stand with me? We won't be far."

I took a deep breath. "Fine," I said at last, and turned back to glare at Rowan. "Don't you dare get hurt. You hear me? I mean it."

He held up both hands. "I would not dare defy the great doctor's orders." And then his smile faded. "You know this is what I must do."

"Yes," I admitted. "I'll be close by."

I let Crinea pull me away. She led me to the side where the nearest centaurs backed away a bit to make a space for us. I was surprised to see Arvid's face, red and scowling, among them, but then the crowd shifted and hid him from my view.

Rowan walked further out, in front of the crowd, to where the rocks did not tower overhead, and the land was flat and red and stretched on and on for what seemed like forever. After going several paces, he stopped and simply stood. He closed his eyes and turned his face toward the sun, his arms loose and hands open at his sides. Waiting. His expression was one of utter serenity, as though the sky whispered something that only he could hear, and the secret message filled him with peace. The sun shone on his tan skin and sparkled off his horns. The red lines had crept all the way up his arms, and now curled around his thick shoulders, but they did not mar his beauty. My heart ached.

I want him, I admitted to myself for the first time. *I want him more than he could ever know, more than he could ever want me in return, no matter what he says. He is too beautiful, inside and out, for me to feel any other way. And I may be about to lose him.*

Suddenly a bang sounded and the ground under my feet trembled. I looked around wildly, trying to trace the disturbance, and I realized as the sound came again that the centaurs had begun, in unison, to stomp on the ground. The heavy thud of hundreds of hoofed feet built into a slow, steady rhythm, their delicate legs rising and falling together in perfect time. There was no other sound, and the mass of faces was focused and intense, every eye on Rowan, every ear straining to hear what would happen next.

The stomping slowly built in tempo and the intensity grew. A small cloud of dust, kicked up by hooves and feet moving together, rose up like a thin cloud from the ground and slowly grew over us. The beat made the ground and air vibrate. The sound was a living thing that wove between everyone standing in that crowd, leaning against us, pushing us, calling out wordlessly for something that did not come.

The chief stood in front of the mass of centaurs, motionless and watching, his face drawn and dark. Rowan had not moved in the slightest, but still stood with his head thrown back to the sun, waiting. Beside me, Crinea had joined with the rhythm of her people, her delicate tan foreleg rising and falling in perfect time with the beat.

Stomp.

Dust stung my eyes, and I squeezed them shut, finding as I did so that the sound was inside me, too. It matched my heartbeat, and then urged it to speed up. Without thinking about it, I lifted my right foot, and stomped on the ground in perfect synchronization with the centaurs.

Stomp.

Please let this work, I prayed. *He has chosen this place, and this battle. Please let him win it. Let this land accept him. Let it be the home he needs to find so badly.*

Stomp.

Suddenly the tempo picked up, and I opened my eyes. The crowd had swelled more. My vision was hazy, but I caught a glimpse of Jason's face, flushed and dripping with sweat, on the edge of the crowd, stomping along with the rest.

Then Rowan raised his head, and opened his eyes. For a second the crowd stilled. Rowan tilted his head a little to the side, his eyes narrow and thoughtful. Anticipation thickened the air. Then he lifted his right foot and brought it slamming down on the ground. A muted cry rose from the crowd, and they took up the beat again, but this time with Rowan as the leader. He urged them on. The pounding grew faster and more frantic.

I stomped along with them. Sweat soon poured down my neck and trickled down my back. Crinea's fine hair grew wet and plastered to her forehead. Hoots and cries rang out, and the crowd moved with the sound. Rowan threw his head back and howled, and a hundred other voices joined his cry, the jagged, raw sound refracting off the rocks and growing stronger and stranger as it echoed back to us.

Suddenly, Rowan ran forward several paces and crouched low to the ground. My breath froze in my throat. He raised his hand in the air and began to pound the ground with his fist. He struck, again and again, his eyes wild as the swelling beat grew until it was practically one continuing, thunderous sound.

The boom, when it came, came from right under the spot where Rowan crouched.

For a second, he and everyone who watched him went utterly still. Then the boom came again, like a fist slamming against a door from just underneath him, echoing up from the ground. A huge cloud of dust billowed up from the earth. Cries of surprise and disbelief rose from the crowd as Rowan stood smoothly to his feet and backed away. A rumble bubbled up from beneath us, and the ground under my feet tilted slightly and then righted itself. Everyone stumbled to catch their balance, many exclaiming in confusion.

The soil in front of Rowan began to crumble inward. Suddenly, where the ground had been smooth and solid just a second before, a small black circle in the ground appeared. A deep, creaking sound filled the air, and the black circle yawned. The hole grew, pebbles and stones cascading down as the boom came again and again. A wind rose out of nowhere, stirring up dust so thickly that it became a constant haze before my eyes.

Rowan watched the widening hole closely and then, for a split second, he turned. His eyes found mine. He looked at me, and there was no mistaking the flash of fierce triumph in his eyes. Whatever came next, he had succeeded in this much at least. The earth had answered his call. I tried to smile back at him, but I couldn't make my lips move. And then Rowan turned his eyes back to the ground. As quickly as it had come, the excitement disappeared from his expression. He closed his eyes and took a deep breath, his fingers flexing at his sides.

He took a slow step toward the hole, and just as he moved, came a great cracking sound. Rowan froze, and something poked up out of the ground.

Long and curved and black as onyx, the razor-sharp claw sheared earth and rock away as it grasped at the surface, pulling more dirt down into the widening chasm. For a second, a beak, huge, white, and curved, broke through to the surface. It snapped and pulled at the edges of the hole, pulling at the ground and breaking it away. Then it disappeared, and the talons re-emerged, grasping at the rock and pushing it aside, like a huge chick breaking out of an egg. A flurry of rocks flew and black feathers gleamed in the sun. The great bird pulled itself to the surface and stretched its wings wide.

It was easily twice Rowan's height, its feathers so black that the muted sunlight tinted them blue. Its yellow eyes flashed and shone. Its white beak looked wicked and sharp. When it flicked its feathers and brought them to its side, the wind clapped in its wings.

Beside me, Crinea jerked back and gave a low cry of wonder and alarm. "What it that creature?" she cried.

In my mind there could be no doubt. I had seen its picture often, had seen a score of artists try to imagine what this long-lost creature might have been. Every mythology of the Badlands sooner or later came down to this; the ancient bird who created the badlands with the carcasses of its kills, the multicolored rocks the long-ago fossilized bones of its prey.

"It's a thunderbird," I whispered, and took a step closer.

Because Rowan was walking right toward it.

The thunderbird bent its head to its chest, adjusting its feathers with its beak, all the while watching Rowan's approach out of the corner of its coal-black eye. Rowan walked slowly up, and stopped before it. He made no other move, but simply presented himself, standing with his hands down by his side and open. My heart hurt as it pounded in my chest, and fear coursed through me.

He was making himself too vulnerable. The least he could do was draw his blade, but he wouldn't. The bird ignored him for a minute, then narrowed its eyes as it looked him over. Opening its beak, it hissed, the sound dry and rasping, and the pink of its narrow tongue terrible as it poked out.

Rowan remained perfectly still, his eyes upturned and expectant.

"What now?" I muttered under my breath as the crowd froze, watching. "Is he supposed to ride it? Get it to eat out of his hand? Wrestle it to the ground? What does it want from him? What?"

The crowd went utterly silent. The only thing that moved was the dust that swirled in the sunlight as it slowly descended to the ground.

The bird hissed again, puffing its feathers up so that it seemed larger than it was. Along the base of its neck several longer feathers, these black striped with gray, stood up like a ruff as it clicked its beak in warning.

Rowan took another step toward it, and the bird struck.

EIGHTEEN

IT HAPPENED SO QUICKLY THAT I DID NOT REALIZE I HAD SCREAMED, or that I had moved at all, until Crinea's hand clamped down on my arm, pulling me back.

The bird had swiped its razor-sharp talons across Rowan's chest. Deep red gashes spread like schisms across the perfect tan of his skin. Rowan made a sound, a deep rumble of pain. As though in slow motion, he fell, collapsing onto his hands and knees before the savage bird. Blood so red that it was almost black streamed from his torn flesh and pooled on the red ground beneath him.

I didn't realize I was fighting her until Crinea pulled me back and wrapped a thin arm, hard as steel, across my chest.

"Let me go, let me go to him!" I gasped.

She shook her head, her teeth clenched together as she fought to hold me back. "It will only kill you, too, Amy. You can't!"

All around us voices cried out, but I didn't care. I couldn't really hear them as much more than a din. Crinea was stronger than I was, and I couldn't pull free of her grasp. Helpless, my eyes zeroed in on Rowan's injury. The cuts went deep, almost to the bone. The flesh curled away from the edges of his wounds. His eyes clamped shut, his face suddenly gray and drawn. He shook.

The bird lowered itself to a crouch, its beak close to the ground as it watched Rowan, shifting its weight constantly from one foot to the next. Waiting to pounce. It gave a thin, high-pitched trill of warning. But it did not strike again.

My whole body vibrated, and the fear was so intense that I almost felt I was floating above myself, watching the scene unfold before me. I took a deep, gasping breath.

Suddenly, I smelled lavender.

I jerked my head around, and at my sudden movement Crinea lost her grip on me. But I didn't rush off in Rowan's direction. Instead I craned my head around further, furiously searching the audience. Someone was using magic.

My eyes moved quickly, but I could see no sign of mages anywhere nearby. Still searching, I took another, deeper breath. The scent of lavender and campfire smoke wove together, filling my head, and I knew. This was no mage magic I sensed—it was Rowan.

Rowan's magic filled the air, sinking into the ground at my feet. Something else was going on, something more than the scene in front of me, a struggle no one could see, and none but I could sense. My eyes flew back to Rowan, and the only thing I saw in his face was agony.

I bit down on my lip to keep from crying out, and forced my feet to stillness. More than anything else, I wanted to run to him, to call up my Truthsight and knit the rent flesh back together. And if every mage in the world fell on me in the same instant, I honestly didn't think I would care. But running up to Rowan now wouldn't help him.

That didn't mean that there was nothing I could do.

I knelt down on the ground and, cautiously, laid my hand against the soil, just as I had seen Rowan do. I didn't need Truthsight now—I needed something different. Rowan had already proved to me that his magic and mine were similar in certain ways. He had walked right into my Truthsight vision. What if I could walk right into his? What if I could follow his magic, use it, just enough to see what was happening to him? To let him know that I was with him, that he wasn't alone? As soon as the skin of my palm touched the earth, I felt the swirl of powers mixing, felt the pulse of Rowan's presence in the very ground beneath me.

It didn't come to me easily, as Truthsight would have. But I had the scent of it, and I knew what I wanted. With my eyes screwed shut, I sought it out, like a chipmunk burrowing deeper and deeper into the ground, nose first. Behind my closed eyes, the darkness deepened and sparkled, and the breath in my chest heaved with effort. But I didn't stop. I followed the trace of Rowan's magic all the way to its source.

Then I opened my eyes, and looked in wonder at his world.

It was true, what he had told me. His magic was wilder than mine. My Truthsight only took the world around me and helped me understand it. With it I could see the place I was in, and the people who were in it, with more clarity. I could use that clarity to take hold of reality and bend it to my will. Rowan's magic was different.

I was in a completely different place. It might as well have been a different universe. The crowd was nowhere to be seen. The hard rock and red dirt were gone. I was deep in a forest, on the edge of a clearing, surrounded by a silence deeper than any true forest could hold. Purple and gold painted the sky above. I looked up at the trees. Strange birds, huge and brightly colored, sat motionless in the branches, looking down at me with knowing eyes. The air was clear, but smelled of the smoke of a good cooking fire. My hand touched my side, and I looked down at myself. I wore coarse linen pants and a long tunic. In reality my hair swung just past my shoulders, but here my pale curls swept against my hips. I looked up and saw the structure that filled the clearing before me. And, suddenly, I knew.

Rowan was a house, built simple, sturdy, and low to the ground.

My breath caught in my throat. I could not be sure how I knew, but I had not the slightest question in my mind. My Truthsight had not touched him in the least. But here, in his own place, he opened as a flower to the sun. The slate-gray stone was exactly the same shade as his hair. Smooth river rocks paved the walkway, and the stately chimney breathed smoke. The windows held the blue of the sky, and in them I saw his own blue eyes looking back at me. I took a step toward him.

Suddenly, just in front of the doorway, came a loud rustling, and a flurry of wind. As though caught in a freak whirlwind, leaves danced up from the earth and swirled wildly together. Beneath them the ground vibrated, then swelled. The dirt and mud began to move, and then to bubble up. The dancing leaves plastered themselves against the clay. A shape took form.

In the swirling leaves and wind, at first I couldn't see it clearly. But after a moment the wind died down, making a strange, low whistle as it disappeared. A small figure stood, looking around at its surroundings.

It was no bigger than a child, its black hair tangled, matted with mud and leaves, and so long that it trailed against the ground. Wise eyes took up most of its face, and a bare belly swelled out round and full. One of the Earth-child's eyes was blue like the sky right after a cleansing storm. The other was as red as the dirt that covered its body. And the red dirt did cover it, from toes to chin, so thick and clinging that I could not tell if it was boy or girl, so red that I wondered if some of it was blood.

The child walked up to the threshold of the house and hesitated.

For a moment nothing happened, and I hung back, not sure what to do. Then the house began to tremble, and slowly the trembling grew. The windows and doors rattled. The very ground shook. Then came a deep animal sound of pain and desperation from somewhere inside the structure. And in one instant, with a wrenching creak, every door and window of the house suddenly flung itself open. For a second the Earth-child simply stood, looking around at the house that now stood utterly open before it. Then it smiled and stepped inside.

I ran up to the house and lay my hand against the cool stone. Instantly, the rock warmed under my hand. The whole house trembled like a living thing in terrible pain, and now that I was closer, I could see tiny fissures inching through the stone. I pressed my forehead against the doorway.

"It's all right," I whispered, somehow sure that Rowan could hear me. "Please, hold on. I'm right here, with you."

Then I heard a clatter, and a sharp wild cry from deep within, and I hurried inside.

"Hello?" I called as I entered. Wind blew through the house, carrying the sound of my words right out the open doors.

I moved slowly, unsure of what to do. The rooms were broad, and sparsely furnished, and all the windows went from ceiling to floor. The sun lived in this place. It swept through it in broad, familiar stripes, spreading out comfortably on the floor and leaning up against the mantle-place. No art hung on the walls, but some were made of stone, and these had been painted over. Large, detailed murals spread from corner to corner, pictures in which thick trees tangled and ivy dripped, and the black, fertile earth sprouted strange, vivid flowers.

A crash sounded, followed by the sound of something shattering. Beneath my naked toes the floor twitched, as though it had winced with pain. I hurried, my bare feet padding silently against the worn wood. Apprehension mounted in my chest as I reached the end of a long hallway and peered inside a large, low–ceilinged room.

The child did not look at me, or seem in any way to notice my presence. A bed stood in this room, and the child jumped on it, bringing its chubby knees up to its chest with its eyes screwed shut. At times it got so high that it risked banging its head on a ceiling beam. The bed creaked and moaned. The sheets that had been light blue were stained and ruined, though the amount of dirt on the child's body did not seem to decrease at all. Before I could decide if I ought to try to intervene, the child bounded from the bed and bolted down the hallway. It trailed grubby fingers along the wall, leaving streaks behind it.

I followed as it ran from place to place. I did not dare to interrupt, but I also could not help but reach out and touch the walls, running my fingers first over rough clay and then over sanded wood. It was the only thing I could do, to try to tell Rowan, with my touch, that I was near, that I was with him. That whatever pain might be coursing through him, or fear that he might feel, he was not alone.

I was not sure how much time passed. Somehow it felt as though time did not exist in this place. But I knew the shaking was getting worse, and I saw tiny cracks spread like deadly vines across the walls. I laid my hands across them, as though I could hold Rowan together from the inside, with nothing but my fingers and my love.

The Earth-child whirled into each room, banging around, picking things up and shaking them. It did clumsy half-cartwheels in the hall. It capered about madly in wild movements that were almost a dance. It hooted a high-pitched cry, clapped its hands, and stomped its feet, tilting its head as if listening to the echoes it made. It found the pantry, and sifted through everything, taking things off the shelf and licking them with a small, blood-red tongue before tossing them away. It leaned out the windows, hefting itself up so that its feet dangled in the air behind it, and tipping forward so that it nearly spilled from the window into the flower beds below.

"Hello," I called to it a few times, with no effect.

I wasn't sure what I would do if it answered me. Did it understand Rowan's peril? Could I somehow urge it to hurry? But it never looked at me, not even when I cried out, "Be careful!" when it picked up a large glass globe and held it high to see its reflection. I was not sure if I was protecting Rowan or the child, who seemed likely to drop the glass right on its head. But it ignored me, and after a minute of sticking its tongue out at itself and making ghastly faces, it grew bored and set the globe back down in its place.

Then it came into a large circular room near the center of the house, and for the first time, its feet slowed. In the middle of the room sat a huge stone fireplace. Orange flame crackled along the logs that filled it. The child stood and studied the fire for a while, watching the flames dance and the smoke curl up and out the chimney. It walked all the way around it, twice, its large eyes suddenly serious. It picked up a poker that leaned against a nearby wall and approached the fire with small, uncertain steps. Then, standing as far back as it could manage, and leaning its face well back and away, it gave the fire a savage poke. The floor twinged beneath me. The child froze, then took a step closer, and poked the fire again.

"Wait!" I cried, lurching forward, but I was too late to stop it.

The floor convulsed underneath my feet, like a man being punched in the gut. The child froze, and looked around it, as though afraid something would happen. When nothing did, it smiled, and threw the poker aside. It leaned its face in close to the flame, so that the fire's lights made strange pockets of light and darkness on its face.

Then, in a sudden, darting movement, it stuck its chubby fist right into the heart of the fire. I cried out and darted forward again. The child only turned its hand from side to side in the flame. It giggled, and stuck its other hand in as well. I stood transfixed, watching as it played with the flames. When it was done, it pulled its hands out and rubbed them together, sighing contentedly and looking around the room with the air of someone making big plans.

The child reached down, and began to push at the thick, sturdy, round stones that made up the fireplace. They flowed beneath its fingers like water, rearranging themselves at just a whisper of its touch. After just a moment's effort the fireplace was completely re-structured. The child had made a tiny stone nook for itself, right by the fireside. It was just the size that the child was, and if it lay down inside it, the fire would warm the stones against its back. It climbed in, turned around three times, and then settled down into the space with a small sound of delight.

Then the Earth-child gazed up at me, and smiled. I found myself smiling back.

I understood then what needed to be done. Leaving the child, I turned and ran back through the house. As quickly as I could move, I pulled shut every open window. I closed every door. As each opening swung shut, the house shook a little less, and I could feel Rowan's pain dwindle. When I had walked through every room in the house, I went back to the fireplace.

The child was stretched out flat on its back, fast asleep, a small smile on its lips.

I let myself out by the front door, which was the only door I left ajar. It seemed to want to stay open behind me.

For a moment I looked around me. The forest, the house, the purple sky, it was all so beautiful. I was almost jealous of the Earth-child. It got to stay here. Then I took a deep breath, closing my eyes as I let go of the scent of Rowan's magic, and reached out for reality once again.

Returning was much easier than going had been, and only an instant later my eyes snapped open. It was as though no time had passed. I knelt on the ground, with Crinea just behind me. Rowan was still on his hands and knees, utterly vulnerable, before the bird who crouched, poised to strike.

Then Rowan's arms gave out, and he fell face first into the dirt. A cry went up from the gathered crowd.

"Oh no!" Crinea gasped.

I stood up, and laid a hand on her shoulder. "Don't worry," I told her quietly. "It will be all right."

Because I saw what they did not. Rowan lay flat on the ground, with his wounds pressed against the earth. His hands stretched out, open and palm down on the soil, his fingers curling down deep into the earth. And where his torn flesh met the earth's surface, there was a slight blur—as though there was no clear line between where his body ended and the ground began.

The earth had accepted him. And it would heal its own.

The thunderbird straightened up out of its crouch and tipped its head up toward the sky, flipping its feathers and crying out once with a shrill, trumpeting cry. A swirl of magic brushed by me like a hot breeze in summer.

And then Rowan pushed himself to his feet, and stood tall and steady. A sudden, disbelieving cheer erupted from the crowd as the sunlight poured down on his healed flesh. The wounds were not completely gone. Stripes now marked his chest, and I knew they would never disappear. They were part of him now; a sign of the trial he had undertaken. But the wounds could have been weeks, even months old, and the color had come back to his face.

The thunderbird settled it feathers. Rowan strode up to it, slow but without hesitation. When he was within arm's reach, he stretched out his hand. The thunderbird bent its head down, and laid his beak against Rowan's open palm.

Again, a cry rose up from the crowd, hoots and cries, and less human sounds of triumph. The thunderbird startled and spread its wings, lifting itself skyward with one thunderous clap of its feathers. It rose into the air and flew slowly, ponderously away.

Rowan stepped forward, and leaned down. When he straightened up, he held something in his right hand, something pitch black, as long as his forearm, and curved like a scythe. He held the thunderbird talon up above his head. The crowd exploded again.

Suddenly the crowd began moving, and a wave of creatures rushed up to him, swirling around him like an eddy.

I hung back, not wanting to press my way through the churning throng, and wanting to let him enjoy his moment of triumph. But then he came toward me. He clutched the talon tightly in his hand, a symbol of the kingship he had won, and a soft smile graced his face.

I stepped forward to meet him, and everyone backed away a little, giving us some space.

My fingers ran over the marks on his chest, my eyes searching his for any sign of lingering pain. "Are you really all right?" I whispered.

"You know I am," he whispered. "You saw. You were there, with me—through everything. How did you do that?"

"I could feel you in the earth and I just ... followed you. You're not upset, are you? I didn't mean to pry. I just couldn't let you go through that alone."

"Asa," he said softly, his eyes lit with emotion as he leaned down to whisper words in my ear that no one else could hear. "You are welcome in my house any day." And he brought my hand to his lips, and kissed my fingers.

Suddenly the moment felt too intense, and I looked away, my eyes darting back out at the crowd.

"They're leaving!" I exclaimed in surprise.

Already most of those gathered had melted away. The group that was left now was mostly centaurs with several pixies still buzzing overhead.

"Yes." Rowan nodded. "The power of the summoning is gone now—its goal accomplished. They have all suddenly remembered that they do not necessarily much like each other. And they certainly do not like to be gathered in great numbers, and exposed in the light of the day."

"But don't they want to...I don't know...meet you?" I asked. "I mean, you're their king now, right? Shouldn't they stick around a little longer?"

Rowan smiled. "That time will come. But though the land has accepted me, my bond with it is still new. It will take a little time before its authority is fully mine. They will come, in their own time and in their own ways, and make themselves known to me."

The chief came to stand beside me, and Rowan reached a hand out to him. They gripped each other's forearms tightly.

Then the chief stepped back. Slowly, he inclined his head ever so slightly in Rowan's direction. I bit back a gasp. I could never have imagined the chief bowing to anyone.

"Welcome back, Dr. Amy," a voice chirped, and I started as a small weight descended on my shoulder.

"Grenalda!" I exclaimed, not able to hide my surprise, not only at her presence, but also at her demeanor. She smiled up at me brightly, with no trace of the wariness I was so used to in her and her kind. "I'm happy to see you. How is your boy?"

"He is healing well and quickly. He is almost back to his usual amount of mischief-making. I heard you had left, and was worried."

"Wow." I really hadn't expected that. I thought of myself as barely tolerated by the pixies. "I appreciate that. I came back just yesterday."

"Yes. My son told me I would be seeing you. And you brought a new lord of the land with you." Grenalda's eyes fixed on Rowan, and she nodded approvingly. "It is good. We pixies have increased in number these last few years. We could not have stayed in a sleeping land much longer. We will be stronger now, and safer."

The chief had a hand on Rowan's shoulder. He smiled at me. It was the most unguarded expression I had ever seen on his face. "Would you both return with us to our home?" he asked. "You can eat, and rest there."

"Please, do come," Crinea said to me, her head poking into view from just behind the chief's shoulder. "I want you to see the baby. He is doing so well."

Rowan reached out and took my hand in his, fingers gently tracing back and forth over my knuckles. He leaned close to whisper in my ear. "If you do not mind, we could accept their invitation. I need rather badly to rest."

"Yes, of course!" I looked up at him, smiling brightly.

His fingers suddenly tightened around mine, closing so tightly that it hurt.

"Rowan?" I asked, "Is something wrong?"

Just inches from my ear, Grenalda gave a high pitched scream of horror.

Rowan's face contorted, his eyes darkening as his whole body went stiff. For a few terrible seconds, I froze, gazing back at him as he stared at me, a sudden intensity in his eyes as though there was something vital I had to understand, but that he couldn't say aloud. And then his face went blank and his body crumpled.

With my hand still locked in his, he fell unconscious to the ground.

NINETEEN

Blood poured out onto the ground all around Rowan, pooling around my feet. I stared at it, not understanding, frozen in disbelief and shock.

I looked up, slowly, and in the space right behind where Rowan had been, a skinny mage with glasses stood, grinning at me.

"You won't be very hard to kill now, traitor," Mark purred. "Without your freak to shield you. Did you really think a gathering this big wouldn't catch my attention?" The knife in his hand was smeared thickly with blood. He stared down at Rowan's prone form, cool derision in his eyes. "Did you really think that any of these animals could protect you from us?"

From Rowan's side, an angry, red wound gaped up at me, and wept blood.

"This is none of your affair," Mark said, his eyes taking in the centaurs that stood clustered around. He sounded almost bored. "This woman is a fugitive, and anyone who stands between us and her will suffer the same fate as that one there." He gestured broadly to Rowan's sprawled form. "Some of you encountered us yesterday —you already know what we can do. But you don't have to be afraid. We have no desire to harm any of you animals. Just leave." He smiled at me. "I'll take it from here."

I heard his voice as though from a great distance. My heart refused to believe what my eyes saw. My chest filled with a slow, agonizing ache. My body wouldn't move.

With a sudden snarl, Mark sprang forward, his knife now pointing at me.

Graceful as a dancer, Crinea darted forward. Her arm flew, pulling her sword smoothly from where it hung across her back. She let out a shrill, high-pitched war cry and brought her sword arching around in a movement as beautiful as it was deadly. The blade swept against the side of Mark's neck, cleaving his head cleanly from his shoulders.

Flesh gave way with a wet sound. Bone snapped. An angry spray of red rose into the air as the corpse fell, twitching, to the ground.

There was a millisecond of silence.

"He thought us no more than deer, to scatter before him and run off into the woods," Crinea muttered, and then she shoved the body out of the way.

I threw myself down onto the grass by Rowan's side.

His chest moved, but I found little comfort in that. The wound in his side was wide and deep, and the blood that leaked from it was the deadly black of fatal harm. A thick, red puddle of blood had already formed in the grass beneath him. As I knelt by his side, the warm wetness soaked through the knees of my pants. And his wounds from the great bird's strike had barely healed.

A buzzing sound, like waves, began inside my ears, and I fought for breath. The pain in my chest burned like lava just beneath my breast bone. I had to think, had to act, but I couldn't stop staring at his slack face. If he had been firmly bonded with the land, if it had been days after his trial, rather than minutes, there would have been good reason to hope he could survive. But this...

"How bad is it?" The chief knelt on the ground beside me, his hand again coming to rest on Rowan's shoulder.

"Bad," I choked out. I couldn't say more. My voice was too unsteady, too close to giving way to tears.

"What do you need us to do?" Crinea's voice was calm, and dispassionate, exactly what I needed to hear to steady myself. I spared her an appreciative glance.

I forced a deep breath, even though it made the pain in my chest worse, and forced myself to think through my panic. "I've got to tap into the Source. It's the only thing that might save him and even then, it's going to be close."

I leaned over and gently pushed the hair that had fallen across his face out of his eyes. His cheek felt cool when my fingers brushed across it. I looked up at the chief. "The mages will come."

"We understand."

He nodded at his people and all of them, moving in perfect, unspoken coordination, drew their blades. Silently, they formed a circle around Rowan and me, turning their backs to us with their weapons outstretched, making themselves into a wall around us.

"Thank you," I whispered.

My vision had already started changing. I didn't reach out for my Truthsight; it sprang forward and fell on me in a sudden, heavy rush of glinting light and burning cold. I didn't even close my eyes as it ran through me. Suddenly the world around me sparkled and changed.

The centaurs grew taller and more terrible, their Truthsight-selves gripping wicked, curling blades that shone with golden light. Crinea stood with them, and she turned her head, her all-black eyes glinting out of a savage face, and nodded down at me. I could hear the Source, bubbling somewhere close by. Everything was different.

Except for Rowan.

I had forgotten. In the panic and the fear, I had made the mistake of thinking I could save him, but Rowan's magic was different from mine. And he was resistant to mage magic. To me. He was pale and still, his chest just barely moving. No more or less than his normal self. I couldn't *see* him.

"No!" I cried, grabbing him by the shoulders. "Rowan! Please—you have to help me see you. You have to let me in!"

But his face was slack and empty. He couldn't hear me, couldn't do anything to help, and I knew I was losing him.

Anger rose up inside me like a wave. "You!" I yelled, and I struck my fist against the blood-stained earth beside me. "He is weakened from *your* trial! You chose him, but you cannot heal him by yourself. Help me! *Do* something. He is a part of you, now. You can't just let him die like this. Show me what to do. Help me understand how I can help him. Please." My voice broke, and I would have broken down in sobs if a small movement off to my left hadn't made the breath catch in my throat.

A small figure stepped out of the trees. I froze, not daring to move or even to breathe as the Earth-child paced slowly toward me. It moved cautiously, stopping every few feet, sometimes looking over its shoulder at the trees behind it with obvious longing. When it got to the ring of centaurs, it walked right through them as though they were made of nothing more than smoke, its eyes huge and round, and focused only on Rowan. I resisted the impulse to call out to it, to urge it to hurry up. With its long black hair and wild, dirt-smeared skin, at that moment it looked to me like nothing more than a frightened child, and I knew, somehow, if I so much as spoke a word to it, it would turn and run away. So I bit my lip and waited until it came to a stop, standing directly behind me.

And then I felt a small hand, soft and strangely warm, settle on my shoulder.

As soon as it touched me, my vision fogged over as though a sudden cloud of smoke had risen in front of my eyes. My fingertips tingled. A second later, when I could see again, Rowan still lay before me. But he was no longer made of flesh.

His body was the dull, dry gray of clay left too long to bake in the sun. Cracks ran through him, deep, aching lines that stretched up his arms and over his shoulders, like arid ground after a terrible drought. His side, where the wound had been, was pale gray dirt that was crumbling away.

He was turning to dust right in front of me.

"No!" I cried. I pressed my hands against the widening gap in his side, as though I could hold him together with nothing more than my hands and the force of my will. But at my touch bits of him crumbled away. I gasped in horror and snatched my hands away.

"What do I do?" I cried.

I looked over at the child, and it stared back at me, silent. I wasn't sure if it didn't know, or if it simply had no words to tell me. Either way, it had done all it could.

"Oh my God," I whispered, looking back down at Rowan, afraid to even touch him, lest I accidentally do him harm. "What do I do now?"

I wished for Meri, for her wisdom, but her voice was nowhere in my head. I wished for Jason, for his trusting presence at my side, believing so earnestly that could I fix anything that, somehow, I found I could.

I wished Rowan would open his eyes. That I could tell him I was sorry for failing.

"Okay," I whispered to myself. "Calm down, Asa. Get it under control. Try to think. His body is made of clay. That's the earth— that makes sense. His father looked the same way. But he's been separated from the land too long, and he's bleeding out. That's why the dirt is so dry." I stared down at him for a second, the pieces falling into place in my mind. "I need water!"

I jerked myself up, meaning to get to my feet and run to the silver water of the Source that flowed not far from me. But the child's hand tightened on my shoulder, its unsuspected strength jerking me back into place at Rowan's side. I froze, and turned around to stare at it.

"What?" I whispered. "I got it wrong?"

It just looked steadily back at me, its face impassive.

Thoughts flashed through my mind with such speed as to be

almost incomprehensible. *Wait. The Source is mage's magic. And Rowan is no mage.*

"He needs something else, right?" I questioned. "Something from the land." I cocked my head. "Can *you* give me water?"

An expression that was almost a smile slid over the Child's face and slipped as quickly off. It pointed at the ground.

I understood, and plunged my fingers into the dirt, clawing at the ground, throwing great clumps of black dirt aside. I could tell the earth was trying to help me, because the soil gave way at my touch, cleaving itself open under the pressure of my hands. Soon I felt a trace of coolness at my fingertips. And then a hint of moisture.

Suddenly the groundwater gushed up, filling the small hole I had made. I cupped my hands and filled them with cool, dirt flecked water. I began splashing it up onto Rowan's body in a frantic rhythm. Every drop that touched him was instantly absorbed, and when it was gone I could see no difference. He needed so much. Every jerking movement I made with my arms sent a sharp surge of pain spiking through my chest, but it didn't slow me. I hardly even felt it. The intensity of my fear was a more effective painkiller than any pill I had ever prescribed in the ER.

The child's hand remained pressed against my shoulder. I could feel its eyes tracking my movements, could hear a tiny hitch in its breath now and then, as worry made its breath uneven. There was some degree of comfort at the solidarity that had suddenly sprung up between me and this strange, feral creature. Both of us had so very much to lose.

I knew minutes were ticking by, but I had no idea how many. Without slowing my hands, I glanced up at the centaurs, still strange and wondrous from the Truthsight, standing as silent sentinels all around. I couldn't have much time left until the mages found me, but there was nothing I could do about that. The only thing I could do was keep throwing water onto Rowan, praying it would be enough.

When I first started to see the difference, it was so slight that I couldn't quite let myself believe. I told myself it was only wishful thinking. But slowly the color of his clay body changed, going from the sickly gray of parched, desert earth to a deeper, rich tone. The cracks that had formed in his arms first filled with water and then, slowly, closed. Finally, he was cool, damp clay beneath my hands, and I began with trembling, uncertain fingers, to try to smooth the ragged edges of his wound together. The gap was too great to simply close over, and after a moment of panic I began scooping up mud from the ground and pressing it against him. I filled the hole as best I could, hoping that was the right thing to do, telling myself that the Earth-child would stop me if I did something that might cause real harm.

The hole was almost filled when the child's hand clamped down tightly on my shoulder. I froze as its grip became painful. Slowly, I looked up at it to find out what I was doing wrong. But the child was not looking at me.

Its face was turned back toward the trees, and its lips were pulled away from its teeth. Its eyes looked at something I could not see, something that made it very, very angry. Strangely colored eyes flashed, and it hissed. Goosebumps rose on my flesh as any feeling of camaraderie between us vanished. Suddenly, I knew myself to be in the presence of something immensely more powerful than myself, something untamed, savage, and mighty. And it frightened me. The child glanced over at Rowan, nodded once to itself. Then it lifted its hand from my shoulder, and was gone.

Cold shot through me, and I tipped over, almost falling on my face. By the time I had found my balance and looked over at Rowan, he was flesh and blood again, his eyes struggling to open.

"Easy," I whispered, putting a hand against his cheek. The wound in his side was still there, but it was no longer life-threatening, and that was all that mattered. "I still need to treat you. Try to hold still."

His eyes cracked open, and the blue of them gazed up at me. I smiled at him, hoping I managed to look calm and reassuring. Then I bent back over his wound. It now appeared to be a surface wound, something I could have treated in my clinic. Moving as quickly as I could, I made a compress of leaves and layered it quickly over the wound to protect it while it healed.

"How soon will the mages come?" Rowan asked after a moment, his voice rough.

I shook my head, my eyes still focused on my work. "That isn't your worry."

"It is my worry," he said, and began to sit up.

"Damn it, Rowan! Stop that," I cried, trying to push him back down. "The centaurs are protecting us. The only thing you are allowed to worry about is not dying. Just let me do this. We will deal with other things later." I locked eyes with him, and couldn't help but smile a little. "Together."

He held my eyes for a long second.

"Very well." He took a deep, shuddering breath, and relaxed back onto the ground. "Together."

I worked in silence for a moment.

"It was here," he said quietly, and I did not need to ask who he meant.

"Yes. And saved your life. I couldn't have done it by myself."

"It remembered you," he murmured. "Knew you could be trusted."

I didn't answer, but focused on my work. Soon I had done all I could for the wound in his side. As soon as I wished for it, my Truthsight had a mug waiting at my side. I filled it with clean groundwater from the hole I had dug, and blew on it. Immediately, the water steamed and boiled. I picked several leaves of the night's foil plant that had sprung up as soon as I knew I would have need of it, and crushed the leaves into the water.

"Do you feel well enough to sit up now?" I asked.

Rowan slowly righted himself, ignoring my attempts to steady him. I handed him the mug.

"What is this?" he asked, after a first, uncertain sip. "It's delicious."

"Night's foil. It'll help your body build new blood. There isn't much else I can do for the loss. Unfortunately, I can't magically produce leshy blood. I could give you a transfusion of mine, and I thought about it, but I'm not really sure what that would do. I don't think we're the same blood type."

Rowan's lips quirked into a smile around the rim of the cup. The red lines on his shoulders and arms were still there, but they were lighter than they had been before. I wished they would fade away completely.

"No. I don't imagine we are." His gaze left mine, looking around at our surroundings. "So this is what your world looks like," he murmured.

"Yes." The adrenaline was fading from my system, leaving heady exhaustion in its wake. I leaned my forehead against his shoulder, and let myself close my eyes for a second. He was warm and substantial. He was alive. "You've seen it before."

"Only once. And then I was so focused on my father that I did not see much else. Even you—I did not realize how very strange and beautiful you appear when you are your truest self."

I shook my head. "I can't see myself, but Crinea told me when I healed her. It sounds so bizarre. I'm a fish in a tree, right? I have to admit that I don't really get what that looks like."

Rowan started.

"What?" I asked, opening my eyes and looking around for what caused his distress. "What's wrong?"

"No," he said, shaking his head. "Is it really possible that you know yourself so little?"

"I don't understand. What do you mean?"

He sat up a little straighter, his face knit with worry. "I too, see a silver fish, held up high in the branches of great tree. But, Asa—the fish is not you. You are holding the fish in your branches."

"What?" I said dumbly, frozen as I looked up at him.

"Asa." He laid a hand against my cheek. "I see you—the true you. You are a weeping willow tree. Your bark is the silver of the Truthsight river that flows beside you." His eyes were full of wonder. "Your roots are thick beneath the surface. I can...*feel* them. Twisting there, deep-planted and strong. You are like a tree spirit, a dryad. Your arms are slender branches, and your hair—cascading leaves. I can see the silver fish, nestled high in your branches. It burns you with silver flames. All around it your branches are broken, and black from the flame." His eyes tightened with anger. "I can *see* it hurting you."

My hand flew to my chest, as sudden understanding flooded me.

"It's Meri," I whispered. "The fish is Meri." Then I froze, as a different memory swam to the forefront of my mind; a silver fish, wrapped round and round with twine. A shining pendant dangling against black cloth.

"Oh, no," I whispered. This was the harsh part of Truthsight, the part that made it almost as much a curse as it was a blessing. The times it forced you to see things you would have given almost anything to not understand.

"I-I have to go, Rowan," I gasped, lurching to my feet. "You're stable now, and healing. And I have to hurry."

"Wait, Asa. What's wrong?" But I was already pulling away from the Source. It hurt to leave it, to feel the clarity and peacefulness peeling away from me. For a second the air around us glimmered, as though suddenly full of falling stars. Then the real world was all around us. The centaurs turned with eyes wide with shock, to watch as Rowan rose onto his feet, steady and nearly whole. Crinea held a hand out to me to steady me as I rose.

"How close are the mages?" I asked, my eyes scanning our surroundings but seeing no trace of movement.

It was Grenalda, who still hovered nearby, who answered, and there was no mistaking the war-like lilt in her voice.

"Close. Those dunderheads are barreling through the trees, not far from here, making an incredible racket. They will be here soon."

At my side Rowan slid his knife from it sheath.

"What are you doing?" I spun to face him. "You are still healing. I don't want you hurt."

"Asa." Rowan gazed at me, his face almost disapproving. "You know me. What have I ever done to make you think I would let you face them alone? That I am capable, no matter what my condition, of abandoning you in such a way?"

"We, too, will stand against them." The chief had turned to watch our conversation, his sword held in steady hands. "We owe them still."

Rowan nodded at him, and I watched as grim understanding slid between them.

"Wait," I said, my mind tripping over itself as I tried desperately to think of something, anything, to prevent an outright battle. "What if there was another way?"

Rowan tilted his head to the side. "Explain."

"I've read stories," I said, talking so fast that my words melted together, "of leshies leading people astray in the forest. Changing the paths, moving trees, keeping them going in circles for hours. Is that something you can really do? Is your bond with the land here strong enough to allow it?"

A smile grew on Rowan's lips. "Two hours ago, the answer would have been no. But now..." He held up his left hand, and stared at his flesh. The lines were so faded that they were barely visible, pale pink lines that trailed across the tan of his skin, a mere whisper of what they had been not long ago. "Now, I think I could do it. I would quite enjoy it, actually." He turned toward the woods. "I hear them coming. I will go and give them something to chase."

"Wait," I said, catching his hand in mine before he could slip away. "There's one more thing."

TWENTY

RUNNING THROUGH THE WOODS, I FELT A FIERCE SENSE OF satisfaction that Rowan had agreed to my plan. I had expected him to object, which he had. But he had also listened. And when Grenalda offered to go with me, he took her offer to ensure my safety quite seriously, despite her small size. She buzzed beside my ear now, occasionally making biting comments about how slowly I moved.

"It would have been easier to stay where we were," she pointed out after a bit, and I nodded.

"I know." I tried to keep my voice steady, but sprinting through the trees was leaving me gasping for air. "But we had to get away from the centaurs. They are eager for a fight, but I've seen enough blood today already." I glanced at her. "Besides, they aren't as tough as you are."

That made her smile.

Soon we came to a clearing.

"Good enough," I announced, putting my hands on my knees and leaning over as I worked to get my breath back. It would have been better to go a bit farther, but the pain in my chest just wouldn't let me move anymore. "We can wait here. It shouldn't be long. We left a pretty clear path behind us. Be careful, once it starts," I warned, knowing she wouldn't like it, but not quite able to stop myself. "This isn't your fight, and I don't want you to get hurt."

"I will pick what fights I like," Grenalda replied, sniffing. "And it seems this might be rather a good one." She darted off into the trees, a bright splash of blue and green that blended seamlessly into the leaves above.

It was good that she left me so quickly because a crashing sound in the brush soon announced someone approached. When my old friend pushed out of the trees, Shanie looked more confused than anything, gazing first at me, and then back over her shoulder in amazement. She had been willing to stab me when Paul threatened her, but nothing could erase all the history we shared. Seeing her sent a pang of guilt and regret surging through my chest.

"Everyone else is gone," she told me, looking dazed, a few leaves sticking haphazardly into her thick black hair. "I don't know where they went."

"I had a friend lead them away," I explained. "I wanted to talk to you alone."

I wasn't sure how she would react when I confronted her. I thought she might be angry, or hostile. I expected yelling, or maybe insults. Instead her face closed down, her eyes hardened, and her lips set in a thin, humorless smile.

"I don't think there's anything to say."

I took a step closer, and she studied me with a coldness in her eyes that hurt my heart.

"Walk away, Asa," she said softly. There was no venom in her words, only exhaustion. "You know I don't want them to find you. As long as you don't tell anyone, we don't have a problem."

I half-laughed. "How can you say that, Shanie? You know what Meri is to me. How could you think I would walk away, knowing that you're holding her? That you're *hurting* her. Every day."

Her eyebrows rose. "And how would you know that, exactly?" she whispered.

"When I first saw you with my Truthsight, I thought it was your grief that was wrapped all around you." I swallowed. "But it wasn't just grief. And your face was so white, as though you had been spending a lot of time away from the sun. Underground. I saw what I thought was a hole in your chest, a wound from the losses you've suffered. But it wasn't a hole at all, was it?"

My eyes fell to the pendant she wore, the small silver fish, wrapped again and again in imprisoning wire. "It was a tunnel." I took a step closer to her. "My Truthsight has been trying to tell me for a while, but I didn't understand it. That's the key, isn't it?" I pointed to her pendant. "It opens the door to the mage-haven where you're keeping her."

Shanie just stared at me.

"I thought Paul had betrayed Meri to the rebels, but somehow it just didn't fit. He can be cruel, but he is also loyal. He sees the world in black and white. He would never turn traitor. Once I realized she was inside a mage-haven, I started to figure it out. The rebels never had her, did they, Shanie? They had only had access to the Source for a few days before Meri disappeared, and mage-havens take months, even years to build. They couldn't have constructed one that quickly."

"Wait," Shanie held her hands up in front of her. "How do you know she's in a mage-haven? How could you unless…"

Unbidden, my hand flew to my chest, covering the place where the pearl nestled.

Her words petered out, as a savage new light lit deep inside her eyes.

"You have it, don't you?" she gasped. "You have the pearl …inside you. I've searched everywhere. I tried everything I could think of to get her to tell me. But you've had it, all this time." She shook her head at me. "How are you still in one piece?"

Moving so fast that I didn't see her coming, Shanie suddenly stood right beside me, her eyes hungry, her hands clutching the front of my shirt.

"Give it to me, Asa," she demanded. "You aren't using it, and holding onto it must be tearing you apart. All these years ...you must be in agony. How can you still be loyal to someone who has put you through so much suffering? Let me have it."

"Don't be a fool!" I cried, trying to pry her fingers away. "I can't take the pearl out of my own body any more than I can perform open-heart surgery on myself. If I tried, I'd just end up killing myself. The damn thing is so powerful—only Meri knows how to handle it safely. I can't take it out, or do anything with it. Get off me!" I shoved her away, and we stood, gasping for breath and staring at each other. "What do you want it for, anyway? Even if you believed you were strong enough to wield it, what could you possibly want to use it for?"

"Isn't it obvious?" Shanie's eyes were lit now, her cheeks flushed with violent red. "Meri was going to make peace with them. Let the rebel mages walk away with everything they'd ever wanted. She told me, as calm as could be, that day that she met with their leader. I didn't really have a choice. I drugged her drink, and then hid her away where no one could find her. I had to do what I did—I had to stop her. All the lives we'd lost, they didn't matter to her. My brothers."

Her voice broke and a moment passed before she went on. "They laid down their lives for her, and she was ready to just forget them. Forget the sacrifice they made. But I will not forget." She jabbed herself in the chest. "It is my responsibility to make sure the rebel mages pay for what they did to my family. To all of us." Her eyes were wide and wild, her breath coming in short hard gasps. "If Meri isn't strong enough to do it herself, then she doesn't deserve to lead us. She doesn't deserve to hold the power to bring those murdering bastards to their knees, if she isn't going to use it. So I'll do it. You had better give me what I want."

I could feel power building in her as she tapped into the Source and prepared to strike out against me.

"Now, Asa!" she screamed. "I don't want to fight you! We've been friends. But I've come too far, and waited too long, to let you just walk away with the pearl. I don't owe you anything. And I've managed to hold Meri prisoner all these years. We both know which of us is the stronger mage."

"I do know," I whispered, not quite able to look her in the eyes. The rage I saw there hurt too much. "That's why I brought a friend." I nodded my head once, sharply.

Suddenly Shanie's hand was at her neck, where a tiny dart, not much bigger than a bee sting, had burrowed deep into her skin.

"What?" she gasped, and her eyes fluttered as she tried to fight back the darkness that shrouded her sight. Then her knees folded under her, and she was on the ground.

"Is she dead?" Grenalda asked, swooping down out of the trees as I hurried over to the crumpled form.

"No," I answered, as I pressed my fingers against Shanie's throat, just to be sure. "Your darts are powerful, but one isn't enough to kill someone of this size. She should be out for a good long while, though."

"Oh." Grenalda's face fell. "Well, it was a good shot nonetheless."

I adjusted Shanie so she lay flat on her back, and moved her hands so they were folded together before I reached down to touch the pendant that still rested against her neck.

"You have to stay here," I told Grenalda. "Only mages can enter a mage-haven; that's part of the way they're built. If you try to come inside, it could be very dangerous for you."

"Follow you where?" Grenalda asked, her eyebrows arching with obvious concern.

No doubt she thought I had cracked under the strain of recent events. But I didn't have time to explain. The fish pendant vibrated slightly as I touched it, my fingers searching for the latch. It only took me a second to find it—there, on the fish's smooth underbelly, a tiny notch. I pressed against it, and the small charm in my hand shimmered and stretched, the fish's round mouth gaping and growing until it was as tall as I was. Grenalda cried out in surprise, but the sound was faint and far away. I was already running down into the darkness, calling Meri's name.

TWENTY-ONE

I SLIPPED WHEN THE ROUGH DIRT UNDER MY FEET MORPHED INTO cool, black stone. Fighting to regain my balance I skidded to a halt, staring around. The entrance led into a round, echoing tunnel that dripped with water and smelled of mold and dust. The mouth of the tunnel opened up into a large, circular cavern. A weak light flickered from the chamber ahead. I had the strongest feeling of being somewhere I had been before.

"Meri?" I called out, my own voice echoing back to me, but there was no answer.

My heart burned with fear like alcohol on a fresh wound. Meri was the most powerful mage I had ever known. Quite possibly the most powerful mage in history. And yet something in this place had managed to hold her down for long years against her will, had left her barely clinging to sanity. I forced myself forward into a darkness so deep I could no longer see. I edged over to the side of the tunnel, running my fingers against the wall as I moved.

Rough gray blocks of stone formed the room. A single light dangled from a domed ceiling high above, giving the place the feel of a decimated, long-deserted church. I stepped sideways into the chamber, keeping my back flush against the wall, trying to move quietly and willing my eyes to adjust to the darkness. The silence was a physical presence, made more sinister by the occasional drip of water hitting the stone floor somewhere not far from me. Everywhere I looked, shadows hung on the walls like gray, sagging skin. Something crunched under my shoes, and I looked down. The light glinted weakly on broken glass that lay everywhere underfoot. My toes brushed against wood that lay splintered on the floor.

What was this place? I couldn't tell, but somehow it seemed so important that I remember.

In the center of the chamber sat four long, horizontal square shapes, raised up on a small dais. Swallowing hard, I inched toward them, my eyes darting around as I moved away from the wall and approached one of the long stone slabs. I leaned down to examine its smooth surface.

The light flickered. Eyes, motionless and staring, gazed up at me from inside the rock.

I gasped and jumped backwards, nearly falling over my own feet in my panic. Then I understood. A picture was carved into the slab of stone, and as I leaned back over it, I realized it was a face I recognized.

There was no mistaking that it was a picture of Shanie's older brother Don, staring serenely up, carved into the stone. Suddenly, I remembered when I had been here before. I had stood here, beside Shanie, when her mother was entombed.

I was standing in Shanie's family crypt.

It was no wonder I had not recognized it. The last time I had been here, so long ago, there had been hundreds of candles glinting from the ceilings and the walls. The air had been thick with incense, and the cave had been crowded with mourners, all singing together, wearing white. Now it was cold, dark, and as silent as the corpses that slept here.

I took a step back, away from the sarcophagus. And my eyes narrowed. Two stone coffins for Shanie's brothers. One for her mother. But four stone slabs lay in the crypt. I darted forward, searching the faces of each stone, finding first her brothers, then her mother. But the very last slab was blank.

"No," I whispered, not wanting to believe it.

But my fingers were already fighting with the weight of the stone, scrabbling desperately to find some purchase on the surface, which was smooth as glass. The weight was incredible. I had to shove against the cover with all my strength, my every muscle screaming at the effort that it took. Finally, the top slid back with a terrible scraping sound, tipping over until it fell on the ground with a deafening thud.

"Meri?"

She was alive, but in a way that only made it more terrible. The form I found should have been a skeleton. Life shouldn't be allowed to go on like that, when it turns into a cruel mockery of itself, when it is nothing but horror and pain heaped on pain. Her bones poked up grotesquely under the gray, lumpy blanket that covered her body. Her eyes were open, staring up at me with not the slightest hint of recognition. I wept as I reached out to her.

"Oh, Meri." I choked, looking down at the ruined face of one I loved so well.

She had always been petite, a small woman who, when she wanted to, could pull in the aura of power that normally flowed around her like a billowing cloak. Using that power, she could shrink down into a slight, unremarkable woman whose flat, lean body could ease in and out of crowds of people without turning any heads, or leaving any impression on unwary minds. But now it was as though she had shriveled, dried out. Her small hands were frozen, her fingers spread wide and clutching at nothing. Her skin was a dull, lifeless gray. Her knees were drawn up to her chest tightly in the fetal position. Even her hair, which I remembered as being long and corn-silk golden, had dulled, gone white, and lay under her head like a pillow of cobwebs. Her mouth was pressed tightly together, as though her lips had been frozen at just the moment when she had been biting back a scream. The only things that moved were her eyes. The brilliant silver I remembered had faded to a dull gray, and her eyes were wide and wild, darting back and forth in the darkness.

I leaned down, gingerly lowering my hand in front of her eyes. She made no response, and I understood. She couldn't see anything in front of her. I could feel the binding spell which kept her in darkness, lying over her whole body and holding her in blind, perpetual stasis.

"I'm going to get you out," I told her, not sure she could hear me.

Somehow the sound of my own voice steadied me. It broke the silence, and this place was too dark, too motionless. I couldn't help but feel that it was waiting for something. That there was something in the darkness just readying itself to spring. I fought back the urge to whirl and look behind me. Instead I reached down and gently ran my hand over Meri's face. Her eyes froze, then fluttered, and she looked up at me.

"Asa," she groaned. "No. Don't. You'll wake them."

I jerked my head up, my eyes darting around the crypt, searching every crevice, every shadow. There was nothing.

"It's okay, Meri," I coaxed. "It's just us. Can you sit up?"

But then the humming started.

The sound rose, a low buzzing that chattered and grew louder, that came, not from behind me, but from inside the sarcophagus where Meri lay.

"No!" she moaned, her voice ragged with terror, her eyes screwing shut.

She lifted her claw-like hands over her ears, and only now did I see the countless long, jagged red lines that stretched from her temple to cheek, where she had scratched at her ears, trying to block out the sound.

"What is it?" I cried, leaning down closer to her, trying to find a source for the sound. When I finally saw, I let out a scream. Despite the love I felt for Meri, and all the years I had hoped and waited for the moment when I would find her, I took an instinctive, stumbling step back and away.

All over her body, hundreds of tiny eyes slit open. Tiny hands adjusted their grip. Countless gray, glinting teeth sank a little deeper into her skin.

I had thought Meri's body was covered with a lumpy, gray blanket. In truth, she was covered with a swarm of small, naked creatures that clung to her like leeches. Each was about the length of my hand, and they looked like minuscule old men. The gray skin hung off their bony, hairless bodies. They lay against her neck like a grotesque necklace, their long, thin fingers biting into her skin, their legs clamped around her arms. Their lifeless phalluses flopped between spindly gray legs. Skin to skin they pressed against her, coating her flesh like fish scales. Embracing her. Some had their needle-like teeth sunk into her skin. Others whispered to her, and the sound of their voices, sharp and grating, rose around her like a swarm of bees.

This, then, was what the boy had been warning me about. "*A hundred mouths, a million teeth. Stone and bone deep underneath.*"

"No," Meri pleaded, her head shaking weakly back and forth. "Please. I'm so, so sorry. Please. Just leave me be."

The begging jolted me out of the shock. I had imagined so many terrible scenarios in the years since I had lost her. In my nightmares, I had found her body a hundred times, knelt over her broken form, held her, motionless, as I wept, over and over again.

But even in my darkest imaginings, my mind had never been able to conceive of Meri begging.

I lunged forward with a wordless cry of rage and grief, seizing one of the creatures, grabbing its cold, clammy body with both hands as I tried to pull it off of her.

Meri shrieked in utter agony. Beady eyes glinted up at me. The creature seemed to smile up at me, as it sunk its pin-like teeth a little deeper into her flesh. I let go of it as though it was suddenly red hot. I stared down at Meri's body with horror. What could I do?

The buzzing sound got louder, as more of the creatures began to speak.

Meri's shriek died into a wordless, wrenching series of sobs and, not knowing what else to do, I leaned closer, and listened.

The creatures spoke in unison, their hissing, high-pitched words almost a song that they crooned, over and over into Meri's ears. She moaned and shuddered, and suddenly I understood. There was almost no magic in the world that could have held Meri down. But the venom of the words these creatures whispered had a power magic never could. Their words shocked me, but I would not let myself reflect on them—not now. Right now, the only thing that mattered was somehow getting Meri free.

Huge, unashamed sobs broke over me like waves, tears running down my cheeks and splashing onto those vile, puckered bodies. If I couldn't get them off her, I would just bring them along. I reached down and gathered Meri in my arms as though she were a child, groaning with effort as I hefted up and pressed her against my chest. My flesh crawled as I felt the tiny creatures' bodies squirming, tightening their grips. She moaned as I moved her, but there was nothing to be done. As fragile as she was, any movement would feel to her like agony. I just had to get her out.

Even though she was wasted away to almost nothing, I bowed and staggered beneath her weight. The creatures that were attached to her seemed to weigh her down. I fought to keep her steady in my arms. The feel of those cold, little bodies pressed tight against my chest made bile rise, hot and searing in my throat. They buzzed angrily, their voices growing louder.

"Asa. Don't do this." Meri's eyes fluttered up at me, and my heart lurched when I realized that at least she knew I was there. That she could recognize my face. "Leave me."

"No." I took an unsteady step back toward the tunnel, which suddenly seemed a horribly long way away.

"You have to," Meri groaned. "They won't let go. Not ever."

"I'm getting you out of here," I grunted. "End of story."

"But Asa." The pure agony in her voice stilled my feet, and I looked down at her face. She was looking up at me now, for the moment fully awake. "Everything they are saying...all of it. It's all true."

"I know, Meri," I whispered, my own tears falling again. "I know it. But the things they are saying are only half of the truth. And a half-truth is worse than a lie."

I took another step.

"They won't let go of me!" she protested.

I nodded, but I didn't look down again. The light of the cavern's opening shone not far away, and I kept my eyes focused on that. With each slow step I took the sound the creatures made grew louder, and their bodies grew heavier, as though there was some magnetic force pulling Meri's body down, towards the ground and out of my arms.

"I know," I grunted. "They are darkness. Parasites that feed on despair, on guilt and hopelessness. They won't choose to let you go, and you can't reason with them. You can't talk your way free. And trying to pull them off one by one will only rip your body to shreds. There is only one thing to do."

Sweat poured down my face, and my legs felt weak beneath me.

"One foot, in front of the other," I gasped, gritting my teeth as I forced my body to keep moving. "We...just... keep...going."

The blackness seemed to be thickening around me, like a dark hand materializing over my eyes, muting the light that emanated from the opening, making it feel miles away. The creatures attached to Meri's body writhed and shouted at her now. Their sharp voices remained in perfect unison, their arms and legs clamped painfully tight against her raw, bleeding flesh.

My foot knocked against stone, and I realized I had made it all the way to the far end of the tunnel, though I hadn't been able to see well enough to tell. I had ended up several feet to the right of the entrance, and I turned, moving with painful slowness to re-direct myself towards the light.

Just at that moment, a dark form came barreling in through the opening. Shanie's face was wild with desperation as she threw herself through the entrance, slipping and falling on the smooth cave floor. For a second I gripped Meri more tightly, sure that Shanie had come to stop our escape—that she would try to wrench Meri's body from my grasp and force her back into the darkness. But Shanie spared us only a glance before scrambling past us on her hands and knees, deeper into the gloom.

"Shanie? What are you doing?" I called out after her, horrified. She still wore the fish pendant, the key to the mage-haven's doorway, around her neck. "You can't bring the key in here!" I shouted to her. "The key is the only link between the haven and the aboveground world! You'll make the whole place collapse in on top of you! You'll die!" But she didn't turn, or seem to hear me.

I looked down at Meri. Her eyes had closed, and her face had gone slack. I was almost to the entrance, and I could see sunlight glinting on the other side of the doorway. Hoisting Meri's body up, straining with the very last bit of my strength, I half-pushed, half-threw her through the opening and out, into the light. She tumbled out of the haven and onto the grass, where she sprawled, unconscious. The instant the light brushed against her skin, the gray parasites screamed. They hurled themselves away from Meri, leaping off of her body like rats abandoning a ship.

Throwing themselves onto me.

TWENTY-TWO

COLD, CLAMMY LIMBS SCRAMBLED ACROSS MY SKIN.

They crawled under my clothes, wriggled up my legs, slid across my belly. I fell backwards, into the darkness, crashing hard onto the stone floor. I didn't try to use my hands to break my fall. I beat at the creatures, trying to push them away from my flesh. But there were too many of them, and they were all over me. Each tiny hand that clutched at my flesh was cold and strong as steel.

Then, tiny teeth, sharp as razors, pierced the skin on the inside of my thigh. As though they all shared one mind, all the little beasts sighed and shivered in simultaneous pleasure.

"We are the night-biters," a high-pitched voice whispered in my ear. One of the creatures had pulled himself up so he could lie across my shoulder with his mouth pressed right up against my ear. "We know you, now. We have tasted your blood. We have sipped your sins. We know the guilt of your heart, the filth of your soul. You are so moist, so full of tears. Better than that dried-up other one."

I looked around through bleary eyes. Shanie had not gotten far. A few of the creatures had found her, and she was curled into a ball against the floor, rocking back and forth with her hands against her ears. But most of them were on me.

"*We can smell the blood that is on your hands, taste the guilt that runs like rivers through your heart,*" they crooned as they settled themselves against me, skin to skin. "*You have caused death. You have ripped lives into raw and bloody pieces. We will count with you, number each life that you have taken. You will weep for each of them, and we will drink your tears. We will help you mourn them. The children they did not live to have, the songs they did not get to sing. Every sunrise they never saw, because of you. You will weep and cry for each and every one, while we nurse at your breast. We will grow fat on the despair you feed us.*"

I stared down at my body, and did not recognize it. The creatures covered me like a second, wriggling gray skin.

"*No one else would hold you, but we will,*" they whispered. But the voice had slowly changed. At first the creature by my ear had spoken in a voice dry and raspy, but it had smoothed out, deepened. The voice they spoke with now was indistinguishable from my own. "*No one else would want you—broken and blood-covered as you are,*" my voice whispered in my ear. "*The world above is full of those who hate you. But you need not fear. We will embrace you. We will keep you close.*"

"Not everyone," I whispered hoarsely. "Not everyone hates me."

"*They call you traitor. They gather together to seek your death.*"

"Some call me healer."

"*Those ones don't know the truth about you,*" the voice answered smoothly. "*They do not know your name. If they did, they would recoil from you. They, too, would name you murderer.*"

"Rowan knows," I groaned. "He has seen me. He knows everything. And he has not turned from me yet."

"*A debt of honor,*" the voice sneered, "*More than fully paid. He is strong again now. He will have no more use for a traitor mage.*"

I made little noises without meaning to. I pressed my lips together tightly, so I'd stop.

"*Traitor,*" it crooned, its voice growing louder as their intensity rose. "*Stupid. Useless. Murderer. So fiercely hated and despised. Who do you have, in the whole wide world, but us?*"

The sound burst out of me then. I couldn't help it.

It was not quite a laugh, but more a snort of scorn and derision.

"Seriously?" I spread my hands out palm down on the ground, and slowly, painfully, pushed myself up to sitting. "Is that really the best that you can do?"

The creature's voice stuttered for a second with surprise, then picked up, growing louder and more furious than before.

"We know you," it hissed. *"You cannot escape us, traitor mage. We know all that you have done. Because of you the innocent have died. Because of your arrogance, your haste, life upon life has been destroyed."*

"Amateurs," I muttered, as I clambered to my feet, swaying where I stood for a moment as I adjusted to the weight of all the creatures that now dangled from me. "Do you really think those words are going to shake me to my core? Do you think I haven't said the same things to myself, a hundred times?"

Shanie huddled against the wall not far from me. Feeling unsteady, as though my body was not fully mine to control, I swung a leg out and moved toward her.

"I've said the same thing a thousand times, alone in the darkness." I stood over Shanie now. Her eyes were screwed up, tightly closed. Two night-biters had attached themselves to her neck, and I saw where a third had burrowed part way under her clothing. "I've said worse to myself," I muttered as I leaned down over her. "I've said far worse of myself, and believed it."

"Shanie." I shook her shoulder, but she didn't look up at me or respond. I heard rock crumbling behind me, and knew we didn't have much time. The haven was beginning to collapse. "We have to get out of here."

The creatures screamed and buzzed, as I gave up on getting her to move, and instead reached down and hooked my arms under hers, pulling her to her feet and dragging her with me as I inched backwards towards the door.

"Traitor," they hissed. *"Murderer. Stupid, useless, and despised!"*

But I had no time to stop and listen.

"What are you doing?" Shanie whispered weakly, her eyes

cracking open. "Why try to save me? You know what I did to Meri. And now the other mages know too. I tapped into the source while I was talking to you…they all saw the truth. They know what I did. If you take me outside, they'll kill me. Why can't you just leave me be?"

"You've been my friend for as long as I can remember, Shanie. I haven't forgotten. The night after my parents died, I slept in a sleeping bag on your bedroom floor. You lent me your favorite doll to sleep with—said it would keep bad dreams away." My throat closed as the memory rose, still clear enough to cut, in my mind. I took another step towards the door.

"That was a long time ago." Her head lolled back and she stared up at the shaking ceiling with glassy eyes. "I'm a different person now. A bad person."

"I don't think that's true, but either way, I don't care. If you want to curl up in the dirt and die, you'll have to do it on another day. I don't leave people behind." I saw her move her lips to argue, and raised my voice to cut her off. "Not even if they deserve it." Then, in an undertone, I said, just starting to understand now that the words were leaving my mouth, "Not even myself."

"*Traitor,*" the night-biters chanted, over and over again.

I grunted and pulled at Shanie's weight, trying to move faster.

"How?" Shanie tilted her head back so she could look up at me, her eyes running over all the wriggling forms that were still holding onto me tight. "With those things attached to you. Whispering to you." She shuddered and closed her eyes again. "I only used them because I couldn't think of any other way to keep hold of Meri. How are you able to move at all?"

I laughed, though there was no humor in the sound. "I guess that's the thing," I said.

We were almost to the door. The creatures knew the light was getting closer, and I could feel them trembling. They hissed at me, calling out terrible things, telling me that everyone I cared about would be better off if I were dead.

"I've been lying awake, listening to my own little voices tell me how worthless I am for what feels like forever. I guess that, after all of this time, I've learned how to survive in the dark."

With Shanie clasped firmly in my arms, I stepped into the light. My foot caught and I fell through the opening, falling out and onto the grass in a tangle of limbs, spilling Shanie out of my arms and onto the ground beside me. The night-biters writhed then slid away, hurling themselves back into the darkness. But a few were not fast enough, and still clung to my neck and side as the sunlight poured down on my flesh. Their bodies shriveled to a horrible sizzling sound. After just a few seconds in the sun nothing was left but empty husks, clinging to my body like cicada shells clinging to a tree.

For a second all I could do was lie prone on the grass, feeling the sun on my shoulders and the clean air in my lungs.

Then I heard him.

"None will harm her!" Rowan's voice was a roar, full of a fury I had never heard from him before.

I felt, rather than saw, him throw his body over mine. He was suddenly on his hands and knees over me, shielding me. That was when I saw them.

Mages were arrayed at the edge of the clearing, just in the shadow of the trees.

"The traitor-bitch came out of her hole!" a voice crowed, and the crowd gave a shout and surged towards me.

Rowan's growl rumbled low and deep in his chest. The ground I lay on suddenly began to change. All around the spot where I lay, thick thorn bushes sprouted from the ground, rising at incredible speed to form a protective wall in front of us. He lifted one hand, and brought it down hard on the ground. The earth rippled like we were in the epicenter of an earthquake. The ground rumbled as it moved, an echo of the thrumming in Rowan's chest, the grass rising and falling like a wave under the feet of the approaching mages, and they were all thrown backwards, off their feet.

In the sudden silence, Rowan rose slowly to his full, impressive height.

"This woman is under my protection," he declared, as a sound like thunder welled up behind him.

Suddenly centaurs poured out of the trees, streaming toward us, taking up defensive positions on either side of Rowan and me. They spread out into ranks with swords drawn and arrows on the string.

The mages muttered to each other, getting back up onto their feet, staring dazedly at the army that had suddenly arrayed itself against them. I took a deep breath and reached up, catching hold of Rowan's hand and pulling myself to my feet. Desperately, I looked around, my eyes running over the scene in front of me. At the moment, the mages and the threat they posed mattered very little to me. All I wanted was to find Meri. When my eyes finally found her, I cried out in anger and despair.

TWENTY-THREE

IN THE NO MAN'S LAND BETWEEN THE CENTAURS AND THE MAGES, Meri lay on the grass. Her body was motionless, her face turned up toward the sun.

The mages weren't helping her, I realized, and fury shot through me. They weren't even looking in her direction. She was naked, her painfully pale skin covered with hundreds of angry red wounds. No one had gone to tend to her. No one had so much as thrown a jacket over her to cover her wretched, torn flesh. They didn't care about her. They hung back, yelling insults, still focused on me and on my crimes. Even with their leader broken and dying on the ground in front of them, they could think of nothing but protecting themselves, and their desire to spill my blood.

"I have to get to her," I whispered to Rowan, who moved his body in front of mine, shielding me from the mages. "She's dying, and they don't care. I have to help her, Rowan!"

Rowan started to respond, but a deep voice cut him off.

"Lord leshy!" The centaur chief's voice boomed down from beside me, and I looked up. The smile I had seen before on his face was gone. His shoulders were thrown back, his chin held up, and he was every bit the stern, angry chief I had first met in the forest what felt like a lifetime ago.

"These invaders bear blood-guilt against my tribe. This fight is ours. I claim the right for my clan to be the one to rise against them and drive them from our home."

"You know what they are." Rowan looked straight into the chief's eyes, his voice smooth and measured. "The cost to you and yours may be great. Do you still choose this fight?"

"I do."

Rowan nodded slowly to the chief.

"Go," he said. "The Earth has taken notice. It, too, thirsts to drive them from this place. It will aid you. Fight well, and with my blessing."

In a movement so fast that it blurred before my eyes, the chief had his sword out and raised high up in the air. His throat bulged as he bellowed a savage war cry that made my ears ring, which count-less other voices immediately echoed. I leaned into Rowan as the centaurs broke around us like a wave, the ground shaking as they moved as one to strike. Some of them leaped up, soaring over the wall of thorns that had grown at Rowan's bidding. Others simply slashed at the thorns with their blades, not slowing down as they rushed through the openings they made for themselves. In the chaos I saw Shanie struggle to her feet and turn and run blindly away into the woods in the opposite direction.

The air filled with cries and small bursts of light, as the mages threw up magical shields around themselves and began to strike back against the centaurs.

"Come," Rowan leaned down and yelled into my ear so I could hear him over the chaos, and together we ran toward Meri.

As I knelt down to examine her, Rowan stood over me, his feet spread wide, ready to spring to my defense. None of the centaurs had trampled her on their way to claim revenge, but there was little else to be thankful for. Her skin felt clammy and cold to the touch. Her breathing sounded so shallow that at first I could not hear it.

When I pressed my fingers against her throat, the heartbeat that fluttered there was weak and erratic. She had more wounds on her body than I could count.

"Meri?" I called, my voice breaking as my hand moved to caress her cheek.

"How is she?" Rowan asked.

"Dying." I looked up at him and shook my head. "We have to get her out of here. To a safe place, where I can treat her."

Rowan knelt down on the grass beside me, as I swallowed and gathered my nerve.

"You'll have to take us," I said, pushing aside the dread that hardened in my belly.

Rowan's brow furrowed. "You are certain?" he asked. "You said you would never travel with me that way again."

"We have no choice," I said, leaning down and wrapping my arms around Meri's still, cool form. "I have to get her to my clinic. It's the only chance she's got."

Lowering my face to her ear, I whispered, "Don't give up now, Meri. You've held on for all these years. I'm here now. I can help you. Just hold on a little bit longer."

I felt Rowan's arms wrap around me, pulling me and Meri close to his chest.

And then we were falling, and the only thing I could do was close my eyes.

I wanted to call out to Meri not to be afraid—that it would be over in a moment, that we were only trying to help. But my voice froze deep inside lungs that would not move, buried in a body that I suddenly could not control.

But I did not shudder or cry, or fight against the lack of sensation. I could feel Meri in my arms, and Rowan's chest was wide and sturdy at my back. I leaned against him, seeking the warmth of his skin in the darkness, as I cradled Meri closer to my chest, and waited for the darkness to pass. After the cave this frozen feeling did not feel quite so difficult to bear.

We broke the surface, and I could see the barn in the distance, the landing lights off and swinging idly in the late day sun. There was no time to feel sick, or try to get my bearings. I staggered to my feet while Rowan reached down and picked Meri up, resting her gingerly against his shoulder.

We ran.

"Don't you have to go back?" I called out as we pelted toward the barn. "Won't the centaurs want you there to help?"

"No," Rowan answered, his voice normal despite the speed at which we were moving. "It would be an insult to the chief if I were to stay and baby-sit his battle. I will know if they truly need my aid."

I didn't answer. I focused on keeping up with Rowan, and trying to force away awareness of the nagging, burning pain in my chest.

"Jason!" I yelled, as we got closer to the lights. I was sure he was there. I had seen the lost expression on his face as he walked away from the summoning, and I knew that, if he was upset or confused, he would have come straight here. "We've got a patient. I really need your help!"

Banging came from within the barn and a second later the door flew open. Jason ran out toward us, stopping at the edge of the trees, his face blank with shock as he took in me running and Rowan with Meri cradled in his arms. We came up to him and stopped.

"She's in really bad shape," I gasped, fighting against the tightness in my chest to get the words out clearly. "I'll get her on the table. I need you to...Jason?" I asked, realizing he wasn't looking at me. "Can you hear me?"

But he didn't answer. He stared at Rowan.

Jason's eyes widened, his face paled, and he crumpled to his knees.

It was as though a terrible weight had suddenly fallen on his shoulders. Even once he was on the ground, he continued to sink down, until his hands and forehead pressed against the ground.

"Jason?" I cried. "What's the matter? Are you sick?"

"He's all right," Rowan answered for him. Eyes locked on Jason, he carefully pushed Meri into my arms. "It is because of me."

Utterly confused, I stood gaping, holding Meri in my arms as Rowan walked over to Jason and slowly knelt down in front of him.

"Changeling," Rowan called softly, putting a hand on Jason's shoulder. "Look at me."

Jason made a strange huffing noise, and didn't move.

"Look up," Rowan commanded, a new, deeper timbre in his voice. I felt a pull in the air, as though the breeze itself were somehow responding to him, and Jason raised his face and stared at Rowan. He shook.

"What's happening to me?" he asked, but the voice didn't sound like the Jason I knew. He sounded small, and vulnerable.

"Nothing bad," Rowan said smoothly. "You have been alone for far too long, with none of your own kind to teach you how to bear the weight of being what you are. Someday, when you are ready, and if you wish for all the good and bad that might be the result, I will take you to your own people, and help you if you wish to join with them. Until then, the land has claimed you as its own."

"And you rule the land," Jason said, his voice unsteady.

"That is true. But you have naught to fear from me." Rowan stood and held out a hand, which Jason took after a second's hesitation. "Come," Rowan said, steadying Jason when he wobbled on his feet. "You have a patient to tend to, and your friend is in need of your help."

Jason stared at Rowan for a moment, before nodding.

"All right," he said. With visible effort, he tore his eyes from Rowan's face and turned to face me. "Let's bring her inside."

He led the way, hurrying as though wanting to put distance between Rowan and himself. As we followed him toward the barn, I leaned over to whisper in Rowan's ear.

"What was that all about?"

"Jason has no tribe, no people. Alone, he falls directly under my authority."

My eyes widened. "I take it that authority is not just a theoretical one."

"No. It is a force as strong as gravity. Jason will be fine," he added, seeing the sudden worry in my eyes. "There are too many things that are new to him, and he is overwhelmed. But I can help him to find his way."

We got to the barn, and the smell of sawdust and wood reached out and welcomed me home. I pushed away all thoughts of anything but Meri as I carefully laid her down on the center table. Without my having to tell him, Jason had run to the supply closet and come back, his arms full of bandages and ointments.

"She's barely got a heartbeat," Jason grunted, moving quickly, his movements complementing mine, as we leaned over her together. "Should I start CPR?"

"Yes, do what you can." I turned to Rowan. "I have to use my Truthsight. Can you shield me?"

Rowan nodded, stepping forward and laying a hand on my shoulder.

I didn't have time to explain to Jason what was about to happen. I blinked, and the silver unfurled in my vision, coating everything around me.

I still stood in the barn, with Rowan right behind me. He was himself, but I knew the Truthsight had changed me. I could feel a difference in my limbs, a springiness to my body.

And I could see Meri.

Rowan took a step closer behind me and sucked in a sudden breath.

"Good God," he whispered. "What is she?"

"One of the most powerful creatures you will ever see," I said, with more than a little pride. "And one of the most ancient."

The barn filled with the swell of discordant music, a chaotic sound like the clamor of a huge orchestra warming up, all the instruments out of time with each other and terribly out of tune.

"What is the noise?" Rowan asked, tilting his head upward and looking around, trying to find its source.

"It's Meri," I answered, but I had no time to explain.

I leaned over, and opened her up.

The outermost layer of Meri's body was a puzzle, the pieces made of wide, interlocking wooden pieces on hinges that flipped forwards and backwards, and snapped securely into place. The wood was chipped and broken, worried away by years of sharp, chewing teeth. But that was just her outermost layer, and not where the darkest threat hid. I folded back the puzzle pieces, opening her up so I could see the terrible mangle within.

Under the outer casing, Meri's body was filled with a web of layer upon layer of long, beaded strings. They wove in and out of each other, forming a design more intricate and fragile than the most breathtaking spider's web. Each bead that hung from the strings was unique. Some bore minuscule paintings of the faces of people that Meri knew, or symbols of powers she held. Some were painted in simple, brilliant colors. But now the webs were broken, and all the cords were tangled into a huge, angry knot. I ran my fingers over them, feeling how truly devastating the damage was. Then I began to mend them.

There was no way to do it except to heal each string individually, and there was no way to make the slow, painstaking work go faster. I knew Meri was dying, knew her time was perilously close to running out, but the beaded strings were her life force, and each had to be pulled out of the knot, and then carefully coaxed back into place. Gently, I pulled one cord free, running my fingers over it so that the beads fell chiming into place, stretching it out inside Meri's hollow form and nudging it with my fingers until it hung just where it was meant to. Then I started on the next. Each string took long moments to put right, and I could feel time falling away from me, like sand running through my fingers.

With each cord I fixed, some part of the discordant melody that floated in the air above us fell into tune. With the first string, what had been a screeching, high-pitched whistle, mellowed to become the sweet, gentle trill of a flute. With the next, the random, occasional slamming sound became the deep, regular, bass of a beating drum. Now I knew that at least her heart was beating. But after working as fast and as hard as I could for untold minutes, hardly daring to breathe, never looking up, her insides were still a mass of chaos.

I pulled at the next cord, and a bead cracked, and fell to pieces at my touch.

I gasped, and stilled. Immediately, Rowan was at my side.

"What's wrong?" he asked.

I shook my head, not wanting to believe the words my own mouth was about to say.

"She's too far gone," I whispered, trying to fight down the panic that swirled in my chest. "The damage is too great. I have hours and hours of work to do, but she's deteriorating too quickly. I can't save her." Rowan's fingers tightened on my shoulder, giving sympathy I wasn't ready to receive. I spun to face him. "But you can."

Rowan frowned. "I don't understand what you are saying, Asa. You know I am no healer."

"Meri doesn't need a healer. She needs to be well enough to heal herself. She is the only one powerful enough to undo this damage. But she is too weak. If she had the pearl, it would give her strength enough to put herself to rights. But I can't remove the pearl from my own body."

Rowan's hand dropped away from my shoulder, and he took a step away.

"Mage magic is different from leshy magic," I said, feeling certainty mount. "But they *can* interact. The Earth-child helped me see you, so I could save your life. And you can walk right in or out of my Truthsight visions. I can't see myself in Truthsight, but you can see me. And you can see the pearl. You can, can't you? You can still see it there."

Rowan's face was drawn and dark, but his eyes flicked upward, and I knew he was gazing at the silver fish that still nestled high up in the branches of a willow tree. That was all the confirmation I needed.

"You have to remove it," I told him, moving a little way away from Meri and sitting down cross-legged on the floor. "Take out the pearl, and give it back to her. Its power may be enough to save her."

"No," Rowan said, his voice climbing as his cheeks flushed. "Of course I will not do this thing, Asa. You told me before that Meri was the only one who could safely remove the Pearl. What you are asking me to do might kill you!"

"What's the alternative?" I shot back. "Letting Meri die right in front of me, after coming so close to saving her? I can't live with that. And if she did die, what then? I would walk around for the rest of my life with a piece of magical power that's the equivalent of a nuclear bomb tucked snugly beneath my collarbone, burning me away from the inside? *No*, Rowan. We have to do this. Every treatment carries risks. Every surgery has potential negative consequences. This is no different. The risk is mine, and the choice is mine. I am choosing to try to help someone I love, to try to free myself from this burden I've been carrying. I need you to trust me, Rowan. And I need your help."

He walked slowly over to me, and crouched down so that his face was just in front of mine.

For a moment he stared into my eyes. Unblinking, I stared right back.

Then he nodded, the movement sudden and sharp.

"You are strong," he said. "You have a warrior's spirit and an unyielding, stubborn soul. You will survive this. I will do as you ask. But you must direct me."

"Okay." I put my hands on my knees and took a long, deep breath. "You can see the pearl, right?"

"You mean the fish in your branches?"

"Yes, yes, that's what I mean. All you need to do is lift it out. Then take it over, and lay it down on top of Meri's chest. The pearl knows her—she is its creator. Once it is free, its power should flow back into her. And Rowan?"

"Yes?"

"Once you've started, don't stop." I closed my eyes, and braced myself. "No matter what."

TWENTY-FOUR

I COULD FEEL HIM, WHEN HE STRETCHED HIS HANDS OUT TOWARD THE pearl. I could feel his hand pressing into me, reaching deeper and deeper into my chest. At first it just felt like pressure. While it was uncomfortable and strange, it wasn't painful. Then the heat started. It began as a flicker, like a jolt of static electricity tickling somewhere above my heart. But it grew, becoming a long, intense sensation.

I will not make any noise, I told myself, pressing my lips together and gritting my teeth. *No matter what, no matter how bad it gets.* If I cried out, Rowan might give up and refuse to do this. I couldn't let that happen.

The heat grew more intense, and soon it morphed into true pain. But the pain was clean and honest, like pulling away a scab that has begun to itch. It was productive pain, and I dug my fingernails into my thighs and refused to make a sound.

Then, suddenly, the pain grew worse. Scorching heat, like the burn of a white-hot poker, pressed flat against my heart. I heard the sound of branches snapping, and smelled ashes. And I screamed. There was no way to stop the sound. My body made it without my permission, an automatic and unstoppable, piercing cry of agony.

"Don't stop don't stop don't stop!" I managed to form the scream into words and to keep my hands clamped to my knees instead of trying to pry his hands away in an instinctive, desperate attempt to end the pain.

"Hold on, Asa," Rowan's voice choked out. He sounded as though he were in pain, too. "It's almost over."

And then it was. The burning sensation didn't stop, but it lessened, and the intense agony disappeared. Instead, my chest felt hollow, and burned with a low, steady thrum of pain. I slumped over onto the ground, opening bleary eyes to watch as Rowan walked over to Meri, something shining and silver held in his hands. He placed it carefully on top of her, then turned and ran back to kneel by my side.

"Asa?" he asked, leaning over me and peering into my eyes. "Are you all right?"

My voice didn't want to work, but I made it. "Take me to her." I couldn't answer his question because I wasn't sure of the answer. Most of my body felt numb. Where it didn't feel numb, it burned. But I had to see Meri, had to see if she was healing.

Rowan placed one of my arms over his shoulder, and wrapped his other long arm around my waist, lifting me effortlessly and supporting my steps over to Meri's side. What I saw there was enough of a wonder to make the awareness of pain fade from the forefront of my mind for at least a moment.

The silver had melted into her, coating and transforming the inside of her body. The cords were no longer strings of beads. They were alive, moving like tentacles with brilliant shining scales, poking around inside until they found the right position and could lock themselves in place. The intricate patterns of Meri's insides rewove themselves as we watched, weaving back and forth, delicately snapping back into place. Above our heads, the music deepened and soared, each instrument back in tune, each chord chiming in perfect chorus with the others.

"Rowan, I need to lie down," I gasped.

The wonder on his face transformed into worry. He lowered me onto the ground, next to Meri, and leaned down over me, his lined face anxious.

"What can I do, Asa? Tell me how to help you!"

But I couldn't answer him. I began screaming again.

The burn had built back up, and I felt like my whole body was going up in flames.

"Rowan, I…"

There were important things, things I needed to say to him, and suddenly I was sure I didn't have much time to get the precious words out. But the pain was stronger than I was, an alien force that had taken over my body and controlled me like a puppet on a string. My mouth was no longer my own, and no words came. I grabbed Rowan's hair, pulling his face close to mine, desperate to see him through the darkness that grew on the edges of my vision like frost creeping across a window and blocking out the light. I had to feel that he was close. I had to see in his eyes that he forgave me for leaving him, because I knew now that I was going, no matter how desperately I wanted to stay.

"Asa!" a voice called, as though from miles away. Even with the pain that thrummed through me, I froze. It was Meri's voice calling to me.

"Shhh, sweet one," her voice whispered. "I will not let you slip away." I saw a hand reaching out for mine. I didn't have the strength to reach back to it, but Rowan took my fingers and pressed them into hers, wrapping his large, rough palms around both of ours, holding us together. And then a cool, blessed chill began to spread, from her fingertips to mine, and down the length of my arm.

The fire went out.

I took, a deep, shaking breath, and turned my eyes toward the sky that glinted above me. Silver snow began to fall. It floated down in thick, shining flakes, coating my skin. The cold pushed the pain away. The music soared. I turned my head to see Meri looking back at me. She did not smile, but squeezed my hand.

"We'll be all right, Asa," she said, in the clear, sweet voice I remembered. "We are survivors, you and I."

TWENTY-FIVE

When I opened my eyes, I lay on the floor of the barn with Rowan's arms wrapped around me. Jason crouched over me, his face drawn with worry, his fingers poking at my chest.

"Ow," I announced, batting his hand away.

"Oh my God, you're awake!" he exclaimed.

"Yes, of course I woke up, with you jabbing me like that. Stop it!" I pushed his hand away as he reached back out for me.

"You are wounded, Asa," Rowan murmured into my ear, his arm warm around me. "Jason fears it will become infected if he does not treat it soon."

"Yes, all right. I understand." I struggled to sit up and push the hair out of my eyes. I was sore, but not in pain. When I fingered my chest warily, it did not burn. "We can take care of it later." Rowan made a disproving sound.

"Soon-later," I reassured him, batting Jason's hand away when he reached back out toward me. "Where's Meri?"

"I'm here."

She sat hunched over on the exam table, her legs dangling over the edge. She looked much smaller than I remembered her. Her face had shrunken and become thin, her body lost in a clean pair of my scrubs that were much too long for her. I must have been out for longer than I had realized, because bandages covered her. While I was unconscious, Jason had cleaned and taped up every single one of her nearly countless wounds. But her eyes were the same silver shade I had always known, and as she gazed at me steadily, they were full of understanding.

I stood up slowly, not sure how stable I would be on my feet. Rowan rose with me, following closely at my side, ready to support me if my legs gave out.

Then Meri held out her arms, and suddenly I ran, my sore chest forgotten.

I had dreamed so many times of finding her, of being able to tell her how sorry I was for everything. With her arms wrapped around me I was suddenly a child again, crying in her arms and hoping for forgiveness.

"I'm so sorry," I whispered to her when I could find my voice. "For everything. I don't know what else to say, Meri, or how to show you..."

"Hush, child," she said, shaking her head. "I could never be angry at you, Asa, for being what you are. It is your nature to heal others, and I could never truly blame you for doing that. Besides, you know everything now. You heard what those creatures were whispering to me, and you know the secret that was so heavy that the guilt of it held me down all those long years. Knowing what I've done, how can you think you need to apologize to *me*?"

I clutched her hands tightly in my own. Her fingers felt cool and fragile. Her body might be in one piece, and her heart was beating, but I was not such a fool as to believe her out of danger. I knew what guilt and darkness could do to a person. "Meri," I said. "It isn't your fault. You didn't know. You cannot blame yourself."

"Of course I can." She wouldn't meet my eyes any longer. She kept her gaze trained steadily on our intertwined fingers in her lap, and as she spoke, her voice was dead and flat. Hopeless. "There is no one else to blame. I should have realized that damming the Source would have far-reaching consequences. I should have suspected there would be effects I couldn't see immediately. But I was over-confident. Arrogant. I was so sure that I, and only I, could make things right. So I played with forces greater than myself, meddled with powers I did not really understand. I was *so* sure, Asa. I didn't ever doubt that I was doing the right thing. That by itself should have been proof that I was wrong."

Tears leaked from her eyes, and she didn't reach up to wipe them away. My heart ached. She was so used to crying—she had been crying for years and years, and the saltwater did not feel foreign on her cheeks. I reached over and wiped her tears away for her.

"I was arrogant," she whispered. "And short-sighted. Proud and stubborn, and cruel." I could practically hear the echoes of the night-biters chant as she spoke. "Until you took down the barriers, I never suspected at all. And even then, I couldn't quite believe it at first. Who could believe that they had done such a thing? Made such a terrible error? When I finally learned the truth, it destroyed me."

"You are *not* destroyed," I said. "You've been through so much, and you're still hurting. Look at me, Meri," I said, and her eyes rose up to mine. "Wounds heal," I whispered. "Yours will, too. You just need time."

She shook her head. "How can I heal from this?" she asked, her eyes wide. She was really asking. "I do not even know the names of all the species that have died out because of me."

Rowan's hand on my shoulder tightened convulsively.

"Asa?" he said, his voice suddenly sounding strangled. "What is she talking about?"

Meri's hands trembled. "Tell him, Asa," she whispered. "He deserves to know—they all do."

I wrapped an arm around Meri's frail shoulder, turning so I could stand by her side and look at both Rowan and Jason as I spoke.

"When Meri dammed the Source, to limit which mages had access to it, she believed what you have always believed, Rowan.

That mage magic is different, separate, from other types of magic, and that her actions would affect only other mages. But you and I have already started to realize that mage magic and other sorts of magic are more connected than we had believed."

Rowan did not answer, but nodded quickly. I could see the tension in the clench of his jaw, in the way that he held himself perfectly still, as though bracing for a blow.

I hated that it would be me delivering that blow.

"When Meri put up the barriers around the Source, she wanted to control which mages had access to its power. She knew that it would harm the mages who were cut off, but she did it anyway. She wanted to prevent mages from misusing their powers, and she believed that it was worth the cost. When I couldn't stand the harm that she was doing to other mages, and to herself, I pulled the barrier down."

I took a deep breath, bracing myself for what came next. "But there was something that no one realized. Meri didn't know it until the barriers fell, and she felt the magic coursing back out into the world. And I didn't realize it until today, when I heard what those creatures were whispering to her in the dark. When Meri dammed the source, it didn't just limit the flow of magic to the mages. Unintentionally, she limited its flow to everything. Even other, non-human species. What she did wasn't enough to cut off the flow of magic to them completely, but it was enough to weaken them. To stunt their growth. It hampered their ability to evolve, almost freezing them. It meant that they were not strong enough to keep pace with humanity. For a long time now, preternatural creatures have been growing weaker. Dying out. This is why."

Rowan's chest rose and fell rapidly as he stared at Meri. I had never seen him out of breath, not even when we had been running for our lives. But this revelation had him gasping for air. His hands clenched into fists at his sides, and his eyes, fastened on Meri's face, began to burn.

"She didn't know," I told him, my voice almost pleading. "No one knew."

"When the barriers fell, I realized what I had done," Meri whispered, her eyes wide but unseeing. "I didn't want to believe it at first, but soon there was no denying it. That was the real reason that I gave the pearl to Asa. When I realized what I had done, I knew that I could not be trusted to hold that kind of power. Asa, who always cared so much for others, who only wanted to heal and to protect people from pain—she was the only one who I could trust. And yet I couldn't stand to have her near me. I didn't want to see her face when she found out the truth. I couldn't stand to watch her faith in me crumble when she realized all the harm that I had done. I didn't want to see her hate me."

She turned her eyes to Rowan. "You despised me before. Now that you know the full truth, I would not even blame you for killing me."

"What good would that do anyone?" Rowan spat, raw fury in his voice. "I have seen you, mage. I know the power you hold. You tell me, weeping, that you have done untold damage to my kind, and to all the creatures I might call my brothers. And I tell you, I have no use for your tears. If what you say is true, then you have a heavy debt to pay. I do not wish to harm you—I want to see you pay that debt." He took a deep breath, and some of the flush crept out of his cheeks.

He looked at me, and I nodded at him. He was right, and though I knew he did not speak for her sake, I also knew that what he said was exactly what she needed to hear. Meri did not need sympathy. She needed a purpose.

"The damage you have done, you did unintentionally," I told her, leaning forward so that I could look into her eyes. "Imagine the good that you can do now, intentionally. I can't lie and tell you that you haven't made mistakes. But you have so much power, so much incredible ability. Who knows what good you can do, once you start trying to put things right?"

Meri's face paled to an even starker shade of white. "I never thought of that," she stammered. "All those years…all those long, dark days. I never thought of that at all."

"How could you, with those creatures hooked onto you, drinking up your tears?" I shuddered at the memory. "But you're free now. And instead of mourning the mistakes you've made in the past, you can begin to put things right."

"But what does it mean?" Jason's voice wavered, and he looked back and forth, wide-eyed, between Rowan and me. "Now that the barriers are down? Will the preternatural species get stronger? Start to change?"

"I think," I said softly, "that they already have. I've even seen it, right in front of me. But I didn't understand what was happening, so I didn't recognize it for what it was. Like the centaurs. I thought the reason the centaur babies were dying was because the species was growing weaker, but really it was the opposite. The babies took a huge leap forward—the problem was just that they changed so quickly that their mothers couldn't keep up. Crinea's baby—he is something new."

I turned to look at Rowan, the wonder still fresh inside me. "Her baby is a shape-shifter. A centaur that can take on human-seeming. I don't know how long he will be able to hold that shape, once he is fully grown. Perhaps for no more than an hour or so at a time. But it will change everything. And Grenalda's son." I took a shaky breath, remembering the feeling that had come over me when his tiny, black eyes had fixed on mine as he sung out his warning. "He ought to be too young to have foresight. But his gift came early. And you, Jason."

I slipped away from Meri, and went to stand in front of Jason. I took his hand in my own, and spoke the next part as gently as I could. "I think that the reason we have had so much trouble figuring out what you are, may be because you are something new too."

"But that isn't possible." Jason shook his head. "This magical barrier that came down—that happened only a few years ago. I'm twenty-seven years old!"

"I know." My heart ached as I spoke. I could only give him guesses, and I knew that they might hurt him. But he deserved to know as much of the truth as I could manage to give him. "But the difference may be that you have survived so long. Maybe you were born different from most of your kind, so different that they thought that your best chance for survival was to be raised by humans. And it could be that, if the barriers had not come down, at some point even that would not have been enough. But the barriers did come down. And here you are."

"It got better," Jason choked out. "My symptoms. Four, maybe five years ago. My skin stopped burning all the time. It was easier to keep down food. I thought it was because there was less stress in my life. I thought maybe I was growing out of it."

"That would fit the time line, more or less," I said softly, and squeezed his hand.

His fingers clung to mine. "You did this," he whispered, his voice rough with emotion, "You are the reason I've been getting better. I knew that you were helping me, treating me. But even before that, it was you."

"Asa!" Rowan's voice was sharp as he pivoted and stared at the closed barn doors. I pulled my hand from Jason's and spun to look.

Rowan strode to the door and cracked it open to look outside.

"Mages are coming," he said, turning to face me.

My heart froze, and instinctively my muscles tensed, as though to run.

Rowan shook his head when he saw the panic in my eyes. "They come," he said, "bearing wounded."

TWENTY-SIX

THE BATTLE HAD BEEN BAD, FOR ALL THAT IT HAD ENDED QUICKLY. The Earth had flooded the centaurs with all the pent-up strength of its many years of slumber, like melting snow flooding a river at springtime's first thaw. The centaurs had swooped down on the mages, crying out for vengeance for the one that the mages had slain, and for the harm that Rowan had suffered. The Earth aided them, cloaking them so thickly in its protection that the mages could hardly see them through the clouds of dust that rose under their hooves, except for the instant of terrifying clarity that came just before a blade struck home.

But the centaurs were warriors, not butchers. Once the field was won, the chief quickly called a halt to the attack, and sent one of his herd as a guide to show the wounded to my clinic. And so they came, stumbling, bleary-eyed, and bloody. And Jason and I threw the barn doors open wide, and did the best we could.

Rowan strode out to meet the young centaur who had guided the battle-weary mages.

"Where are your own wounded?" he asked.

The centaur shook his head and stood taller, answering with obvious pride. "We took only minor injuries, my Lord. And the chief thought it best that we not overburden the good doctor. We will be fine on our own."

"Very well," Rowan said, nodding his approval, even as I took a deep breath of relief.

The twenty or so mages who were waiting for treatment were already more than enough patients to treat.

"Well fought. Tell the chief I will come to speak with him in the morning."

He clasped forearms with the young centaur, who inclined his head before galloping away.

I had never had so many patients at the night clinic at one time before, and suddenly the barn was full to bursting. We put two in every patient room, and two in the library, and laid the most severely injured out on the exam tables that ran down the center of the barn. A few threw themselves down on the floor and leaned up against the base of the fountain, forcing me to pick my way through a tangle of limbs whenever I needed to get supplies from the back. Those with the lightest injuries had to lie on the grass outside and wait till we had time to tend them.

Even using my Truthsight, there were still two who were beyond my help by the time they arrived. The first was a young mage I did not know, who had stopped breathing before they even laid him down before me. His face was so peaceful that it was hard to believe that he had felt the cut of the blade that had sliced so cleanly through his midsection.

The second was Alice.

I leaned over her anxiously for long minutes, even though deep down I knew, from the first moment that I saw her, that there was nothing I could do. She had fought ferociously, and the blood that caked her arms and clothing was not all her own. Her eyes never opened while I was trying to save her, and she clutched her son's knife in her hands when she died. I left it there as I pulled a clean sheet over her face, still twisted with anger. There are some wounds of the body, and of the heart, that even Truthsight cannot heal.

I saw a look of perfect understanding pass between Rowan and Meri as the mages first began to pour into the clinic, and knew that one of them would be always by my side. It was Rowan mostly, who glowered over my shoulder at each and every mage I touched, the stormy expression in his eyes a warning that none try to harm me while I did my best to help. I didn't think any would have even thought to attack me, hurt and tired as they were, except perhaps for Paul. He made no comment as I tended him, staring straight up at the ceiling, a pained look on his face that I believed had more to do with the brush of my fingers than the head wound that had dyed most of his face red.

"Do not think that this means you are forgiven, traitor," he rasped when I was done and about to turn away.

I wiped my hands off carefully on a towel, and did not bother to look at him as I responded. "I did not heal you to gain your forgiveness, Paul."

"Right," he scoffed. "Now that Meri's back, you've no thought to worm your way back into her affections. You are doing all this out of the kindness of your black, rebel-loving heart."

"I do this because I am a healer. Because I know who I am," I replied, and turned to walk away.

Paul's hand snaked out and grabbed my elbow. Despite the way his hand shook, his grip was still tight enough to hurt.

"I do not forget so easily," he whispered. "And even with Meri back, there are plenty in the clan who still want your blood. We may have to wait, but we have waited already, and we are good at it now. The time will come when Meri's affection wavers, or her power wanes. And we will be ready. I may not be the head of the clan any longer, now that she is back. But I am still powerful enough to hurt you."

"You," Rowan's voice cut in before I could think of a reply, "are a petty tyrant, and a fool. And you are about to be a dead one." He had not raised his voice, but there was again that new, deep timbre to his words, and suddenly the whole barn went silent.

Meri straightened up from the wounded she had been leaning over. She pivoted slowly to look at Rowan, her eyes narrowed and thoughtful as she watched him.

"I tell you again that this woman is under my protection," Rowan said, his eyes moving to include all the mages in his gaze. "You would be unwise to make yourself my enemy."

Paul's face froze. Slowly, he released my arm. I turned my back on him and, together, Rowan and I stalked away.

Greg was the last one to be treated because it had taken him the longest to get to the barn. His ample body was covered with long black and blue marks, where he had been struck repeatedly with the broadside of a sword.

"You're lucky," I told him, as I watched the last bruise fade away under my fingers. "The centaur who was fighting you must have thought it unsporting to actually attack you. He chose to give you a beating, but left you alive. If even a few of these blows had cut into you, we wouldn't be having this conversation."

"Are you implying that this centaur saw me as somehow less than a worthy opponent?" Greg snorted, grimacing a little as the last sting faded from his skin. He wiped away some of the sweat beading on his beet-red face with the back of his hand. "I can't imagine why."

I smiled. "Just give yourself a day or two of rest in your sleep number bed, and you'll be good as new."

"That," Greg exclaimed, "is the best idea I've heard in ages."

I was already walking away when his voice called out after me.

"Hey, Asa?"

"Yes?" I turned, surprised. It was the first time any of the mages but Meri had actually called me by my true name.

"Thanks for helping me out," he said, not quite looking me in the eye. "I appreciate it."

I blinked back a sudden stinging in my eyes. "You're welcome," I responded, my voice only cracking a tiny bit. "Any time."

It was dark out when the mages began to pick themselves up and talk of leaving. I had spent some more time healing Meri, and as she crossed the barn floor to find me, there were no more bandages covering her skin.

"You have done all you can for tonight," she told me, and I nodded in agreement, shooting a covert glance in Jason's direction.

He stood close by, his arms folded as he leaned heavily against the wall. He might not need to sleep, but that didn't mean he could work indefinitely. His haggard expression told me that, if he didn't sit down soon, he would probably fall. Rowan stood just behind me, his eyes alert as he continued to keep a distrustful eye on the mages as they began to straggle out of the barn. They stood outside the barn doors, in the pool of light that spilled out into the dark, talking to each other in muted, tired voices and milling around.

It was dark outside, but other than that I had no concept of what time it was.

"I think," Meri said, smiling as she stretched out her hand to clasp mine, "that it is finally time for us to go home."

"You're right," I agreed, rubbing the back of my neck.

"Do you want to gather up some things, before we leave?" Meri asked. "I can send someone to help you, if you like."

I had thought Jason too tired to be paying much attention to anything, but at Meri's words he gasped and stood up straight.

I took a deep breath. There was something wonderful about the idea of going back with Meri. Of being wanted. Of taking care of her again, and allowing her to take care of me.

"Thank you, Meri," I said, and meant it. "But I can't come with you."

Meri's eyes widened with surprise. "What are you talking about?" she asked, almost laughing. "You can't stay here. Hidden away, in the middle of nowhere." Meri's brow furrowed as she looked around her, at the rough-hewn wood of the exposed beams, the dangling paper lanterns and the brightly painted patient rooms. "This has been a good place for you to hide. I'm very glad that you've had it. But you belong with us—at home, where we need you."

"I can't go back to the Clan, Meri. Surely you have to understand that. Too much has happened."

Meri smiled, and it was the expression of a parent calming a frightened child. "I won't let them hurt you, Asa. You don't have to be afraid. I know it has been awful, but all that is over now. It's in the past. And besides, I need you."

She dropped her voice to little more than a whisper. "You know you're the only one I really trust. There is so much to do now. The Clan is in shambles, and has to be pieced back together. We have to make some sort of real, lasting peace with the rebels. There are so many things I have to put right." Her smile faded, and I saw real fear peeking out from deep within her eyes. "I need you," she said. "By my side. Helping me."

I squeezed her fingers tightly in my own. "I can't," I whispered back. "I've changed too much to go back. This is my home now."

I looked around, at the clinic I had built with my own hands, the place where I had found so much comfort and meaning. "I belong here. Where I'm wanted. Doing what I'm meant to be doing. For so long, I've thought that I was watching all these beautiful species fading out, and disappearing forever. But now I know that isn't true. The barriers are down, and everything is going to change. My patients are going to need me, and I want to be here for them. To be a part of what happens next."

"You can't mean that, Asa," Meri protested. "You'll be so lonely here. Cut off. It is lovely to make friends with other creatures but, at the end of the day, you're a mage. You should be where you belong."

"Don't worry," I told her, smiling.

I reached my hand out behind me. I didn't have to look back to know that Rowan was there, or that he would immediately wrap his fingers around mine. He enveloped my fingers in his palm, and I leaned back, letting myself rest against the warmth of his smooth, broad chest. "I am."

THE END

Thank you for reading! Did you enjoy?
Please Add Your Review!

And find book two of the Outcast Mage novels, WINTER'S MAGE, and discover more from author Miriam Greystone at www.miriamgreystone.com

---

A strange new danger is stirring in the forest . . .

As a healer for supernatural creatures, Amy isn't afraid of things that go bump in the night. But curing one of her patients comes at a potentially fatal cost. With every passing night bringing her closer to a terrible fate, even the help of her supernatural friends may not be enough to save her. The worst part is her sealed fate finally brings Rowan, the leshy she loves, back into her life.

And there's another danger lurking in the trees, something...unnatural. It is a magic beyond Amy's understanding, or even Rowan's power to control.

As time runs out and danger mounts, Amy must test her strength and her courage, if she has any hope of saving her friends, or herself.

Please sign up for the City Owl Press newsletter for chances to win special subscriber-only contests and giveaways as well as receiving information on upcoming releases and special excerpts.

All reviews are **welcome** and **appreciated**. Please consider leaving one on your favorite social media and book buying sites.

For books in the world of romance and speculative fiction that embody Innovation, Creativity, and Affordability, check out City Owl Press at www.cityowlpress.com.

ACKNOWLEDGMENTS

I am so grateful to so many people who have been a part of bringing this book to life. The first thank you must go to Heather McCorkle, who was the first one to spot Truthsight and believe that it could be something special. Throughout the editing process she has been a dream to work with, and her patience, smart suggestions, and gentle advice have made the book immeasurably better. I am also deeply indebted to Tina Moss, who has provided wonderful guidance, and done so much to help make this book shine. I am also grateful to Yelena Casale and the rest of the City Owl family, who have been so supportive from the very first moment that I joined the flock.

Grace Sikorski and Michelle Markey Butler, what can I say? You have read countless drafts, patiently reading the same scene over and over until I got it right. You have given me so much priceless advice, feedback, and counsel. You have brainstormed with me for hours when I felt stuck, and then forgiven me when I threw everything out and started from scratch. Truthsight wouldn't be the book it is today without your help, and I wouldn't be the writer that I am today without your mentorship and friendship. Thank you – we are the best critique group ever!

I also benefited tremendously from the help of several expert beta-readers. Many thanks to Leah Cypess, Adina Rishe Gewirtz, and B.K. Stevens for taking the time to read the book carefully, and give me such amazingly helpful comments and advice. Many thanks also to Anita Mumm, for her insightful suggestions. I think it is safe to say that, without the help from each of you, this book would never have made its way onto the shelf.

I have been lucky in my life to have the joy of having three sisters: one by birth, one by marriage, and one because we simply have been sisters, ever since the day we met. Rachel, Kerry, and Yocheved, thank you to each of you for being my friends, my confidants, and my role models. I love you guys! (Also a big thank-you to my brother-in-law for all his support, too.)

Thank you to my mother and father for being my parents, my role models, my teachers, and my friends. Everything good in my life is rooted in the childhood full of love that you gave me.

To M, Z, I, and E: Whatever else I may do in life, and whatever I may accomplish, there is nothing that will ever matter half as much to me as the joy and privilege of being your mother. You are each indescribably precious, and I love you more than words can say.

And a final thank you to my husband. You are my happy place. Thanks for being my partner and my friend. Love you always.

ABOUT THE AUTHOR

Miriam Greystone writes urban fantasy stories filled with magic, romance, and the occasional centaur. She fuels her creativity with an insatiable appetite for reading and frequent episodes of *Doctor Who*. She lives just outside of Washington, DC, with her husband and children. When she isn't hunched over her laptop, she can often be found baking or going on long hikes with her family.

Facebook: www.facebook.com/miriam.greystone

Twitter: www.twitter.com/MiriamGreystone

Website: www.miriamgreystone.com

ABOUT THE PUBLISHER

City Owl Press is a cutting edge indie publishing company, bringing the world of romance and speculative fiction to discerning readers.

www.cityowlpress.com